LAST SHOT

Second Edition

LAST SHOT

Second Edition

Mike Faricy

Library of Congress Control Number: 2023914500
paperback ISBN: 978-1-962080-01-9
e-book ISBN: 978-1-962080-02-6

MJF Publishing books may be purchased for education, Business, or promotional use. For information on bulk purchases, please contact the author directly at mikefaricyauthor@gmail.com

Published by

MJF Publishing
https://www.mikefaricybooks.com

To Teresa
"The nightmare woke him again.
It was from the distant past yet still frighteningly real,
but this time he knew he was safe because she was
there next to him."

Acknowledgments

I would like to thank the following people for their help and support:
Special thanks to my editors, Kitty, Donna and Rhonda for their hard work, cheerful patience and positive feedback.

I would like to thank Ann and Julie for their creative talent and not slitting their wrists or jumping off the high bridge when dealing with my Neanderthal computer capabilities.

Special thanks to Ann for her patience.

Last, I would like to thank family and friends for their encouragement and unqualified support. Special thanks to Maggie, Jed, Schatz, Pat, Av, Emily and Pat for not rolling their eyes, at least when I was there, and most of all, to my wife Teresa whose belief, support and inspiration has from day one, never waned.

One

nnie was a petite blonde with large brown eyes, who stood barely an inch over five feet. We'd casually linked up from time to time over the past couple of months. Up until now, all of our meetings had been spur of the moment, meaning she called, and I suggested maybe she would like to come right over and 'chat.'

Tonight's 'chat' was different. For the first time, she invited me over to her place. We feasted on undercooked spaghetti with little cut up bits of hot dog floundering in a runny ketchup sauce. Apparently, the kitchen wasn't her strong suit, so the bottles of wine I showed up with helped us survive her lack of gourmet skills.

It was drizzling softly outside when we finally took a break. Annie was lying next to me with one of her gorgeous shapely legs draped over mine. She was tracing four-letter words and triple-X suggestions across my chest with her fingertip, giggling. We'd been frolicking up in her candlelit bedroom for a couple of hours, a room I'd never been in before. During our break, I was beginning to check the place out.

The walls were painted a dinged-up off-white. A large oak double-chest of drawers with a matching mirror that covered most of the wall was wedged in next to the door. About four dozen Mardi Gras-style beaded necklaces hung from either side of the mirror.

A smaller dresser, once painted olive drab now chipped and scratched, stood at the end of the queen-size bed. A flatscreen TV sat on top of the dresser and half-covered one of the two-bedroom windows. It all made for tight quarters, and I'd had to turn sideways just to squeeze around the end of her bed.

Six-foot mirrors on the bi-fold closet doors reflected our image as we lay in bed. Next to the closet, the clear imprint of a heavy-treaded boot, about ten sizes larger than Annie's demure little feet was stamped on the wall.

"Did you play a lot of sports in school?" I asked.

"No, not at all, I was a pretty geeky kid. About the only thing I played was the clarinet in the school band, and I didn't do that very well."

"Then where'd you get all the trophies? There must be a couple dozen up here, looks like you're into ballet or dance or something. What about all those medals and ribbons in the two cases on the wall? Are they from your school band?"

"All that junk belongs to Lydell."

"Lydell?"

"He was my boyfriend. Well, until I broke up with him."

"And he left all this stuff here?"

"Well, I only sent him the text last night."

"The text?" I asked and rolled over to face her.

"Yeah, telling him we were through. I really didn't feel like talking with him. He gets so dramatic, and he's kinda got a temper."

"You didn't tell him in person?" I was getting a warning sign flashing inside my thick skull.

"How could I, Dev? He's out of town," she said, suddenly sitting up and looking down on me.

"Out of town? You mean just across the river in Minneapolis or like way far away out of town?" I sat up to face her.

"Relax, he's in Chicago," she said, bouncing her surgically enhanced chest from side to side.

I completely forgot what I was going to ask next.

"He's such a big baby."

"Chicago?"

"Yeah, that stupid UFC."

"UFC . . . is that where he goes to school?"

"No, dopey," she said and pushed me down. She straddled me and began to lightly run her nails down my stomach, smiling in a leering way. "It's his crazy obsession, baby, that idiotic Ultimate Fight Club. God, I'm so sick of it. He trains all day long, lifting his big, dumb weights and drinking all those smelly old protein drinks. Five days a week, he spends at least an hour in a cage sparring with some other obsessed animal."

"Sparring in a cage?"

"Yeah, he—" Her iPhone rang at that moment, and she reached over to grab it off the top of the double chest of drawers. "Oh, God, can you believe it? Go figure!"

"What is it?" I asked.

"Hello, Lydell?"

I attempted to sit up, but she pushed me down again. "Shhh-hhh," she said, signaling with her index finger to be quiet.

"So, you got my text message?"

I could feel my heart beginning to pound, but then again, he was in Chicago.

"No, we've talked about all this before. No, I don't care. This time I really mean it."

I wasn't sure she should be sitting on top of me during this conversation.

"What?" she said. "You did? When?"

Whatever it was, Lydell had her attention. I was guessing a tattoo with 'Annie' emblazoned across his heart.

"No, Lydell, this time I'm not kidding," she said, sounding like she really wasn't.

I was thinking maybe some of the passion and romance in the air from just a moment ago was beginning to dissipate.

"Fine, go ahead! So what? Oh, really? Is that supposed to be a threat, Lydell?"

Oh-oh.

"I don't care if you are parked out front. Besides, this just isn't a very good time for me."

Out front?

"Well, you should have called me first."

Not what I wanted to hear.

"Don't you talk to me like that, and it's really none of your business."

Alarm bells were sounding in my head.

"Well, just go ahead and try. See if I care. Anyway, I had the locks changed."

Not good.

"Don't you dare! You kick that door in, and you're going to pay for it. I'm warning you, Mister."

I took that last line as my walking papers. I rolled out from underneath Annie just as a loud boom sounded downstairs.

"God, I just hate it when he goes crazy like this. He gets so worked up he's liable to do anything. You probably should leave, Dev," she said, then slid off the bed and tossed her phone onto the pillow.

I heard wood splintering in the door frame downstairs.

"Oh-oh, might be better if you just went out the window." She made it sound like it wasn't the first time someone had fled by that route

"Annie, damn it," a voice roared from downstairs.

"Better hurry," she half-whispered, then motioned me away with her hands before she peeked into the hallway.

I raised the window and stared into the wet night. God, it was at least a story and a half drop. There was some large bush spreading out right below the window. A light flashed on in the house next door, and I could see a little high school girl filling a glass of water at the kitchen sink.

"Annie, where the hell are you?" Lydell roared. It sounded like he was stomping through the dining room, making his way into the kitchen.

"You gonna be okay?" I asked.

"Don't worry. He does this every once-in-a-while. Soon as he sees me with my clothes off, he'll calm down and get all apologetic, but you better go," she whispered and nodded toward the open window.

"Annie," he screamed as he stomped back into the dining room.

I figured a 911 call wouldn't get the police here fast enough. What the hell, just a story and a half. I was out the window, hanging from the sill, dropping. Ouch! Snap, crackle, and pop! I landed on my feet and tried to do the crouch, tuck, and roll just like I'd learned in the Army, but I'd never done it naked before, and then there was that damn bush. I heard something break as I tumbled into the mud. Fortunately, it was a branch on the bush. I didn't care to contemplate a misplaced limb.

I'd barely landed when my jeans and T-shirt flew out the window. One of my shoes sailed out next. Then the other, hastily tossed, landed on the roof of the back porch next door.

The high-school girl at the kitchen sink stared at me wide-eyed as I picked up my T-shirt. She looked up toward the ceiling when my shoe thumped across her roof, but I really couldn't worry about that just now. I was more concerned about that Ultimate Fight Cluber, Lydell, flying out the window after me. I couldn't find my boxers and didn't have the luxury of time to search. I pulled my T-shirt on over the mud and scratches then quickly stepped into my jeans, zipping them up on the run.

I only had one shoe. Fortunately, my wallet and car keys were still in my jeans. I limped across the backyard and out to the alley so I could circle the block. The high school girl had moved from the kitchen window to her backdoor and watched me as I faded from view under the alley light.

Luckily, I had parked across the street and down a couple of doors. A bright red pick-up truck had skidded to a stop after barreling fifteen feet through the hedge into Annie's front yard. The thing had dual rear wheels and an Ultimate Fight Club bumper sticker that said 'Go Ahead - Take Your Best Shot.' The driver's door was still open with some country chorus blaring 'Death before Dishonor.' Pretty safe guess the vehicle belonged to recently returned Lydell.

As I drove past, I could see the back of a broad-shouldered muscular guy with a shaved head standing in Annie's front entry. His head looked like a shiny globe and appeared to be hanging in abject surrender on his muscle-bound body. He was nodding slightly, and it looked like he had already been reduced to the apologetic mode. I could just see Annie from the knees down, standing halfway up the stairs. Hopefully, she'd make him sleep on the floor against her ruined front door.

I drove home scratched, muddied, but still alive.

TWO

auley Kopff was a ninth-grade dropout, a doper, a failed petty criminal, and, in general, a lifelong disappointment to anyone who had the misfortune to come in contact with him. Even worse, he still owed me close to two hundred bucks for some investigative work I'd done at his behest a while back. Like all things where Pauley was involved, someone got stiffed. In this case, me. I figured two hundred bucks wasn't worth the trouble of dealing with Pauley again.

Unbeknownst to me, he was currently working at Karla's Karwash. Fortunately, I'd seen him first and had successfully hidden in a retail aisle amidst packages of naked-girl air-fresheners and devil's-head gearshift knobs until I had to step up to the register and pay for my carwash.

Pauley stood no more than five-foot-six if you included his ridiculous gel-spiked hair. He held the door as I walked outside to my car. He somehow seemed to always have a wiseass look pasted across his face, and I felt the immediate urge to hit him, hard.

"Thank you for getting cleaned up at Karla's, please … Hey, Dev Haskell, right? Is that really you? Didn't recognize you with all those scratches. Did someone change her mind?" he said, then laughed just a little too loudly. "Get it? Change her . . ."

There were too many witnesses around for what I had in mind, so I decided to ignore his comment.

"Hi there, Pauley. When did you get out?"

"Two months and twenty-six days ago. I only had to pull two years on a four-to-six. Good behavior," he bragged as if it was somehow an over-the-top lifetime accomplishment.

"Congratulations, Pauley. I hope things continue to work out for you," I said, still on the move, trying desperately to put more distance between us.

"Got another four days, six hours and thirty-nine minutes and I'm out of that half-way house. But, who's counting?" He chuckled after me.

I figured the folks at the half-way house were counting the seconds and crossing the days off their calendars. The entire staff probably had a party lined up to celebrate Pauley's imminent departure.

"Good for you. Sounds like things are getting back on track. Keep up the good work, Pauley," I said, all the while, hurrying toward my car. I slid behind the wheel and tried to pull the door closed.

A woman stepped between the car door and me. She had shoulder-length auburn hair pulled back in a ponytail. She pretended to wipe the doorframe dry then caught me trying to look down her T-shirt. There was a gold chain around her neck, but it had slipped inside her

T-shirt and gotten lost somewhere in that healthy cleavage, so I couldn't see what lucky medallion dangled on the end.

She stared up at me with brown eyes before she whispered, "I could really use your help, Mr. Haskell."

"Do I know you?"

She visibly blushed, then glanced around quickly to see if anyone else was listening.

"No." She shook her head. "But Karla told me about you. She's a friend of mine. I heard Pauley say your name. Will you give me a call, please? Promise?" She handed me a card that advertised a dollar off my next carwash. Her name and number were hastily penned across the back.

"Gee a dollar off…how can I refuse?"

"Promise?"

"You're Desi?" I asked, reading the name scrawled across the back of the card.

A car honked behind me. Pauley was behind the wheel, slowly rolling forward with the driver's door open. He sprayed glass cleaner on the inside of the windshield then honked the horn again.

"I'm finished here at three," she said softly, then stepped away and closed my door.

"I'll give you a call," I said, nodded and checked her out in my sideview mirror as I drove off.

I left a message on Desi's phone around dinner time.

I'd fallen asleep later that night on the couch watching the Twins lose. I had no idea what time it was or who was on the other end of the phone when it rang.

"Hi, Mr. Haskell, I hope I'm not calling too late," the voice said after my hello.

"No, not a problem. I was just going over some paperwork here. How are things on your end?" I asked, fishing for some clue, trying to determine who in the hell I was talking to.

"Fine, I guess, as long as you don't go into any real detail."

"Okay, I won't. What else is cooking?"

"Well, Mr. Haskell I…"

"Please call me Dev, okay?"

"Okay, Dev. Look, I wondered if we could get together and talk about my, ahhh situation. Karla said you were pretty good."

Got it, Desi from the car wash.

"Pretty good? That covers a lot of sins." I chuckled.

"I'd like to meet so I could maybe get your opinion," she said, ignoring my attempt at humor then added, "Some public place." Apparently, Karla had told her about me, and she was playing it safe.

Today was the seventh or eighth, and other than Jameson night next Thursday at The Spot bar, I had an open calendar for the rest of the month, so I asked, "What's your week look like?"

"I'm working from noon till seven at night for Karla, and I picked up a bartending gig at Nasty's on the weekend, nine 'til close. Other than that, I'm pretty much free."

"You know Nina's?"

"That coffee place?"

"Yeah. Right, I could make some calls and reschedule things to meet you, say tomorrow morning? Does that work?"

"You sure? I mean, I don't want to cause any problems. I'm guessing you're really busy."

"I think I can move some things around. Let me get to a couple of people. I don't anticipate any difficulty. I'll see you at Nina's, nine-thirty tomorrow morning."

"Thank you, Mr., I mean, Dev. I'll see you there."

Three

I walked into Nina's ten minutes early. Desi was already seated at a far table and gave me a wave. Her auburn hair was like a flashing beacon in a sea of 'not-quite-awake' folks surgically attached to their coffee. As I approached, seeing her away from the noise and blur of the car wash, I noticed she had a figure that garnered a double-take.

"Hey, I guess the early bird gets the worm. Been here long?"

"Only a minute or two. I just sat down," she said.

If she'd just sat down, she must have drunk her large coffee standing up. Her mug was empty. She was dressed in blue jeans and a v-neck T-shirt. The T-shirt had sharply creased sleeves and looked to have been ironed. A Claddagh dangled from the gold chain around her lovely neck; hands holding a heart with a crown, the Irish symbol for friendship, love and loyalty.

"I'm gonna get a coffee. You want another or something to eat? I was actually thinking of ordering some breakfast."

"A coffee would be great. Just black, nothing else for me," she said.

There was something in her look. I'd been in these situations before and maybe picked up on her starving eyes. If we were dating, she would have wanted just 'one little bite' of my dessert then inhaled the entire thing. I got two coffees, ordered two omelets and a caramel roll.

"Thanks for the coffee," she said as I sat down. "Wow, that looks really good." She nodded toward my caramel roll.

Oh-oh.

"I hope you don't mind. I took the liberty of ordering you an omelet. I didn't want to be my usually piggy self and eat in front of you. Here, you gotta try half of this. They're really good," I said, cutting the caramel roll in half.

"Oh, no, I really couldn't," she said at the same time she grabbed the larger half.

"Go ahead . . . the omelets should be out in just a couple of minutes."

"You sure you don't mind?" she said, then crammed a good portion of the caramel roll into her mouth, not waiting for my answer.

"So, you mentioned a situation. How can I help?"

Desi quickly chewed, then swallowed and glanced longingly at her remaining portion before looking up at me.

"Well, see, I didn't always wash cars and tend bar at a strip joint."

I shook my head and gave a little shrug suggesting it wasn't important where she worked or what she did.

"No, really, I was somebody. I went to school and even made the Dean's List in grad school. I was an architect here in town. I was making something of myself."

"An architect?" I didn't mean to sound so surprised.

"Yeah." She nodded then shoved the rest of the caramel roll into her mouth.

"Why aren't you working as an architect now?"

"Have you read the papers? You remember that little thing called the great recession? No one was building anything for about five years, let alone looking for someone to do design work."

"So, you went from being an architect to washing cars?" That sounded pretty drastic, and I wasn't quite following.

"Not quite that direct a route, but then that's what I wanted to talk to you about. Karla said you were someone who would understand."

"You two friends?"

"We were friends in high school but drifted apart when I went off to college and then grad school. We were out of touch for years, then when I hit rock bottom, Karla was one of the few who didn't turn their back on me."

Two large omelets arrived. Desi held back from immediately stuffing hers into her mouth. "God, this looks absolutely fabulous, but I'll never be able to finish it all," she said.

"Well, do your best. They're even better than they look. Dig in. So you were telling me about learning the car wash business from the ground floor up."

She smiled a sad smile, shoveled a forkful of omelet into her mouth and chewed for a moment.

"I graduated from Clemson and got hired by a firm in town, Touchier and Touchier."

I nodded, pretending I was familiar with the firm.

"You know them? Most people don't, but then again, I suppose in your line of work you would."

"Give me the short version," I said.

"Well, as you know, we were into the security thing, financial institutions, a couple of high-security detention facilities, the occasional federal building."

I nodded knowingly, not having the slightest idea what she was talking about.

"Anyway, that's where I met Gas. He was one of the senior partners."

"Gas?"

"Gaston Driscoll," she said off-handedly like the name needed no explanation.

"That rings a bell, but I can't tell you why."

"Probably because I was charged, tried and convicted, and that bastard got off without so much as a slap on the wrist."

I suddenly got it. "Does this have something to do with the security system at the Federal Reserve Bank?"

"That was part of it, along with the security system at the Federal facility down in Rochester."

"Minnesota?"

She nodded and shoveled another bite of omelet into her mouth.

"Oh, yeah, there was an escape or something. That sound right?" I said.

She nodded, followed with another forkful, then said, "Yeah, literally a genius. The media called him Little Jimmy Fennell. He was some kind of savant, only about four-foot-three. I don't know what the politically correct term is, height-challenged, or something. Anyway, he'd been transferred to the Federal Medical Center in Rochester for health reasons."

She stuffed another forkful of omelet, chewed a moment, thinking and then swallowed.

"I could say he escaped. Actually, that's the official story, but the truth is he just walked away from the Federal Medical Center one day. No one thought him capable of ever getting out of his wheel chair. Apparently, he'd been successfully fooling everyone for a couple months. Then one day, he just got up and walked out the door wearing an orange jumpsuit. I guess there was a car waiting for him."

It was ringing a bell. The story was like something out of a bad movie.

"Yeah, I remember this. Someone ends up with the security plans to the Federal Reserve Bank, right? They bypass security with that Little Jimmy guy's help, make a big haul, but didn't something strange happen to this Little Jimmy character?"

"Yeah, he's found on the top steps of the Cathedral, prostrate and dead. It was around the time of that book, The Da Vinci Code, and people went crazy thinking there was some message because of the way he was laid out. I think in reality, he was just a guy who'd eaten one too many White Castle's and happened to be walking past the Cathedral when he suffered a major heart attack."

"But the money was never recovered, and it was a lot of money," I said, remembering.

"Millions," Desi said, then scraped up the last bit of omelet from her plate and looked longingly at the remaining portion of my caramel roll.

"Go for it," I nodded.

"Thanks," she said, quickly stuffing it into her mouth. "Anyway, right. In fact, if not for his association with bank security systems, there was a good chance no one would have even linked Little Jimmy to the robbery."

"But didn't they find money on him?"

"Yeah, nine crisp one hundred dollar bills with consecutive serial numbers. Poor little fool had them hidden in his sock. They suspect he probably passed one at the White Castle, but they never found it."

"And your involvement? How did you know this guy?"

"I didn't know him at all. I just read about him in the paper. My involvement? I can sum it up in two words, Gaston Driscoll. We had a little thing going, at least, that's what I thought. Turned out, he was just using me as a delivery girl. Well, and his mistress."

"Was this a one-time get-together over too many drinks, or was it more of a relationship?"

"It was a relationship, definitely a relationship," she said, then seemed to reconsider. "At least, that's what I thought at the time."

I was treading carefully. More than one guy I knew didn't realize he was in a relationship after an alcohol-fueled wrestling match in the backseat of a car.

"How long did the relationship last?"

"Until the day he had me fired. He had me escorted out of the building by a woman from HR who seemed to be about as thrilled with the situation as I was. Jesus, we were both in shock and tears."

I just nodded.

"Gas and I had been together for maybe ten months if that's your question. He told me he was making plans to divorce his wife. He told me he'd been trapped in a loveless marriage for years, and I was like an open window that let the sunshine in. Of course, I wasn't adding two and two. Jesus, they still lived together. They were actually on vacation in Florida when he had me fired."

"Did he ever try to contact you?"

"Since the day he had me fired, I haven't heard so much as a peep from that creep."

"Can you prove any of this?"

"The mistress part?" she asked and then brushed a strand of hair off her pretty face. "You mean, do I have love letters or the home videos he took of us making love? A book of photos from our beach trip? No. He bought me gifts, lingerie, a lot of lingerie. He gave me a set of pearls one time. He surprised me with diamond earrings on Valentine's Day. He promised to take me to Ireland, where my grandparents were from. But no, nothing I can document."

I nodded and continued to listen. Desi was looking at me, but I didn't think she could see me. She was remembering candlelight dinners and that crazy, wonderful head-over-heels infatuation that came with falling in love. The fact that you just couldn't believe your incredible good fortune at finding the world's most wonderfully perfect partner, that was usually just before everything went to hell in a hand-basket.

"Funny, my grandparents came from a little village in County Sligo, Ireland. Turns out his family came from the same area, in fact, he owns a house over there. Well, at least that's what he told me. He pointed it out to me on the map one time. Course, stupid gullible old me, I thought it might be some celestial sign like we were made for one another." She was looking through me seeing something else, something not actually there. Her lips formed a slight smile, yet somehow she looked sad. Then she blinked and seemed to come back to the here and now.

"When the bank foreclosed on my home, I still had his favorite wines laid out in my pantry. The CDs he liked were still in my living room. Oh, and a giant jar of chocolate topping was in the drawer next to my bed," she said but didn't elaborate.

"The map of Ireland was spread out on the dining room table with my grandparent's village circled and a red heart I'd drawn around the town his family came from. He told me we were going to travel there once his divorce was final, not that he ever filed for divorce. It was going to be just the two of us loving it up in Ireland for a couple of weeks. Maybe we'd begin to decorate the house he owned. You know, make it our own little private vacation spot. Jesus Christ, sorry." She sniffled then blinked back her tears.

"Anything you can document?" I asked, moving on.

"He's got a tattoo of the Ace of Spades on his ass. I used to think that was really cute."

"He's a poker player?"

"Not really. It was from when he was in Vietnam. I guess they used to leave an Ace of Spades on enemy bodies. At least that's what he told me. Anyway, that's about the only private info I have on him. He's got a white scar on his chin…shrapnel he said, except he lied about everything else, so I can't be sure. I didn't realize it at the time, but he was pretty cautious. I've come to understand I probably wasn't his first love scam and certainly not his last. I was the latest stupid head-in-the-clouds girl falling for a rich, sexy older guy. I just think I'm the only one who ended up going to jail because of it."

She said this very matter of fact, with no emotion, like she'd had plenty of time to think about it. Time served, I guessed.

"And you mentioned you were the delivery girl?"

"In layman's terms, the plans for secure federal facilities are kept under lock and key. Gas basically prepped me so I could override the firm's security using his access code, copy the plans, deliver them to his contact…oh, and then take the fall. I lost my job, my home, everything I'd ever worked for. I was charged, tried, convicted, and did six years of a ten-year sentence in a woman's facility. I've got nine years and two months left to go on probation."

"Nine years and two months," I said, doing the math and thinking that rounded up to an even decade.

Desi nodded. "Nine years of going in once a month and peeing in a cup. Nine years of reporting every month to a probation officer. Nine years of idiotic interviews and stupid questions about why I'm washing cars and tending bar in a strip club. You tell me, Dev. Would you hire an ex-con to help design your hundred-million-dollar secure facility?"

"So, what would you like me to do?"

"I suppose I couldn't ask you to kill him." She laughed, but I had the sense she was only half kidding. "I want you to get the goods on Gaston Driscoll. I want him to be charged. I want him to go down like I did. That creep laughed all the way to the Federal Reserve Bank, or from it. He set me up, and I want him to feel what I have to feel, lose what I've lost. He took everything from me, Dev. My folks died thinking I was a criminal. I've lost everything," she spat out this last bit in a harsh whisper, verging on tears that caused a couple of nearby heads to turn. Her eyes had watered again, and she attempted to blink them clear.

"You want revenge," I said.

"You're damn right, I want revenge," she hissed the words out.

"Desi, you seem like a nice woman. But I'm not in the revenge business. Besides, just looking at it from my end, it's quite possible I could spend a lot of time and energy on this and not come up with a damn thing. You could be talking thousands here, tens of thousands of dollars in fees, and absolutely nothing to show for it."

She glanced around to make sure she wouldn't be overheard then softly whispered, "Karla mentioned you might be amenable to me working off the debt," she said, and gave a little shrug.

I immediately thought, 'Thanks for keeping our secret, Karla.'

"Look, Desi, not that I don't find you attractive. You're very attractive as a matter of fact. But like I said, I think an investigation of this sort could go on for quite some time. And to be—"

"I don't care how long it would take. And I could figure something out to get you the money if that's the problem," she interrupted.

"Actually, it's not the money. To be honest, this is out of my league. If you need to find out if this Driscoll guy is stealing cars, into insurance fraud, or taking bets on the Super Bowl, I'm maybe your guy. But the level you're suggesting, I don't really swim in those waters."

"But if you don't take this, there's really no one else I can ask. You were my last shot. I don't know, but I just have a feeling."

"A feeling?"

"Relax, it's nothing," she said, shaking her head while pushing back her chair. "I'm sorry to take up your time. Look, what do I owe you for breakfast?" she said, reaching for her purse.

"How about you work it off sometime?" I joked.

She looked up at me and stared for a long moment. "Actually, I would have liked that. Well, thanks for listening." She stood up, draped her purse over her shoulder and put her hand out to shake. "I better get to work. A lot of people probably need their cars washed. Thanks for listening, Dev."

I shook her hand, then watched her walk out the door and disappear around the corner.

Four

As per almost always, I beat Louie into the office. He washed up on shore a little after the noon hour.

"Late night?" I asked.

"No, midmorning court date. I had to plead two DUI's."

"You got nailed twice?"

"Gimme some credit," he said, tossing his computer case on his picnic table desk. "Clients. Seems the grapevine is finally starting to work, and I'm becoming the go-to-guy for driving-under-the-influence charges in town."

"You get them off?"

"You kidding? Maybe in another lifetime, fifteen, twenty years ago, but that ain't happening nowadays."

No need to comment. I knew exactly what he was saying.

"You working on anything?" Louie asked, already knowing the answer.

I had been waiting and looking out the window, hoping some good-looking woman would stand at one of the bus stops, so I could check her out. I'd drawn a blank for over an hour. Just then, a woman crossed the street and waited on the corner. She looked to be maybe late thirties, early forties. I'd seen her before and put the binoculars up to continue my research as I spoke.

"Actually, I turned a case down this morning. A big one," I said.

"Turned it down?" Louie asked. He'd just poured himself a coffee and was seated with his feet up on the picnic table. His first sip dribbled coffee down his white shirt and across his tie.

"God damn, that's hot. How long has that pot been brewing?"

"What? Oh, now that you mention it, ummm, I guess since yesterday. I was in a breakfast meeting, so I didn't make any this morning. Unless you came in earlier?"

"Yesterday?"

"I guess." The bus pulled up, and the woman climbed on. Not bad, not bad at all. I lowered the binoculars and looked at Louie.

"So you turned down a case?" he said.

"Yeah, I still feel kind of bad about it. Nice girl, but it just wasn't my gig."

"Insurance?"

"No. You remember that guy they found dead on the steps of the Cathedral a couple years back?"

"If it's the one I'm thinking of, it was more than a couple of years, and he was some escaped savant with cash on him from the Fed or something."

"Yeah, that's the deal."

"Hadn't he escaped from where, Rochester?" Louie attempted another sip of coffee.

"Yeah, Federal Medical Facility. Actually, I think he just walked away when no one was watching."

"So, who and what?"

"There was a young woman architect who got nailed stealing security plans for the Federal Reserve from her firm and apparently passing them on to the bad guys."

"I kinda remember," Louie said.

"That's who I met. She claims she was railroaded and wants to nail the guy who did it. She'll never be able to work as an architect again. I mean, Christ, she's washing cars at Karla's and bartending at Nasty's, if that gives you any indication."

Louie nodded.

"Anyway, she wants to nail a guy. Apparently, she was in a relationship with him, and she maintains he set her up. After thinking about it for fifteen or twenty seconds, I turned her down."

"Because?"

"Because even if she's correct in her assumption, it's going to take a lot of time and energy to be able to prove anything."

"And you're obviously very busy," Louie said.

I was back to staring through my binoculars, studying a woman pushing a stroller with two little kids in it."

"Yeah, well, that and the fact she didn't have any money."

"I never realized you were that mercenary."

"I'm not. I just got a negative vibe on the whole deal, to tell you the truth."

"Negative vibe," Louie said, shaking his head.

"I'm not taking her case, man. I don't need that kind of trouble. Whatever it is, I don't need it."

"Probably the wise move."

"No, there's no probably about it. It was definitely the wise move."

Five

A couple of days later, I got a call from Karla.

"Haskell Investigations."

"Hi, Dev, Karla."

"Karla, been a long time, lady. What can I do for you?"

"Did you ever meet with that employee of mine, Desi Quinn?"

"Quinn, is that her last name? I guess in the course of our conversation, it never really came up."

"So, you did meet with her?"

"Yeah, didn't she mention it?"

"Actually, I haven't seen her for the past few days. She never misses work, so I let the first day go. Yesterday I was really worried and called her a couple of times, but never got an answer. I'm tempted to call the cops, but she's been such a sweetheart I don't want to get her in trouble with her parole agent. I'm not sure what to do."

"Has this ever happened before?" I asked, not liking the sound of it.

"No, she's been a model employee. I'd have her doing something else if I had the opening. I mean, with her education and she's washing cars alongside my collection of deadbeats, not that she ever complained. Anyway, she didn't say anything to you?"

"No, she explained what she wanted me to do, and basically, I turned her down."

"Turned her down? Why? She's so sweet."

"No doubt, but as I explained to her, I could spend a lot of time and energy, not to mention her money, and still come up with nothing. I couldn't begin to guess what the bill might run, and I just figured she was better off dropping the whole thing now, rather than ten grand down the road."

"She was willing to work it off."

"Come on, Karla, it's one thing when we're dealing with an employee of yours doing a workers comp scam. Desi's deal was in a whole different league. Not a reflection on her, by the way."

"God, I don't know. I really hate to call the police. I don't want to get her in any kind of trouble," she said, then just let that last statement hang out there.

I waited what seemed like an exceptionally long time, hoping Karla would blink first. She didn't.

"Look, you want me to check on her?"

"God, would you mind? Are you doing something right now? I mean, maybe I should just drive over to her place and see?"

"Karla—"

"I don't know. I'm kind of nervous going over by myself. I suppose I could get my sister or my mom, one of them to come—"

"Karla. I'll go over to her place and check it out. Give me her address. I'll call you back if I find anything. No, wait, better yet, I'll call you back either way."

"Thanks, Dev. I owe you. Maybe I'll have to work it off, you know?"

"Yeah, by the way, thanks for mentioning our little secret to Desi. You tell anyone else?"

"Maybe just a few dozen of my closest friends," she said.

"What?"

"Somehow, I didn't think you'd mind that kind of advertising."

I hung up with Karla and drove over to Desi's address. She lived in a nondescript apartment building that looked like it had been built about 1960. It was a three-story structure with long thin bricks and large square picture windows. It was probably very trendy in the middle of the last century, but like the surrounding postwar neighborhood, it had clearly fallen on hard times.

The house next door was vacant and had been boarded up. Red and blue city inspection notices were posted on the grey sheet of plywood covering the front door. Two phone books sat on the front stoop. Yellow and weathered, they looked to have been there for months.

In today's world of triple deadbolt locks, security systems, and passwords needing upper and lower case letters plus at least a four-digit number, Desi's building was a rarity. There was no security, absolutely none. I pulled the front door open and just walked in.

The hallways needed airing. On second thought, they needed a lot more than that. There was graffiti either spray painted or scribbled with a large marker all over the stairwell. It was almost illegible and looked to resemble some form of Arabic. I hated that. What appeared to be a torn mattress was leaning against a wall down at the far end of the hallway. I could hear a rheumy cough rattling from somewhere behind a closed door.

Desi's unit was 204. As I climbed the stairs, I grabbed the wrought iron banister. The thing wobbled in my hand and felt like it could break loose at almost any moment. I made a mental note not to slide down the thing on the way out. I could say the stairway carpet was worn, but that would be an understatement suggesting there was actually a semblance of carpeting left. What remained was grimy, threadbare, and could probably serve as a Petri dish at the Center for Disease Control.

There was a baby crying in one of the second-floor units, and either someone had the television on too loud, or a domestic was heating up in another unit. There were two overflowing white trash bags next to one of the apartment doors, the smell of garbage suggested they needed to be taken out yesterday or the day before.

Desi's door was the second one on the right. Slightly off-center adhesive numbers identified the unit, although the '2' had been partially torn off. An area the size of a dinner plate around the doorknob was coated from a half-century of grimy hands rubbing against it. There were a number of scuffs and two large boot prints on the lower half of the door. I momentarily thought back to the night Lydell made his memorable entrance at Annie's by kicking in her front door.

I placed my ear to the door, but couldn't hear anything. I knocked, waited, then knocked again. Still no response. I turned the knob, and the door pushed open. This was definitely not the sort of building where I would choose to leave my door unlocked.

"Desi? Desi, it's Dev Haskell," I called out.

She didn't answer back, but I knew she was there. I'd smelled death before. I was suddenly aware of the flies, lots of flies, and the sound of buzzing. I had a momentary flashback to a hut we'd opened up in Iraq where we found a family. I would have given anything right now to have an M-16, and a-half dozen guys backing me up. As it was, all I had was my phone, so I made the call.

Six

Aaron LaZelle asked me again, "Tell me again, how was it you were here?"

He was a lieutenant in homicide and a long-time pal. We'd known one another since kindergarten, played hockey together, got dumped by some of the same girls. He'd pulled my feet from the fire more than once, and I could only hope I'd done the same for him on occasion. We were standing in the parking lot next to the overflowing dumpster outside Desi's building. It was warm in the sun, and in between the noise from passing buses and trucks, you were able to catch the odd bird chirping.

"Like I said, her employer called me. Said she was worried because Desi hadn't been at work for a few days. She didn't get an answer when she called and asked me to stop by and check on her."

"You knew her, the deceased?"

"Desi Quinn? Not really. I met with her the other morning for breakfast. She wanted me to look at her case, the circumstances of her conviction. I took a pass. It was out of my area, plus I told her it would cost a hell of a lot, and frankly, I didn't think she had the money."

"So you told her 'no.'"

"Yeah. Actually, I told her she sounded like she was looking for revenge, and maybe she should just move on or something like that."

Aaron nodded and sipped from a Starbucks cup.

"You giving sensible advice, when the hell did that start?"

I ignored his comment. "There is one thing. She said something like she had a feeling."

"A feeling?" Aaron said. "Like what? Was she being watched or followed? Someone threatened her?"

"She didn't elaborate. Just said she had a feeling, and then I told her I wouldn't help, and she walked out, said she had to get to work. Oh, yeah, and she said I was her last shot."

The unlocked front door to the building swung open, and a gurney with a black rubber body bag strapped to it was rolled out by two medical examiners dressed in navy blue trousers and short-sleeved white shirts. One of the guys headed our way and nodded at Aaron when he got closer.

"How's it going, LT?" he said, then handed a clipboard to Aaron.

"Good, Doc, any conclusions?" Aaron asked as he scribbled his name across a line at the bottom of the form and handed the clipboard back.

"Looks to be a small caliber. If I had to guess, I'd say maybe .22 short or a .25. Whoever it was, they wanted to make sure. One to the side of her head and another beneath her chin. We'll have a little more definitive information once we autopsy."

Aaron gave a slight nod.

"Just guessing here, and you can check the pictures your guys took, but the way she was on the bed, it doesn't seem to be a forced thing. No real abrasions on her wrists or ankles that we saw. No outward indications of a struggle. Like I said, I'll be able to give you more detail tomorrow after the autopsy work up."

"Hazard a guess?" Aaron asked.

"Good chance she probably knew whoever it was. Maybe they pulled the gun on her and made her lie down. Small caliber, so it could have been a novice, or it was just small by design, keep the noise down. I don't know. That's your job. See you tomorrow. I'll email you on the time. We're sorta light right now, so unless something awful happens tonight, we're probably looking at a morning exam." He gave a nod then caught up with his partner standing next to the gurney.

They shoved the gurney onto a track and rolled Desi into the back of the M.E. wagon, slammed the door closed, climbed in, and drove off.

The building door flew open again, and Detective Norris Manning came out. As he walked toward us, he puffed out his cheeks as he exhaled, then began to peel off one of his latex gloves. He shook his bald, pink head as he approached and kept his eyes focused on Aaron.

"Haskell." He nodded after he came to a stop then snapped a piece of gum between his teeth like he was preparing to bite me. "Other than the body, we're not coming up with much. They should be finished there in another hour, hour and a half."

"You knew the deceased?" He turned toward me, and his eyes seemed to suddenly morph into blue lasers.

"Not really. Like I told Lieutenant LaZelle, I met her the other day for breakfast to talk about a case, but I really didn't know her. I was checking on her for her employer."

"I'll fill you in," Aaron said, taking me off the hook. I was already tired of repeating the story, and I'd only told it to Aaron.

"She worked at Karla's Karwash," Manning said.

"Yeah, and she said she'd picked up a weekend gig bartending at Nasty's," I added.

"So between those two places, if we take all the characters she'd meet on any given workday, we'll have more than enough suspects," Manning said.

I shrugged and noticed Manning's mustache was glistening. It dawned on me it was from the Vicks Vapo-Rub he'd applied under his nose in an attempt to mask the smell of death in Desi's apartment.

"Like I said, I'll fill you in," Aaron said, then turned to me. "You call Karla with the news?"

I shook my head. "Not yet."

"I think we're going over there in a bit. You want to give her a call, now would be the time."

"Yeah, about Karla . . . listen, do you guys have any problem with me going over there in person? I don't like the idea of telling her on the phone. Obviously, she was concerned," I said.

Aaron shook his head and looked at Manning. Manning snapped off the remaining latex glove and gave a slight shake of his head.

"Shouldn't take more than a few minutes, but I just think it would be better if I did it this way. I think Karla genuinely wanted to help this woman."

"Sure, we've got some things to tie up here before we go over. Maybe ask her to have employment records available so we can take a look once we get there."

I nodded.

"You think of anything else?" he asked Manning.

Manning shook his head, then looked at me and attacked his piece of gum. "Sorry, Haskell, hopefully, we'll find whoever is responsible and soon."

I nodded, but thought they didn't seem the least bit optimistic.

Seven

The drive to Karla's Karwash went way too fast. I seemed to be there in just a few minutes. I sat behind the wheel and tried to think long and hard about how I was going to present this, but I couldn't seem to come up with any good answers. After a while, I climbed out of the car, took a deep breath, and forced myself to go inside.

Karla's office was through a white-enameled door labeled 'OFFICE' in blue letters, then up a flight of stairs to the second floor. I stepped into a carpeted reception area complete, with a smiling grey-haired receptionist.

"May I help you, sir?" She smiled coldly and flashed some overly large teeth.

"Karla, please."

"Do you have an appointment, sir?" The 'sir' was more or less tacked on there as an afterthought. I guessed in my sandals, shorts and T-shirt she figured me for just another lowlife looking for a job washing cars.

"She asked me to stop by," I said, not really paying attention, still concentrating on how I was going to break the news.

"She's involved in a meeting just now." This time she left off the 'sir'.

"Could you phone her or send in a note? It's pretty important."

"I really can't leave the desk here. Maybe if I took your name and, sir, sir!"

I was halfway down the hall, glancing into offices along the way. There was a fat guy in a golf shirt sitting behind a couple of computer screens in one of the offices. He looked up as I drifted into his doorway.

"I'm looking for Karla."

"Think she's in the conference room, end of the hall." He indicated my route with a nod of his head.

"Thanks." I nodded back and made my way toward the far end of the hall.

The conference room had floor-to-ceiling glass panels with beige curtains that facing me. She was talking to a half dozen people seated around the table. She looked up and spotted me in mid-sentence. I motioned to her with my hand, and she nodded, excused herself, and walked out into the hallway.

"Dev?"

"Can we go to your office, Karla?"

"Oh, dear . . . it's not good, is it?"

I shrugged. How do you tell someone nicely that their friend had been found in bed shot twice in the head?

Whatever the people still sitting in the conference room had been discussing was put aside, and they had all turned to look at us.

"Is she going to be okay, Dev?"

I started to speak, but suddenly choked up and all I could do was stand there, shake my head and then I started to cry.

"Oh God! No, no! Please, not her, not Desi!"

"I'm— I'm sorry, Karla."

"No, no," she said quietly and then wrapped her left arm across her chest and covered her face with her right hand. Her shoulders began to shake, and she started to sob.

I didn't know what to do, so I took a step forward, wrapped my arms around her, and held her. She seemed to melt into me, shuddered, and sobbed quietly for a short moment, then suddenly pushed away.

"Oh, dear, dear. Poor Desi. God damn it! Here, come on into my office, I need a Kleenex. Jesus Christ!"

I followed her into her office. It was large enough to house her desk, three chairs in front of the desk, a file cabinet, and not much more. The Kleenex box was on the edge of her desk. She pulled out a fist full, handed one to me then blew her nose.

"What the hell happened?" she asked, stepping behind the desk and settling into her office chair.

I told her what little I knew. I mentioned that Aaron and Manning were going to be here shortly and would want to see Desi's employment records.

"Murdered? Shot? Twice?" she said a few moments later.

I nodded.

"God damn it. Did you pick up on any of this when you met with her? Did she say she was in any danger? Was she frightened? Did she—"

"No, Karla, nothing. She wanted me to find something on this Gaston Driscoll guy, but—"

"That bastard! He ruined that girl's life, and now he's killed her."

"Well, we don't know—"

"He's involved, Dev. Believe me."

"I'm not trying to be difficult, Karla. But if he's involved, Aaron LaZelle and Detective Manning will nail him. They're good."

She shook her head. "They won't be able to touch him."

"They're good. I've been on both sides with them. Believe me, they don't miss much."

Karla just shook her head. "Jesus Christ, murdered. The poor thing. Oh, Desi . . . " she said and then just let that drift off.

"They should be here shortly. When you talk to them, let them know your concerns. Any information you can give them can only help."

Karla just looked at me and shook her head like she didn't believe me. "I'm sure they're good, Dev. But people like Driscoll get to play by a different set of rules than you and I have to follow." She bit her lower lip and seemed to be thinking.

"They'll get whoever did this, Karla. I'm pretty sure," I said, but suddenly I didn't seem to sound too convincing.

Karla shook her head, then pulled open a desk drawer and said, "No, I want you on this. I want you to nail that bastard, Driscoll."

"Karla, this is way out of my league. I deal in cheating spouses, fake insurance claims, or the occasional dog-napping. This is a murder, and we don't even know if Driscoll was involved. Let's just let the police handle it."

"You owe it to Desi, and you're going to owe it to me," she said, pulling out a checkbook and beginning to write.

"Karla, that's really kind. But don't you think it would be better not to screw up the police and their—"

"I haven't got the time or the inclination. Besides, it's just become very personal for me. Here," she said, reaching across her desk to hand me the check.

"Karla, come on, five grand? Think for a minute. This is a hell of a lot of money."

"Then you had better get to work. I'll expect an accounting of your expenses. Keep me up to date at least a couple of times a week."

"Karla? I really can't—"

"I don't want to hear it, Dev. Get on it and nail this bastard. Now get your ass out of my office before the cops show up."

Eight

Louie took another sip of Jameson and threw his dart. He missed the board by a good foot. The dart lodged in the oak trim around the office window with a loud crack. "Help me out here."

The late afternoon heat in the office had left the two of us drowsy. Or was that from the Jameson? It didn't really matter. Louie had opened the window a half-hour ago, but I thought it only served to increase the room temperature and add a heavy dose of bus exhaust to the immediate atmosphere.

"I think you should stop trying to multitask and either drink whiskey or throw darts. Together it just doesn't seem like it's the best combination," I said, then pulled Louie's dart out of the woodwork.

He nodded in agreement, dropped the remaining three darts onto his picnic table, then refilled his glass from the Jameson bottle. He took a sip, settled back into his office chair, put his feet up on the picnic table, and proceeded to pontificate.

"Now, help me out here. This Karla woman writes you a check for five grand, and suggests there's more where that came from, should you need it. So, tell me, exactly why this isn't a good thing?"

"It's not the money."

"Problem number one," Louie said and sipped.

"The investigation Desi wanted me to do may have nothing to do with her murder."

"You really believe that?" Louie said and sipped again.

"Maybe. What I do know is that if what Desi told me is true, and I stress the word *if*, then this Gaston Driscoll guy is far too clever to march over to her apartment and shoot her twice."

"But what if he was behind it? What if he felt she was going to find something out, and he just sent someone, paid someone to make the hit?"

"Yeah, but where do you find a good hitman when you need him?"

"I don't think it's that far fetched, buddy." Louie drained his glass and looked longingly to the Jameson bottle resting on the far end of the picnic table.

"Make you another?" I asked.

"No, you don't have to," he said, pushing the empty glass in my direction and getting a little more comfortable in his chair. "It just strikes me as a major coincidence that this woman meets with you, tells you her tale, tells you she has a feeling, and she's found dead a couple of days later."

"The problem with all that is I didn't talk to anyone about our meeting. Well, except for Karla, but that was this morning, three days after the fact. Karla didn't even know I'd met with Desi, so she didn't tell anyone. That just leaves Desi. I can't believe she went around town boasting I didn't take her case."

"Possibly," Louie said, then gave me the nod as I handed him another drink. "Thanks."

"Possibly? Now you're on even thinner ice. You think that after Desi met with me over the course of the next couple days, she ran around telling people I wasn't going to take her case? No doubt she talked to every one of the guys she washed cars with, and then she mentioned it to all the customers at Nasty's since they decided they wanted to go to a strip joint and talk to the bartender more than they wanted to watch all the strippers. Come on, man, that can't be what went down."

"Not exactly," Louie said.

"You think? Then according to your theory, one of these losers has a direct link to Gaston Driscoll and calls him. Gaston gives his hit man a ring and sends the guy to Desi's. She likes the look of this hitman. So she suggests, wouldn't it be a good idea if she got all comfortable on the bed before he blows her brains out? That about it?"

"Are you through?"

"You tell me?" I asked.

"Oh man, and I'm the one drinking," Louie said, shaking his head.

"Yeah, I know."

"Look, Dev, what if someone knew she was going to talk to you or maybe just knew she wanted to pursue an investigation? Maybe that was enough to set things in motion, and it was merely a coincidence that she spoke with you. I mean, you said she told you she had a feeling. What caused that? Did she get a phone call or maybe a note? Was some idiot following her?"

"I don't know."

"And you may never know. I'm just saying it might be interesting to check into it. And, well, as long as you got that five grand sitting in your back pocket, maybe it could be worth your while, too."

"I suppose it couldn't hurt to at least Google the news articles. See what happened seven years ago."

"While you're Googling, maybe you could make me a refill," Louie said and drained his glass.

Nine

I had a legal pad next to my laptop and was making notes as I read a number of articles. I began with the discovery of the robbery at the Ninth District Federal Reserve Bank over in Minneapolis. That led to articles on the elaborate security measures which led to the architectural firm Touchier and Touchier, which led to the death of Little Jimmy Fennell prostrate on the steps of the St. Paul Cathedral. When Little Jimmy died, he had nine consecutively numbered one hundred dollar bills stuffed in the athletic sock on his right foot. That, in turn, somehow led to Desi and her purported stealing of the security plans.

One of the first things that struck me was that it seemed amazing there wasn't the slightest mention of Desi's purported lover, senior partner Gaston Driscoll. Well, except for his one comment.

"We at Touchier and Touchier do our very best to vet and run substantial security checks on all our employees. Despite our best efforts, as well as those of the Federal government, it would seem an individual such as Miss Quinn, who apparently lacked basic moral fiber, somehow managed to find a way to sneak through the cracks in the system. Sadly, Miss Quinn's shortcomings reflect poorly on all of us who constantly strive to do our

best. We are cooperating at every level with Federal, State, and local authorities to bring this sordid affair to a logical and speedy conclusion."

Not exactly the ringing endorsement one would hope to hear from a lover. I had to give old Gaston this much. He was pretty good at denying.

By this time, Louie was snoring contentedly in his office chair, and I called Aaron to see if I could have a look at the Little Jimmy Fennell file.

"Which one?" he said. There was background noise that sounded like a bar or maybe a restaurant.

"The file where he ends up on the steps of the Cathedral for starters, then maybe whatever else you have just to give me some background on the guy."

"Actually, it's a bit sketchy. You're right, that's where he was found dead, but that was ruled natural causes. If I recall specifically, he died of a cardiac arrest. It's entirely possible he just dropped dead there, not that it would really matter all that much anymore. This wouldn't have anything to do with the Desi Quinn murder, would it?"

"I just want to make damn sure I'm doing the right thing by not getting involved."

"Oh, believe me, you're doing the right thing, Dev. You've never been more right in your life. Here, hold on half a second, someone wants to talk to you."

I heard a voice ask, "Who is it?"

Then Aaron said, "Dev Haskell. Give him your honest opinion and maybe some additional incentive to stay away from our investigation."

"Haskell?"

The gum-snapping across the phone line identified Detective Manning. I visualized him sitting wherever they were with his bald head gleaming in the dim light of a bar, then his face suddenly changing from pink to an explosive crimson when Aaron told him I was on the line. He spoke slowly, but with an edge to his voice, like he was explaining something to a wayward child and on the verge of completely wigging out.

"Haskell, I want you to listen carefully. I'm going to reserve our worst cell for you down in the holding unit. There might be one or two other serial rapists, probably a deranged butcher in there as well, but you know, birds of a feather and all. Course they won't like the interruption caused by your arrival, but that shouldn't worry a top investigator such as yourself. You just keep on screwing up our work. After all, that's what counts, right? Oh, and one other thing, listen to this," he said and then hung up.

I was tempted to phone back and tell him we'd been disconnected but thought better of it. I wasn't ready to go after Gaston Driscoll, yet. But my interest had been piqued to the point where I wanted to have a look at the case files for both Little Jimmy Fennell and Desi Quinn.

Ten

Madeline Siedschlag had worked in records at the police department for at least as long as I could remember. I thought she'd been hired during Roosevelt's New Deal. I was told she was a pretty hot number at one time, but a hundred years of sitting on a chair and working in the lower dungeon of the police department seemed to have a way of changing that.

The records room was actually a series of rooms replete with a musty, damp basement smell that seemed to permeate everything. Concrete walls painted an Igloo white and lowest bid beige carpet, lacking a pad beneath, did nothing to enhance the charm of the place. Madeline's office furniture, such as it was, resembled remnants from a time prior to computers or even touch-tone phones. I figured the file room was most likely the final resting place for outdated office equipment before it simply got tossed in a dumpster.

I had been standing in front of Madeline's empty desk for close to fifteen minutes, waiting for her to return. I'd had more than enough time to examine the four framed photos of her holding five different cats. The photos sat on a government issue green desk with a grey linoleum top and a bead of chrome trim running around the edge. Her faded purple office chair was pushed in against the desk with a note folded over the top that read, *'Back in 3 minutes.'*

"May I help you?" A smoker's voice rasped from behind me.

Madeline lumbered back behind the counter and set a thermos on her desk. She took me by surprise, first because she'd been behind me and secondly because she didn't resemble the woman I remembered. She'd put on weight, a lot of weight, and there were purplish double bags under both eyes that stood out from her pasty white skin.

The woman I remembered as fastidiously unattractive looked to have not brushed her hair in a while. Maybe she was going for the dreadlocks look. She certainly had the 'dread' part down. Her dress was wrinkled and spotted with food stains. She'd become a female version of Louie, only about ten times his age.

"May I help you?" she asked again, then moved behind the counter to steady herself and stared across at me.

"Hi, Madeline, I don't know if you remember me. I'm Dev Haskell."

"Dev Haskell," she said, obviously thinking about it for a long moment.

I caught the tell-tale whiff of alcohol and wondered about the thermos she'd set on her desk. It wasn't quite eleven in the morning.

"Dev Haskell," she repeated before a light suddenly went on. "Oh, well, yes, of course. Dev, how are you?"

"Fine, Madeline, just fine. You look, well, you don't seem to have changed one bit," I lied.

"Oh, you, stop." She giggled, then waited for me to tell her more.

"Madeline, I was wondering if I could look at a couple of closed case files. They go back, well, almost ten years and I was hoping—"

"Are you with the department now, Dev?"

"Not exactly. See, I'm looking into the—"

"Well, then unless you have express permission from one of our investigators."

"Actually, Lieutenant LaZelle in homicide suggested I come down and review a couple of these files."

"He didn't happen to give you a review card, did he? They're supposed to fill one out."

"Gee, no, he didn't. But I know he was busy. He was just rushing off to somewhere as a matter of fact. I bet he just forgot, Madeline."

As she picked up the phone on her desk and started pushing buttons, she said, "Let me just call up there and see. He's usually so good. He— Oh, Lieutenant, glad I was able to catch you before you dashed out the door. Madeline, down in records. Mr. Haskell is down here and it appears you forgot to sign off on our review card. Department policy." She chuckled. "I'm afraid I'm going to have to send him back up."

"I'll just go," I half-whispered.

Madeline signaled me to wait a moment.

"Oh, Lieutenant, you don't have to do that. I'm sure Mr. Haskell wouldn't mind." She smiled, nodded at me, and held up an index finger. I noticed there was dirt under her nail.

"Oh." She shrugged. "You're so kind," she said and then hung up.

"Everything okay?" I gambled.

"Yes." She smiled, but then added, "He's on his way down and said for you to just wait. He's always so darn sweet. Why don't you just have a seat over there? It should only be a minute." She indicated a line of card table chairs against the far wall.

Eleven

Fifty minutes later, Madeline said, "Goodness, some emergency must have come up. He's usually so prompt,"

"Maybe I should just run up to his office," I suggested.

"Oh, I'm afraid you better not. That would be exactly the time he'll come down, and you'll miss him," she said. "Would you excuse me? I'm just going to run to the ladies room for a moment," she said, then picked up her thermos and quickly walked around the counter.

If I'd known their filing system, I could have pulled the files myself. It wasn't like I was going to take the things home with me. I just wanted to read them and get up to speed.

"What the hell do you think you're doing?" Aaron asked a moment later. He was standing in the doorway, watching me stare at my feet.

"Look, Aaron, I'm sorry. I just wanted to get up to speed on some background stuff relating to Desi Quinn."

"So, you decided that the best way to try and get up to speed was to pull an end-run on me, is that it?"

"No."

"Oh, that's good to know. Now I guess I don't have to worry. What the hell are you doing down here? And where's Madeline?" he asked, looking around.

"I think she went out for a drink," I half-whispered.

That didn't seem to faze him. "You want to look at our files, just ask me. They've been closed for seven or eight years. I would have let you take a look."

"That's not the impression I got when we spoke on the phone yesterday."

He seemed to think about that for a moment. "You can't leave this room with anything except your own notes. Clear?"

I nodded.

"I'll have you locked up and turned over to Manning and his serial rapists if you even think about taking anything out of one of the files."

"What could I possibly take?"

"I'm not sure, just don't. Okay? Madeline usually has some damn form to fill out around here," he said, looking behind the counter. "Here we go. Okay," he spoke as he filled in the form. "You stay here with those files. When you're finished, you report back to me up at my desk before you leave the building. Clear?"

I nodded.

"I'm not kidding, Dev."

"I got it."

Madeline lurched back behind the counter about twenty minutes later. She looked glassy-eyed and the alcohol smell seemed stronger.

"Lieutenant LaZelle came down and filled out this form," I said, handing it to her.

"Oh, isn't that just the way? I'm gone for two minutes, and he breezes in and out."

"He said I should read the files down here. I guess maybe in one of those cubicles," I said, trying to get things moving.

She waved a hand dismissively. "Sure, dear, whatever you want."

I was hoping she was just talking about the files. I handed her a slip of paper with Desi's and Little Jimmy's names written on it. "How about I wait in a cubicle for these files?"

"Perfect." She smiled, then seemed to stagger just a half step while she examined the names I'd written down, then she turned the sheet over to see if I'd written anything on the backside.

I waited in one of the cubicle's, wondering for fifteen minutes if I'd ever see a file or Madeline when all of a sudden she rushed in. "There you go, Mr. Hastings," she said, making a grand gesture as she deposited about a foot high stack of files on the desktop where I was seated. "All neat and tidy. Does Sir desire anything else? Anything?" she asked, raising an eyebrow and making a grand sweeping gesture with her right arm.

"No, thanks, Madeline. This will keep me busy for quite a while."

"Very good. I bid thee farewell and anon, my prince," she said and then rushed back out of the cubicle.

I started with the smaller set of files first, Little Jimmy Fennell. I could go through all sorts of minute detail, but suffice to say Little Jimmy died of a heart attack, cardiac arrest. He'd apparently climbed up thirty-seven granite steps toward the front doors of the Cathedral, where he collapsed. The coroner's report suggested he was most likely dead by the time he hit the ground, not that far a fall for a fellow who was barely four-foot-three.

The medical examiner's photos had him laid out with his arms spread as if he was awaiting crucifixion. It was surmised this may have been the prank of some warped individual who happened across Little Jimmy's still warm body. The image, a version of which ran on the front page of the Sunday paper, is what led to all sorts of Da Vinci Code type speculation. Much of which was investigated and none of which seemed to hold the least bit of credence. To date, James Fennell, aka Little Jimmy, remained the only known member of the gang who actually robbed the Ninth District Federal Reserve Bank, and now Little Jimmy wasn't talking.

I stood up, stretched, and looked around. I spotted Madeline with her head down on her desk, apparently asleep, which was probably a good thing. Her thermos lay on its side at the foot of her desk. It was apparently empty because there didn't seem to be any trace of a puddle on the floor.

I returned to my seat and began to review the Desi Quinn files.

Twelve

Desi had told me the truth. She had been an architect for Touchier and Touchier. Her address was listed, at least in the file I was reading, as being in the seven hundred block of Fairmont Avenue in St. Paul. A trendy older section of town comprised of large three-story Victorian homes.

She'd apparently been a model college student, made the Dean's List in grad school at Clemson, and had been employed at Touchier for three years. She was on track to be made a partner in the next three or four years, and by all accounts, was an excellent employee. Her employee reviews, all signed by Gaston Driscoll, described her as a credit to herself and to the firm. She had no known prior offenses. Not even so much as a parking ticket.

How she came to steal Driscoll's access codes and what she did with the funds that she presumably received as a payoff, was never determined. Other than withdrawing the one set of files, there was never any record of her tampering with firm security. There were no bank records showing a large deposit, no evidence of a change in her spending patterns, nothing.

She was on record as having withdrawn the Federal Reserve files from the firm's vault. Upon closer examination, it was determined that she had used Gaston Driscoll's access code when withdrawing the files. At the time, Driscoll was conveniently out of town, enjoying a three-week vacation retreat with his wife. The Driscoll's had traveled to Sanibel Island in February, just as they had for the past eleven years.

Desi maintained Driscoll instructed her to deliver the files to an office in Town Square Court while he was out of town. The office was located in the twenty-seven story Bremer Tower. The office suite she delivered the files to, suite 2405, had been vacant for over a year, and in fact, remained vacant at least up to and during her trial.

Her story had credence from the standpoint that in order to gain access and remove the Federal Reserve files, she needed Driscoll's security codes. Desi had her own personal code, but her security clearance wasn't as high as Driscoll's. Interestingly enough, she followed procedure and signed her name, registering her removal of the Federal Reserve files. She did not obtain a delivery receipt when she supposedly delivered the same files to the non-existent office.

I was beginning to believe Desi's story. The thing that was really convincing me was that Driscoll just happened to be away on his annual vacation. It could be a coincidence, but then why would Desi sign her own name and insist she had delivered them to an office suite? She wasn't an idiot. She had to have known that the office suite was a point, a key point that could be verified. She was either completely naïve or . . .

Desi's desk calendar was included in the file I was reviewing. There was a one-word notation on February 14, Valentines Day interestingly enough. The notation read *'Files.'* Two days later, on the 16th was the notation *'Gas.'* Then written on the 17th was the notation *'Call Gas!! 1st thig!'*

Was she feeling some pressure by the 17th? Had someone discovered the files were missing? The robbery didn't occur for almost another two weeks. Dropping the 'n' on what I presumed should have been the word 'thing' . . . did that suggest she was feeling pressure and possibly making mistakes? Or, was she just busy at that particular moment and writing quickly?

The file indicated Desi was terminated on February 26th. A full five days before the Federal Reserve Bank was even robbed. The reason given for her termination was simply 'poor performance' which seemed to run contrary to her three years' worth of exemplary performance reviews. Up until that time, she'd been a model employee, the golden child. What the hell happened?

Her termination had been personally handled by Gaston Driscoll via the phone, which seemed a rather cold and heartless method for anyone to be subjected to. I noted an individual from the firm's Human Resources Department had also been present on the conference call, a woman named Helen Olsen. I made a note. There were probably a few thousand Olsen's in the phone book. If Helen was under fifty years old, there was a strong possibility she wouldn't even be listed in the phone book. I'd have to call her at Touchier, and if she was still employed there, try to set up an appointment.

I flipped back a page and looked at the reason for termination, 'poor performance.' It didn't seem to add up.

Over the course of the afternoon, I continued to wade through the file. At no time did there ever seem to be a major focus on Gaston Driscoll. If Desi looked to be a model employee, Driscoll was a sterling citizen. The little that was in the file mentioned he was a wounded Army veteran, highly regarded professionally, as well as socially. He sat on the boards of four separate non-profit organizations, as well as half-a-dozen corporations. Hell, the guy even volunteered monthly at his church to cook and serve food to the needy.

He'd testified in court, and a portion of the transcripts had been included in the file. Reading the transcripts, Driscoll came across as reluctant to say anything negative about Desi. He'd been at the opposite end of the country when she'd 'stolen' the files. In the file transcripts, it was presented that it would not have been a difficult thing for Desi to obtain the files since she was aware Driscoll's security access code was written on a card in his Rolodex.

It would not be a far leap to conclude that Desi waited until lily-white senior partner Gaston Driscoll was out of the office for a week, used his access code, and stole the files. Of course, that still left some serious questions. Why would Desi sign her own name? And when confronted, instead of denying the fact, why would Desi not only admit she took the files, but then provide the address of a vacant office suite as the location where she delivered them?

Nowhere in Desi's case file was there a hint of a sexual relationship between her and Gaston Driscoll. I understood Driscoll not wanting to bring it up, but you'd think Desi would have said something about it in her own defense, maybe mentioned the Ace of Spades tattoo she'd told me about. At least the tattoo was something that could be verified and suggested a more intimate knowledge of the guy than any other casual employee might have.

It was late in the afternoon. I had a few pages of notes and scribbles, some of which I could actually decipher. I replaced everything, closed the files, and walked out to Madeline's desk. She was nowhere to be found. Her thermos was still on the floor next to her desk. There was a container of aspirin with the lid torn off where last I saw her sleeping. I left the stack of files on her desk and took the elevator up to Aaron's office on the fourth floor.

After asking to see him, I waited for another ten minutes before he came out of the secure homicide area.

"You finished down there?" he asked, stating the obvious.

"Yeah, I got about all I can get from your files at this point. And that's not much."

He nodded, like he understood. "Any conclusions?" he asked.

"Conclusions? No, not really. But maybe some suspicions."

"Such as?"

"Well, I don't know. Desi told me she was in a relationship for the better part of a year with Gaston Driscoll. He fires her a few weeks before the Federal Reserve robbery on the grounds of poor performance. Maybe she thought at the time he may have taken up with another woman, and she was going to make life difficult for him."

"There's no mention of any of that in the case file or the court transcripts. Christ, the guy is Mr. Civic Responsibility," Aaron said.

"Yeah, I know."

"She have any proof?"

"She told me he had a tattoo," I said.

Aaron shook his head. "Hell, you know as well as I do that could just be something she picked up at the water cooler. Even if it's true, it doesn't prove anything. I don't recall any mention of her ever bringing any of this up when she was being interviewed or on trial. You'd think at some point it would have crossed the defense's mind to at least mention it."

I nodded my head, agreeing with Aaron. "I didn't read anything that suggested she brought it up. But she did know about the tattoo."

"A tattoo? Jesus Christ just about everyone has one. Even if she guessed she's got about a seventy-five per-cent chance of being right. And it doesn't prove a damn thing. Tell you the truth, it sounds like she got the advice of some jailhouse lawyer while she was in for six years stewing about this Driscoll guy," Aaron said, shaking his head. "No, I don't like it. I can't quite see it."

"I didn't say he did anything, Aaron, other than to take her to bed."

"I don't like that either, based on what we know of the guy. Like I said, he's Mr. Civic Responsibility. I just don't see it.

"Yeah, I know. Look, thanks, sorry if I pissed you off earlier. I—"

"You didn't piss me off, you just tried to pull an end-run, and I don't like that, that's all. Still friends?" He laughed.

"Yeah, and I suppose it's my turn to buy."

"It will be, but not tonight. I'm jammed. See you later."

I didn't feel like going home. I didn't feel like sitting at The Spot. To be honest, I was feeling kind of down. I phoned Heidi.

"Hello?" she answered with a question like she was amazed her phone rang.

"Hi, Heidi, you sound like you're surprised someone would bother to call you."

"Oh, hi, Dev," she said. Her tone didn't hide her disappointment.

"You doing anything tonight?" I had hoped to get
together with her, but if she was going to be in one of her
downer moods, I would just as soon stay away.

"No, nothing, I guess."

I was picking up the signs, and none of them were
good.

"Just thought I'd call and see if you wanted to go to
a movie. There's a new sequel out, Car Chase Four. I'm
thinking of going." Heidi hated guy movies and hated
car chases even more.

"Oh, I don't know. Where is it playing?"

"A little place out in St. Paul Park." She wasn't a
fan of that side of town.

"Oh."

"But I'd have to swing by now. The thing starts in
about thirty-five minutes." She hated to be rushed, so I
was banking on getting credit for at least asking, and she
could continue her private session of the blues.

"I think I might just give it a miss," she said and then
let loose with a sigh.

This was where I was supposed to ask was something wrong. Then, when she said 'no,' I was supposed
to ask three or four more times until she eventually came
out with it. Once the cause came to light, I could show
up with a favorite takeout dinner and a couple bottles of

wine to the tune of about eighty bucks. Then, at the end of the night, she'd tell me it was time to go home because she just wasn't in the mood. I had a better idea.

Thirteen

The bartender, a brunette about forty-five, looked to have been around the block a few times. The music coming from the stage area was just loud enough that she had to raise her voice so I could hear when she said, "Hi, what can I get you?"

"Better give me a Summit Extra Pale," I half yelled.

She was back with my beer in about two minutes, and I slipped her a ten. I was the only guy at the bar. The music was loud, the light was dim, and the carpet was a sleazy leopard skin pattern. The other customers were placing their orders with cocktail waitresses half-dressed in a black lingerie kind of uniform.

Nasty's patrons, all male, were mostly seated at tables, hunkered down in their own private world. The exception being the guys along the edge of the stage with dollar bills folded in front of them, watching the strippers. The girls would give them that little extra bit of attention, maybe a couple of winks and a smile, then blow them a kiss before they bent down and picked up the cash.

"Anything else?" she asked, sliding four ones across the bar, my change. She seemed a little surprised I hadn't turned to watch the entertainment.

"Keep the change," I said, thinking six bucks for an eight-ounce beer, Jesus. "Actually, maybe there is one thing. I'm checking something for a friend, trying to get some information. Maybe you can help me?"

"A friend? Yeah, sure you are, pal. Look, company policy, we don't give out the names or phone numbers of the girls. We sure as hell don't give out addresses, and we don't deliver notes. That just about cover any information you're looking for?"

I was suddenly thinking I might have been better off bringing dinner over to Heidi.

"No, that's not what I want—"

"We don't have pictures or videos of them, and we don't sell their thongs either. And, no, we don't allow you to photograph on the premises. All the girls here are private contractors. If you can get one of 'em to talk to you when they come around, whatever you line up is between them and you. Got it?"

"Hey, calm down, will you? I just wanted a beer and some information on a friend of mine who used to work here."

"Sure you do. If she's such a good friend, why don't you just give her a call?" she asked, then crossed her arms, leaned back, and glared.

I was usually a polite guy, but I'd just about had it with the attitude.

"Believe me. I'd love to give her a call, love to hear her voice. But see a couple a days ago some asshole put two slugs in her head."

"You knew Desi?"

"I had breakfast with her that morning. I'm a private investigator, and I'm trying to find out whatever I can. She told me she'd just started tending bar here, pulling a couple of weekend shifts. She was busting her ass over at Karla's Karwash during the week. I thought she was getting everything back together, and then someone shot her," I said. I took a card out of my pocket and pushed it across the bar.

She took a moment to read my card, turned it over probably to look for a message, or to see if she'd won a prize. I wasn't sure which.

"Okay, ask away," she yelled just as the music stopped. A couple of heads turned to look at us, but everyone stayed seated. A male voice suddenly came over the sound system.

"That's one of our favorites, Misty. Give a round of applause to the gorgeous and talented Misty."

Naked Misty was down on all fours, picking up dollar bills from the stage. She seemed to ignore the two guys applauding. She stood up, collected the red lingerie she'd tossed in the corner, and walked off. A thin smattering of applause and a shrill whistle followed her off stage.

"I don't know where to start. Anything you can tell me, anything she may have said could help. Was there ever an incident or maybe an altercation? Maybe something that stands out?"

"Well . . ."

"And now let's welcome back the popular Brandi," the male voice said as a brunette in a cowboy hat, boots, and a very small thong pranced on stage riding a hobby horse. Some nondescript music began to blare from a static-filled speaker, and I had to lean across the bar so I could listen to what she was saying.

"She didn't seem to have any trouble here, at least that I know of. She was a pretty careful girl. Didn't really stand for no guys chatting her up, ya know."

I nodded like I knew.

"Yeah, she was a good little worker, too. Got some nice tips. Far as I can tell, she never had no problems here. Girls all seemed to like her, I guess."

I nodded again then asked, "Did anyone ever come in to see her? She ever leave with anyone?"

She shook her head. "Na, nobody come in here lookin' for her, ever. Far as leaving with someone . . . If she picked someone up, they must a got together outside, off the premises like."

I nodded again. "She ever tell you anything about her situation?"

"Her situation? Honey, we all been nailed a couple of times. Comes with the territory. Me, I got popped with an assault charge a few years back, couple three solicitation charges. They reduced the last one down to just loitering with intent, dumb bastards. I guess old Desi was in the big leagues. She pulled some heavy-duty time, 'bout five or six years' worth, I think. Not the bullshit county stuff I done. But she never talked none about it. Least ways as far as I know."

I nodded and couldn't think of anything else to ask.

"You find the bastard, you bring em down here. Me and the girls will deal with him. He'll be able to hit all them high notes by the time we get done." She gave a little cackle that quickly barked into a heavy cough.

I nodded, then asked, "She ever mention someone named Gas?"

"Gas? Like what ya put in your car? Naw, that don't ring no bell. Gas? No, sorry, can't help." She shook her head.

"Thanks, you've actually been a big help," I lied. "Hang onto my card, and if anything pops into your head, please give me a call, okay?"

She nodded and read my card again.

"You mind if I ask some of the other girls?" I motioned up at the stage and toward a couple of girls giving lap dances out in the crowd.

"I got no problem with it, long as you behave. Just like everyone else, keep your hands to yourself and no pictures."

"I think I can handle that," I said.

"And it might cost you, honey. Time is money to 'em, ya know."

I set my beer on a table close to the bar and sat down. The tables on either side of me were unoccupied. A black girl with burgundy hair walked over before I'd taken a sip.

"Looking for some personal enjoyment?" she asked. Her left hand rested on her hip. Her hips were cocked at an angle, and she looked like she was getting ready to read me the riot act for not having my homework done.

"Join me?" I motioned to an empty chair.

"I'm working for a living here. You gonna appreciate me, baby?"

I pulled out a twenty and set it on the table. She sat down in a nano-second, flashing her long fake burgundy eyelashes at me once she stuffed the bill in the side of her thong.

"I'm Moana. What'd you have in mind, Sugar?" she said and fluttered her eyelashes again as she ran her tongue back and forth over her bottom lip.

"Maybe just some information," I said, then watched the walls go up and the freeze set in.

"You a cop? I'm up to date with my parole office. You don't need to come in here bothering me at my place of business."

"That's not it," I said, and grabbed for her wrist as she stood up.

"Don't you go putting your damn hands on me, Mr. Police," she shouted.

I let go just as a large figure drifted alongside me. "Sir, we have a no-touching policy. I'm going to have to ask you to leave."

"I'm aware of your policy. I was merely attempting to explain—"

"This Mother says he's a cop, Benny."

"No, I didn't say that I—"

"Said he was gonna lock me up again if I didn't treat him right," she yelled loudly enough so that most of the audience turned around toward us, ignoring Brandi and her hobby horse galloping across the stage. Everyone seemed to be focused on giant Benny and me. They were all probably hoping he'd pick me up and toss me through the blacked-out window.

"Sir?"

There was no point in arguing. I simply nodded, stood up, and headed toward the door. Benny shadowed me all the way.

"See you, Sucker," Moana yelled, then cocked her hips, crossed her arms and glared.

The bartender shook her head and watched me as I made for the door.

"Probably be a good idea, we don't see your ass for about a month," Benny called to me as I made my way across the parking lot to my car.

"Not to worry," I called back.

Fourteen

I glanced over at Louie and said, "Talk about a collection of unhappy campers. I don't think I'll be darkening their door for a while."

We were sipping coffee in the office the following morning. Louie was checking his watch every other minute because he had another DUI court date at eleven. The courthouse was only a five-minute drive away.

"Yeah, that pretty much sums up the place. Last time I was there, the beer was warm, and the employees were cold."

"Pain in the ass is what they were," I said.

"No argument, just think how it would be to work in that joint. So what's your next stop?"

"Next stop? I'll check with her former neighbors, maybe go up to that office suite in the Bremer Tower. I don't know."

"You going to talk to that Driscoll guy?"

"I don't see any point, at least not until I can get a little more background information. As it stands now, what can I say to him? A woman you fired over the phone for being unprofessional stole files from your firm. She's dead now, but before she died, she told me she was in a relationship with you eight years ago and that you have a tattoo. Not exactly earth shattering and let me just make a wild guess that old Gas wouldn't talk to me anyway. She did steal files. He does have a tattoo. So what? As much as I may believe what she told me, there is nothing in Desi's version of the story that I can prove."

"Doesn't sound too promising," Louie said.

"You think?"

Louie headed off to the courthouse a half-hour later. I decided to dial the number for Touchier and Touchier, only because I couldn't think of anything else to do.

"Gaston Enterprises," a perky voice answered.

I was caught off guard.

"Oh, I'm sorry, I must have misdialed."

"Were you attempting to reach Touchier and Touchier architectural firm?'

"Yes, I was."

"Our name was changed a few months ago. The name change still confuses a few people," she said.

'Still confused' seemed to cover me on just about any morning.

"How may I help you, Sir?"

"I'm trying to reach Helen Olsen in your HR department."

"Helen Olsen?"

"Yeah, in HR. Well, at least she was in HR a few years back. Maybe she's moved to a different area."

"I'm sorry, Sir. I'm not aware of anyone by that name in our organization. What was this in relation to?"

I didn't think 'murder' was a suitable response. "Maybe if I could speak to someone in your HR department?"

"Certainly…connecting you now, Sir. Enjoy your day." Click.

Whoever the polite, perky receptionist was, she wouldn't have fit in at Nasty's. My transferred call was picked up on the third ring.

"H.R. this is Dawn Miller."

"Hello Dawn, my name is Devlin Haskell. I was attempting to reach a woman, who at one time, worked in your HR department. I'm wondering if perhaps she moved to another area or possibly married and changed her name."

"Who were you trying to reach, sir?"

"Her name is or was, Helen Olsen."

It was suddenly a repeat of the previous night. I could feel the freeze coming through the phone. "There is no one by that name in our organization."

"Maybe she changed her name and…"

"If she had. I would certainly be aware of that, sir. No one by that name is employed by this organization."

"Was she at one time? If there was a way I could get hold of her I—"

"I wouldn't have that information, sir. And even if I did, our privacy policy would prohibit me from providing that information to you."

"But she did work there, at one time, in your Human Resources department?"

"Your name again, sir?"

I couldn't see any benefit to alerting this woman, Gaston Driscoll or anyone else for that matter to who I was.

"Thank you," I said and hung up.

I took a wild shot and Googled Helen Olsen. The first hit I got was a woman living in the United Kingdom. I stopped searching after seven pages and hadn't even scratched the surface. I'd have to refine my search.

I left the office and drove over to Fairmont Avenue. Desi's former home was in a trendy area of town loosely referred to as Crocus Hill. I knocked on eight doors and got three answers. The first woman had moved in two years earlier and knew nothing. The second woman had lived there for fifty-six years and knew even less.

The third woman was attractive, looked to be in her mid-fifties and appeared to have all the time in the world to talk. She introduced herself as Libby. She thought a moment then said, "She was the one who got into all that trouble, right?"

We were standing on her front porch, a wood-floored thing that ran across the entire front of the house with a white porch swing hanging at the far end. The house was three-stories tall, cream-colored with green trim, and a flowered-pattern stained glass window above the large front picture window. Her front door was actually a pair of heavy, dark-stained oak doors with a glossy finish and shiny brass doorknobs. She was leaning against the door that was still closed.

"She was involved with the removal of some documents from her place of business," I said. "The documents were never recovered. There was a question regarding proper access to the documents." I thought it a good idea to skip over some of the more negative aspects of Desi's situation.

"Well, you left out the little fact of a bank robbery. The Federal Reserve no less. Then there was that bizarre situation where they found that little character on the steps of the Cathedral. If I recall, the money, millions, was never recovered. If it wasn't the largest robbery in the state's history, it certainly ranks in the top two or three."

"That's probably correct."

"Sad…we were all quite surprised. She was quiet and kept to herself. An architect, right?"

I nodded.

"If architecture is anything like the legal profession, she worked long hours. My husband is a lawyer. He used to come home and work some more, collapse, then right off to work again. It's no wonder we never saw the poor thing. Are you representing her?"

"Not exactly."

"Please give her my best. The whole situation seemed rather strange. I still have a difficult time believing she was involved." She looked across the street and up two doors to the house where Desi used to live.

"Can you give me any idea of what she was like? You know, when she was living across the street from you."

"Actually no, I can't. We waved at one another, but I really only saw her maybe a couple times a month. I can't recall ever having a conversation. She always looked like she was either going to or coming home from work. We maybe chatted about something at a neighborhood Christmas party for a brief moment, nothing memorable. You know how it is."

"Did she ever have any visitors?"

"Visitors?" she asked, and gave me a look out of the corner of her eye.

"Boyfriends, girlfriends, did she throw parties?"

"No, nothing of that sort. At least that I'm aware of, like I said, she was very quiet and kept to herself. Then one day, there was a For Sale sign out front, and she was off to Federal prison. Honest to God, St. Paul, I'll tell you," she said, shaking her head.

I thanked her for talking with me, gave her my card, and drove down to the Bremer Tower. It was a sign of the times in downtown St. Paul that I was able to get a parking space right across the street from the building.

Back in the seventies, the city, in its wisdom, connected most of the downtown buildings with a series of second-story pedestrian walkways known as the Downtown Skyway System. The idea was to provide a way to walk around downtown without having to deal with the climate extremes of Minnesota.

This helped to accomplish two things. In maybe eighteen months, it killed off most of the street-level retail businesses. Then it dawned on people that a good portion of the office workers lived in the suburbs. In the morning, they drove into work. At the end of the day, they quickly fled the scene, and in the process, it killed most of the retail business on the skyway level. Now, other than the occasional insurance or state office, the only things left were luncheon food courts and white-washed windows hiding empty retail space.

I rode the elevator alone up to the twenty-fourth floor of the Bremer Tower. Suite 2405 was a short walk down a very quiet hall. The suite was empty, and the door was locked. There was a window of reinforced glass along the lefthand side of the door. A sign with rental contact information was taped to the inside of the glass.

The suite seemed to consist of a small central reception room with entrances to maybe three offices. Beige carpet, lighter beige walls, and dust along the window frame gave the place a blank canvas look. It appeared to have been empty for quite some time and wasn't the only empty unit on the floor. I counted four on my return trip to the elevator.

I was back in the office, thinking about my wasted day and wondering if it was too early to head over to The Spot when the phone rang.

"Haskell Investigations," I said, then waited a long moment. "Hello?"

"May I speak to Devlin, please?" a woman asked.

"You got him."

"Are you the guy who was kicked out of Nasty's last night?"

"I'm not sure I was kicked out, maybe just nicely asked to leave. It was a misunderstanding. Who's this?"

"Devlin, my name is Marsha Norling. I got your card from Evelyn, one of the bartenders on duty last night."

"Oh, yeah, the always charming Evelyn."

"Usually not how she's described. Anyway, she said you had some questions about Desi. Maybe I can help you."

"Marsha, I'd love to talk with you. Could I meet you somewhere? Tonight or maybe sometime tomorrow?"

"I could do this afternoon. I'm dancing eight to close this week."

"You tell me when and where."

"You know Dunn Brothers Coffee?" she said.

"There's a couple of them. Which one were you thinking?"

"Grand Ave?"

"You name the time, Marsha, and I'll be there."

Fifteen

I was waiting for Marsha in the Grand Avenue coffee shop. The place sat within sight of Macalester College. A school full of accomplished academics I maybe could have gotten into, but if I had, I would've just flunked out.

The inside of the coffee shop was crowded with people who seemed to have nothing to do and all day to do it. Every other table had someone on a laptop scanning Facebook or playing a phone app. The people talking were waxing eloquent with big impressive words, in voices just a little too loud and devoid of any hint of a Midwest accent. Marsha said she'd be wearing white shorts and a red top. I didn't see anyone like that when I entered, so I got a cup of coffee and grabbed a table toward the back of the place that allowed me to watch both doors.

I recognized her the moment she strutted in. Okay, she was the only woman with white shorts, tight white shorts, and a red top from which her figure was fighting to burst free. Remove the perfect makeup, give her an oversized ratty knit bag large enough to hide a Volkswagen in, and she could be a college student. She was missing her cowboy hat and boots, not to mention the hobby horse. Last night, when I'd seen her prancing around on stage at Nasty's, she was using the name Brandi.

She placed an order at the counter and then looked around while she was waiting for her coffee. I gave her a wave, and she nodded in my direction.

"Mr. Haskell?" she said a moment later, setting what looked like a latte on the table and extending her hand.

"Please, call me Dev. Thank you for getting in touch with me earlier."

I noticed a couple of overly educated patrons appraising her white shorts from the rear. One very slight woman with a not-so-slight mustache shook her head as if she found attractive young women with drop-dead figures offensive.

"Have you had much luck?" she asked, sitting down across from me.

"Depends on what you call luck. I've eliminated a number of questions and people to talk to, but there hasn't been that lightning bolt from the blue that suddenly provides you with all the answers. Then again, in my line of work, there rarely is."

She smiled and nodded. "Private Investigator, it just sounds so cool, so exciting, so very dangerous."

"Don't believe everything you see on TV or in the movies. Most of what I do is very boring."

"I'll bet," she said, then flashed her eyes over the rim of her Latte.

"Your stage name is Brandi." I said it as a statement, not a question.

She nodded, sipped, then said, "Yeah, at least at Nasty's. I'm Kellie at Lickety Splits, Desire at the Beaver Hut, and Temptation at Buns and Roses. Then I've got a whole different bunch of names when I'm on the road. It makes for more bookings. Did you catch me last night?"

"I saw the beginning, you and the hobby horse, but not much more. I was in the process of talking to Moana when I was asked to leave."

She smiled and took another sip. "Oh yeah, Moana. How'd that go? That girl has some issues."

"You think? Anyway, enough about Moana tell me what you know about Desi."

"Desi? Well, unfortunately, I'm afraid it's not that lightning bolt you mentioned. She was worried someone was watching her, following her. She mentioned it to me a couple of times. Again, nothing definitive…at least that I'm aware of. Just a feeling she had."

"Did she ever mention who she thought might be following her or why?"

"No, unfortunately. I know she had Benny walk her to her car a few times, but we all do that from time to time. It just comes with the territory, so it's really not all that unusual. Although, now that you mention it, she made a casual remark one night about running into an ex, but she never said anything beyond that."

"An ex?"

"I took it to mean an ex-boyfriend, husband, lover . . . you know, someone like that. But it was a throwaway line. Matter of fact, I think I probably started it. Some guy I used to date came in drunk and acting like a total jerk, so they threw him out."

"Well, I know how that goes."

"No, that wasn't your fault last night. Anyway, I was feeling embarrassed about this idiot who came in, and Desi was her usual nice self. Said she'd run into her ex a day or two before on the street, and he was a jerk, too. Pretended he didn't know her, couldn't wait to get away from her. You know the type."

"Did she tell you where this happened?"

Marsha seemed to think for a moment, then shook her head. "Not that I can recall, except that it was on the street. The way she said it made me think it was a surprise to both of them, not like some guy was stalking her, and she caught him."

"Did she ever mention her private life?"

"No, not really. I'm not aware of her dating anyone or working, if that's what you mean."

"Working?" I asked.

"You know, getting paid for a date, escorting, whatever you want to call it."

"There a lot of that going on?"

Marsha seemed to eye me cautiously for a moment then stared into the distance. "You look like you know what happens in this business. You swear you'll never do it, but then there's a guy with some money, he may even be cute, and you've got the rent due or a car payment. You get paid, and he gets a smile on his face. No problems, no strings attached. Sometimes I even enjoy the moment," she said very matter of fact.

"Did Desi ever mention anything about being an architect?"

"Actually, I never knew anything about that until I heard it on the news the other night. I was pretty surprised."

"Did she ever mention a guy named Gas or Gaston?"

"No, other than the one comment about running into her ex, nothing remotely along those lines. Like I said, I never knew if it was a husband or a boyfriend or who she ran into. She never mentioned a name." Marsha smiled and seemed to laugh at a private joke.

"Something funny?"

"I'm just thinking of Gaston in Beauty and the Beast, the Disney movie. It was one of my favorites as a kid. Gaston is the handsome, strong hero of the village, and everyone wants to get him into their bed except Belle. Everyone thinks he's so wonderful, but he turns out to be the real villain."

"Get him into their bed? I guess Disney's changed from what I remember."

"Well, they put the little girl spin on it, but we catch on a lot sooner than guys do. We have to."

"Yeah."

"Anyway, I really wish I had more to tell you. I don't know if I helped, but Desi was really nice, and she was especially nice to me. I'm gonna miss her."

"How so?"

"Oh, nothing dramatic. I just needed my hand held, and she did it. It was sweet. She didn't want anything, didn't ask for anything. She was just a nice person, and she sure didn't deserve what happened to her. I just wish I had that lightning bolt you mentioned. Sorry." She gave a big shrug, and a number of heads turned for a quick follow-up glance.

"Marsha, I really appreciate your help. Here," I said, pushing a card across the table. "You think of anything else, please give me a call, anything."

"I just wish I could help you out more," she said.

"I'll buy the coffee next time," I said as she stood up. Heads turned throughout the place. Mustache lady shook her head in disgust and appeared to make a side comment to her heavyset girlfriend.

"You got a deal." She smiled and held my eyes for a long moment.

Sixteen

I was on my way back from the bathroom, a little after two in the morning, making my way down the dark hallway. I'd been out with pals earlier, and I was hoping to get back into bed before I fully woke up when the phone rang.

"Yeah," I answered cautiously. Anytime the phone rang after about ten at night it usually wasn't to deliver good news.

"Hi, Dev, hope I'm not getting you up," a woman said, then giggled at the inside joke. Her voice sounded familiar, but I didn't know who it was. My phone displayed the number as 'Unknown.'

"No, no problem."

"I was wondering if you were maybe interested in getting together?" I had the sense she was concentrating on her words, trying not to slur them.

I was awake at this point. "Sure, I'd like that. What did you have in mind?" I asked, thinking dinner, drinks. My nights were wide open for the rest of the week.

"Great, I'm just leaving now so I could be over there in ten minutes. Well, I mean, if you're not already entertaining."

"I'm just cleaning up after the party. I should have it pretty much under control by the time you arrive," I said, coming wide awake.

"Okay, see you soon." Click.

There were a couple of women it could be, but I doubted it. I thought the first thing I should do was to put some clothes on.

A few minutes later, my phone rang again.

I answered and heard giggling.

"Hello."

"Oh, sorry, I'm so screwed up. I forgot to ask where you live. I'm just turning onto East Seventh now."

I gave her directions St. Paul-style. We don't use a lot of street names or specific distances. We use landmarks. "Stay on Seventh to the Xcel Center, take a right and go up the hill. Left at the first light and drive past the Cathedral, then take a right on that corner. I'm a few blocks down on the right side. I'll have the porch light on for you."

I had the porch light on with the living room light off. I was standing in the dark, watching the quiet street and waiting for a car to pull up so I could see who had called. So far, the only traffic had been a taxi cruising past about three minutes earlier.

A few minutes later, a car drove past, stopped two doors down, backed up, and parked in front of my place. Marsha climbed out of the car wearing the same red top, a pair of jeans, and her cowboy hat. I opened the front door just as she stepped onto my porch.

"Hi, Marsha, thanks for calling. Come on in," I said.

She smiled and gave me a peck on the cheek while I held the door.

"You weren't doing anything, were you?"

I could tell her I'd been in the bathroom or sound asleep, but neither one seemed conducive to furthering the direction I was hoping for. "No, no . . . you know, just up reading and thinking about maybe hitting the sack. Can I get you a little something?" I asked as we walked into the living room. Marsha made a beeline for my couch.

"I'd have another shot of Cuervo. Cuervo Gold if you got any," she said.

"I think I do have some, but I'm all out of limes," I said, walking into the kitchen. I grabbed the fifth of tequila out of the cupboard and picked up a shot glass off the counter.

I had an incident with tequila some years back, and let's just say it was no longer my poison of choice. Nonetheless, I did have a bottle of the stuff, and it was Cuervo Gold. I made it back to the living room in record time. Marsha had already settled into the corner of my couch, kicked off her sandals, and looked to be settling in for a stay.

"Nice digs, Dev. No offense, but I figured you for a typical kind of slob guy. Umm, thanks. Wow, unopened," she said as I set the bottle and shot glass down in front of her on the coffee table.

"Sorry about no limes. You want some salt?"

"No, don't worry. You're not going to join me?" she asked, leaning forward in anticipation.

"I have a tequila thing, so no, I better not. Plus, I've got an early morning meeting I can't miss," I lied.

"Is it about Desi?" she asked, then poured a shot and tossed it down without blinking. It clearly wasn't her first of the evening.

"It may be. I'll know more when I get out of the meeting."

She pushed her cowboy hat back then poured another shot. "I was thinking about her all the while I was dancing tonight. Did you hear from any of the other girls?"

"No," I said.

She tossed down the shot and let out a satisfied little gasp a moment later. "I was thinking…you know you mentioned this guy from Beauty and the Beast and, well, I was thinking."

"Beauty and the Beast?"

She waved her arm a little clumsily then poured another shot as she spoke. "Don't you remember? Gaston, from Beauty & the Beast, the Disney movie. He's the hero who's really the villain. Remember? I told you all about him, I think."

"Oh yeah, of course. Jesus. How could I forget?"

She nodded like she wasn't surprised, then tossed her next shot back and gave another little satisfied gasp.

"So?"

"So I was thinking, maybe I could help you catch this dude."

"You've already been a big help, Marsha."

She shook her head while she poured another shot then inadvertently slammed the bottle down on the coffee table.

"You're not getting it. You're not picking up what I'm putting down." She giggled then quickly tossed the shot back, causing her cowboy hat to fall off. A little drip rolled down her chin and hung there for a moment until it became large enough that it fell onto her red top. She appeared completely unaware.

"I'm a pretty slow learner. Maybe you could tell me what you're thinking."

"We use my ass as the bait," she slurred, then slid her glass onto the table and poured another shot. This time the glass overflowed, and the tequila ran onto the table.

"Whoopsie." She giggled, then pushed the shot glass to the side, got down on her knees and proceeded to slurp the tequila off the top of the coffee table. As she sat up, there was a larger tequila stain spreading across her top. Her eyes suddenly seemed to take on a glazed stare where you're not sure she was able to see past the tip of her nose.

"So, you were saying we use you as bait?"

"No, my ass, Den. I've got a great ass, you know," she said, then reached for the bottle and began to pour more tequila into the full shot glass.

"Careful not to waste, Marsha," I said, gently taking the bottle from her.

"Watch it, you're spilling!" she said, then downed the shot and tried to set the glass on the table. She knocked the glass over in the process, and it rolled in a large circle.

I placed the bottle on the floor, out of her sight.

"Hmm-mmm…" She watched the glass roll back and forth until it stopped.

"So, your plan?"

"I've got a great ass."

"Yes, you do, Marsha. And maybe you can tell me all about it in the morning, okay?"

"Perfect, I can show you." She giggled.

"I'm gonna hit the lights in the kitchen, and I'll be right back."

She found the bottle I'd set on the floor and had poured some of the tequila into the shot glass. She'd poured a larger amount onto the coffee table. "I think I should have a little bitty nightcap before you take me to bed," she said, then dodged my reach and downed the shot before I could get it out of her hand.

"Okay, but that's going to be the last one. You're going to have a pretty bad headache in the morning."

"Probably. Come on, let's get started." She giggled.

I helped her up the staircase and walked her into the bathroom.

"Where's the bed?" she asked, unbuckling her jeans and sitting down.

"In the next room. I'll wait for you in the hallway. Call me when you're finished, and I'll help you."

"You're so sweet," she slurred.

I knew where this was headed. She had maybe two minutes of life left in her, and she was going to be in the bathroom for at least fifteen. I turned on the nightlight in the upstairs hallway then I got the guest bedroom prepared. I turned the bedside table lamp on, pulled the sheets back, and placed an empty wastebasket by the side of the bed.

She didn't call me. I just heard her fall down in the bathroom about ten minutes later. When I opened the door, she was on all fours, giggling, with her jeans around her ankles. I rolled her over, pulled her jeans off, then helped her into the guest bedroom where she more or less collapsed on the bed. I raised her up, and she sat there, weaving with her eyes closed while I pulled her top over her head. As her top came off, she fell backward onto the bed with a smile on her face. I lifted her legs up onto the bed and pulled the covers up over her shoulders.

"You want to be on top, Dave?" she slurred.

I folded her jeans and the red top and placed them on the dresser. Marsha was already snoring as I turned off the lamp on the bedside table. I left the bathroom light on and then headed back to bed.

Seventeen

The next morning I returned what was left of the Cuervo Gold bottle to the cupboard and washed Marsha's shot glass. The finish on the top of my coffee table had bubbled up from the spilled tequila, and I attempted to wipe up the damage. The top of the table was ruined and would have to be stripped, sanded, stained again, and then refinished— not the best start to the day or a tryst.

Marsha was still upstairs asleep, so I made coffee and breakfast. I made myself a sandwich at lunchtime. After a while, I went upstairs to wake her. She was still sleeping soundly with her head under the pillow. I'd been in the same position myself once or twice, and I didn't have the heart to wake her. So I just left her a note saying, 'Close the door on the way out and give me a call when you feel up to it.' Then I drove to the office.

Louie wasn't in when I arrived, but he'd been there. The coffee pot was empty, but the burner was still on, and the office smelled like an electrical fire. I turned the burner off, opened a window, and drummed my fingers on the desk, thinking about Marsha and the fact that no good deed seems to go unpunished. Louie huffed and puffed his way up the stairs and into the office about a half-hour later.

"Something burning?" he asked as he stood in the doorway and wrinkled his nose.

"You left the burner on and the coffee pot empty."

"Oh." He shrugged in a 'that answers it' kind of way like it was just a daily occurrence. "Still working the Desi thing?" he asked, then settled into his office chair and set his feet on the picnic table.

"Right now, I just seem to be eliminating options. Nothing at the Bremer Tower, that particular suite was empty or still empty. I spoke to neighbors where she used to live before she was convicted, nothing there. I talked to a couple of co-workers at Nasty's, but they didn't have any information." I didn't feel the need to elaborate about Marsha. "I've still got to check with the people at Karla's, but I'd be surprised if they were able to tell me anything."

"You talk to the rental people at the Bremer Tower or the maintenance staff?" Louie asked.

"No, I probably should and will, but their testimony was in the case notes. They had no record of anyone being in that office suite."

"Sounds like that old movie with Robert Redford and Paul Newman…not Butch Cassidy. What the hell was it?"

"The Sting?"

"Yeah. They make that betting place look like the real deal, then fold it up and get out of town in about fifteen minutes."

"Seems like an awful lot of work," I said.

"Not when you consider the millions someone got from the Federal Reserve."

My phone rang, but I didn't recognize the number.

"Haskell Investigations."

"Dev, I am so sorry."

"Well, at least you got my name right. How's the head, Marsha?"

"God," she groaned. "At first, I was afraid I was going to die. Now I'm afraid I won't."

"I guess there's hope then."

"I'm not so sure," she said. "Listen, Dev, I really, really apologize for the way I acted last night. At least the part I remember. You didn't deserve that, and I certainly didn't help matters. I'm so sorry."

"Relax, it happens."

"I would still like to talk to you. I have an idea."

"This doesn't have anything to do with your really great ass, does it?"

There was a pause before her groan. "Oh, God, I said that, didn't I? I halfway remember, but I was hoping I'd just dreamed it. I'm so, so sorry. Please give me a chance. I want to help."

I was thinking Marsha really wasn't the kind of help I needed right now.

"I know, I know, you're probably thinking this isn't the kind of help you really need right now, but just give me a chance. I promise no tequila ever again in my entire life."

"Okay, look, I'm at my office now. Can you make it down here later this afternoon?"

"I'll be there. Let me just grab a shower and get cleaned up."

"There are spare towels in that closet at the end of the hallway," I said.

"Actually, I'm at my place. I followed your directions and locked the door behind me when I left."

"Thanks."

"Is your office still at the address on this card?"

"Yeah."

"I'll see you in an hour, and I'm so sorry for everything. And, well, for what didn't happen," she said and then hung up before I could ask for a rain check.

"Last night's entertainment?" Louie asked.

I told him the story, finishing up with Marsha's half dozen apologies.

"Well, you're a better man than me. I would have sat there and finished the tequila with her."

"Not what I need to be doing right now. She said she's gonna grab a shower and be here in about an hour."

"You believe that?" Louie asked.

"Yeah, I'm sure she'll feel better once she has a hot shower and just—"

"No, I meant the hour part?" he said.

Eighteen

Louie's point was well taken. Marsha washed up on shore about two and a half hours later. Amazing what a hot shower and a couple hours of makeup can do to a hangover. She looked a lot better than anything I'd seen that day. She carried a bag stuffed with jelly-filled doughnuts from Wuollet's Bakery and two large Starbucks coffees. Great breakfast fare, but unfortunately, it was close to five in the afternoon.

"What can I say? I'm in the entertainment business. We're on a different clock than the rest of the world," she said after I pointed her timing out to her. Louie already had the better part of a jelly doughnut crammed in his mouth.

"I suppose I could take the doughnuts back if you think that would help," she said.

"No, no, not a big deal, these things are great. I love 'em," Louie said, then reached for another.

"Grab a seat, Marsha. You want some coffee?" I asked.

"No, I'm on a sugar high just to chase away my hangover. You shouldn't have gotten me so drunk last night."

"Actually—"

"Relax, I'm kidding," she said, then shrugged.

"So, you mentioned a plan on the phone?"

She took a moment to lick sugar from her fingertips, while Louie and I just stared, mesmerized.

"What? Oh, God, you two are such pervs."

"Your plan?" I said, coming back to reality.

"I'm just wondering if maybe this Gaston guy would hit on me if I flirted. Maybe that would help."

"Interesting. But I don't think hitting on you would be considered a criminal offense and, how, exactly, do you propose getting in contact with him? I've only seen the guy on TV."

"I was thinking I could do something unusual like maybe find him at his office. Try something clever and unexpected, like maybe call and make an appointment."

"An appointment?"

"Yeah, never seems to fail."

She had me thinking or at least trying to think. "But then what?"

"He'll want to take me out to dinner and woo me into his bed. Somewhere along the way, I'll learn about Desi, and I suspect a number of other women."

"The guy is happily married."

"Is that what they call it? Even better. From what you've told me, he sounds like the type who keeps score. Probably lies awake at night trying to remember the names of all the women he's conquered over the course of his life."

Louie swallowed, licked some jelly off his lower lip, and said, "The guy's a model citizen. He serves on boards and donates to charity. He's a wounded veteran, a pillar of the damn community."

"Aren't they all?" Marsha said and paused, not looking at either one of us. She gave the distinct impression she was thinking far beyond our immediate conversation.

"You left out the part where he had Desi as a mistress for close to a year. That he set her up, watched her take the fall, let her do time in prison, lose virtually everything, and never even bothered to lift a hand. As far as anyone can tell, he never even bothered to ask if she was okay."

"I'm not disagreeing, but at best, it would be viewed as hearsay, tough if not impossible to prove at this stage," Louie said as he attacked another jelly doughnut. He seemed oblivious to the glob of red jelly that had dribbled down across the front of his shirt.

"Take it from me, just knowing a little about human nature and certain men," Marsha emphasized the word 'certain.' "Desi wasn't this creep's first little dabble on the side. She's just the one we know about. There were most likely women before her, and there have been women after her. In fact, if we found out he brought her on board for the express purpose of being the delivery person of those files and taking the fall, it wouldn't surprise me in the least. This guy's a real schemer."

I couldn't disagree, but I still couldn't see how Marsha getting in the way of my investigation was going to help.

"We're still back to the same thing, trying to prove any of this ever happened. As it stands now, this is all nothing more than unfounded rumors. Might as well be something we just made up. Old Gaston, being attracted to a gorgeous woman like you, Marsha, is one thing. Proving he set up Desi to take the fall is quite another, a huge leap."

"I'm going to make an appointment with Mr. Driscoll. Not if, but when he places his follow-up phone call, that will be the first indication we're on the right track."

"Marsha, the guy is something like a hundred years older than you."

"Which just makes my job that much easier. He'd like nothing better than a younger woman to remind him he's still got that old magic. A pillar of the community? Spare me. Pull his pants down, and it's all about him. Look, I'll keep you posted. I gotta work tonight."

"You got time for dinner?" I asked.

"Don't take it personally, but no, Dev. I don't. I'm still a little bit in the recovery mode from last night. Besides, I want to call this guy's office after five, so I have to leave a message, then I'll call him again tomorrow. I'll take a rain check though on the dinner offer."

"You got it."

She stood, brushed some imaginary sugar off her front, then gave me a peck on the cheek, and looked at Louie.

"You've got jelly on your shirt." She nodded to the blob that had landed on his stomach.

"I'm saving that for later," he said.

Nineteen

Marsha phoned the following afternoon, my first call of the day. Louie was napping in his chair, and I was staring out the window daydreaming while I waited for buses to begin unloading working girls at the end of their day.

"Haskell Investigations."

"Hi, Dev. Guess what?"

"You're back on tequila?"

"Oh, icky, no. But I have an eleven o'clock appointment with the infamous Mr. Gaston Driscoll tomorrow morning."

"You're kidding?" I was more than a little surprised.

"I told you."

"What are you supposed to be meeting about?"

"I just said I was considering making a career change, and a friend mentioned him as a top man in his field, someone I should talk to."

"And that got you an appointment with him the next day?"

"He said he could only give me ten minutes."

"Ten minutes? You'll have to wear a raincoat with nothing on underneath."

"That's what I was planning to wear for the second meeting."

"So, what do you think he'll do?" I asked. For some reason, I wasn't thrilled about her getting an appointment with Driscoll.

"What will he do? He'll sit there and tell me how absolutely wonderful and successful he is while I bat my eyelashes. Then, he'll either ask me to lunch, call me later in the day or both. I'll give him my personal number."

"Your personal number?"

"I use an answering service, sometimes," she said but didn't elaborate.

"Marsha, will you call me after you get out of that meeting. Please? I just want to know you're all right. You said you're meeting him at his office, right?"

"No, Dev, a pay-by-the-hour hotel room, did I forget to mention that? Yes, I'm meeting him at his office. I'll call you when I'm out of there, but don't wig out if I'm not calling you ten minutes later. He may be busy or something and I end up waiting. On the other hand—"

"It's the '*on the other hand,*' that worries me."

"Oh, that's sweet. I'd make a good private investigator. Wouldn't I?" She laughed.

"Just be careful and call me when you're out of there."

"I promise. Bye," she said and hung up.

"She got an appointment with Gaston Driscoll?" Louie asked. He was tilted back in his office chair with his feet resting up on the picnic table. His eyes remained closed, arms wrapped comfortably across his belly. There was a reddish-pink smear across the front of his shirt from the jelly he'd dribbled yesterday. I'd thought he'd been asleep through my phone conversation.

"Yeah, she's meeting him tomorrow, but only for a few minutes. She thinks he'll either ask her to lunch or call her later on. I don't know. It sounds pretty slim to me."

"Well, first things first, she got the appointment with him."

"Yeah, she got the appointment. Say, I'm going to try and do a little research on a name. You interested in meeting at The Spot later on?"

Louie still hadn't opened his eyes.

"What time were you thinking? I'll see if I can fit it in."

"I'll call you," I said and headed down to police headquarters.

I'd phoned Aaron LaZelle in advance, and he had the proper form signed and supposedly waiting for me at the Sergeant's desk.

"Haskell, Haskell," the Desk Sergeant said. His nametag read Suel, P. I knew him as Petey. "No, not seeing anything like that in the file here, Dev."

"Lieutenant LaZelle said he would have it down here waiting for me."

"Nope, sorry. Nothing with Haskell on it."

"You're kidding."

"No, nothing here. Got one addressed to Hassle. Could that be you?" He smiled.

"Probably. Very funny, Petey," I said, taking the envelope from his hand. It was an 8 x 10 manila envelope with 'Hassle' scrawled across the front in black marker. I checked inside. It was the form I needed, and amazingly my name was spelled correctly on the thing.

"We can't be too careful, Dev. You never know what kind of lowlifes are going to wander in here off the street."

I couldn't tell if he was referring to me. I thanked Petey and took the elevator down to the basement catacomb level, where Madeline Siedschlag drank in private. That musty basement smell hit me the moment the elevator door opened. Madeline was seated at her desk, and fortunately for me, still awake. I couldn't spot her thermos anywhere.

"Hi, Madeline. How are you this sunny day?"

"Not that you'd know it from down here. Not so much as a window to save my soul. It could be snowing out there, and I'd never be the wiser."

I really didn't want to get into the various bleak aspects of Madeline's life down here below ground level, so I just smiled and handed her my properly signed form.

"I just need to hop onto one of your computers and review some information."

She half grunted without looking up then said, "Cubicles two and four are available. Don't forget to sign-in. The logbook is on the counter, and sign out when you leave. I can't leave here until four-fifteen." She made it sound like a sentence, which in a way, I guess it was.

I settled into the second cubicle, pushed aside the Milky Way wrapper left on the keyboard, and logged in. Aaron had given me an ID and password to log in with. I supposed giving me access to state and federal files wasn't quite following chapter and verse, but on the other hand, everything I looked at could be monitored and reviewed. I was denied access to ongoing investigations and a variety of sensitive files. My mission today was to try and locate Helen Olsen, formerly with the HR department at Touchier & Touchier. I wanted to talk with her regarding Desi's dismissal and frankly any other information I might be able to obtain from her.

In short order, it became pretty apparent the conversation was going to be brief and rather one-sided. Helen Olsen was residing in Resurrection Cemetery. She'd died tragically six-and-a-half years ago at age thirty-seven. Apparently, she'd driven her car out onto the ice on Lake Minnetonka at about three in the morning on the sixteenth of March. One day before St. Patrick's Day. The vehicle had fallen through the ice. A follow-up article listed her blood alcohol content as 0.29, almost three times the legal limit at the time. It was amazing she had been conscious enough to even drive.

It turned out a lake resident became suspicious about the large hole in the ice, and a day later, on the 17th, her car was located by the authorities. If it had snowed or temperatures had dipped that night, she might never have been found. The vehicle and her body couldn't be recovered for another week until the ice went out on the twenty-third of March. When the vehicle was pulled from the eighteen feet of water, an open bottle stashed under the front seat was recovered.

I used my pen and did the math on the inside of the Milky Way wrapper. Helen Olsen's accident would have been about a year and a half into Desi's sentence. Maybe a coincidence, maybe not. She went through the ice on a lake located on the far side of town, a good half-hour to forty-minute drive from her St. Paul home. It led one to at least pause if not question.

I read her obituary. Helen's picture showed a fairly attractive, slim woman with Scandinavian features, sharp blue eyes, reddish-blonde hair, and prominent cheekbones with a slightly upturned nose. Other than four years away at college, she seemed to have lived her entire life in St. Paul.

She was single, a graduate of the University of Wisconsin, Madison, and had received an MBA at the University of Minnesota. She was survived by a younger sister, Catherine Lindquist, living in Minneapolis. I made a note. Helen had apparently been involved in her church choir, local girl scouts, and volunteered in the Big Brother's and Sister's program. One had the impression she was a disciplined individual who would have taken her employment rather seriously.

The picture I got from her obituary and the follow-up articles presented a contradiction. On the one hand was a serious, accomplished, dedicated, successful woman. On the other, a woman who was miles from her home at three in the morning, all alone, drinking and driving with an open bottle. So intoxicated, she was almost three times beyond the legal limit. She drove her vehicle out onto the lake a full month after ice fishing houses, and everything else in the entire state of Minnesota had been ordered off the ice.

At a time when everyone in the upper Midwest was welcoming warming temperatures and the melting of snow and ice, this woman, born and raised here, obviously smart, thought it would be a good idea to drive out to the middle of one of the larger lakes in the region. Maybe she was just drunk and stupid. Or maybe there was something more to the story. I remembered Desi mentioning that the day she'd been fired, Helen Olson had seemed very uncomfortable escorting her out of the building. It seemed like it might be a good idea to talk with Helen's sister, Catherine Lindquist.

Twenty

I read through the rest of the online information regarding Helen Olsen, then started to wade through the volumes regarding Gaston Driscoll.

In the negative column, I didn't find so much as a ticket for jaywalking. Born and raised in the city, he had served or was serving on most of the boards of directors worth serving on. He was the quintessential successful businessman, a senior partner at Touchier & Touchier, one of the region's most highly-regarded architectural firms and now called Gaston Enterprises. He was an elder in his church and served on the school board. He donated time, money, and his expertise to a variety of community organizations. He supported, funded, and advised the local and state arts community. He'd been a stalwart of the business community for years and, in general, seemed to represent exactly the sort of individual any city would love to brag about.

It turned out Gaston was also widowed. His wife, Bernadette, had died in a solo boating accident about five years back. The accident was attributed to the unfortunate combination of a cigarette and a leaky fuel line. Interestingly the accident had occurred at night out on Lake Minnetonka, the very same lake where Helen Olsen's car had gone through the ice just a year-and-a-half earlier. It was a large lake, used by a lot of people all year round, but still a curious coincidence. I decided to learn what I could about Bernadette.

I found a grand total of four articles from which to glean Bernadette Driscoll's information. One was her obituary. She'd been born in Buhl, Minnesota, a small town up north on the Mesabi Iron Range. It seemed her claim to fame in life had been she was married to Gaston Driscoll. Where Gaston was an extrovert with a thumb in uncountable pies, Bernadette Driscoll, from the little I could find, seemed to come across as damn near a recluse.

They had been married for forty-two years. No children. Apparently, she loved her English Springer Spaniels. Other than her obituary, she was mentioned only in passing in three other articles. Based on what I read, her most notable accomplishment had been her attendance at an American Kennel Club show back in 2007.

My cell phone rang, and as I answered, I stood and glanced over the grey cubicle walls to see if I could spot Madeline. I could not.

"Haskell Investigations."

"Hi, Dev, I'm just checking in so you can relax. I'm out of my meeting," Marsha said.

"How'd it go?" I asked then checked my watch. It was close to two.

"What a charmer!"

"Really?"

"Yeah, if you're into that kind of thing. I'm not, especially under these circumstances."

"So he took you to lunch?"

"Actually, no, he didn't. He tried, but I told him I had an appointment, then we proceeded to chat. Let me rephrase that. He proceeded to wax eloquent about how wonderful he was. I just had to sit there and pretend to be interested, for the better part of an hour."

"You learn anything?"

"Only that he's a more pompous butt-head than I thought. I expect to hear from him in a day or two."

"You made another appointment with him?"

"No, but I gave him my card and wrote my private number on the thing while he tried to look down my blouse. He'll call."

"How can you be so sure?"

"Because you're all the same. The only time he took his eyes off my boobs was when I was crossing my legs."

"He was probably trying to figure out what bra color you were wearing."

"Red, date underwear, not that it's any of your business."

I was beginning to understand why Marsha was so sure Driscoll would call her back.

"Look, I just wanted to check in and give you the update. You learn anything?"

"Maybe, nothing earth-shattering, but I think I'm beginning to see some coincidences, and I don't really believe in coincidence. Driscoll mention his wife?"

"No, but I really didn't expect him to. Why?"

"She died in a boating accident a few years back. Might just be an unfortunate incident, I don't know."

"Gee, just like on CSI. Cool. Look, I'm dancing the dinner hour, four 'til midnight so I better run."

"Dinner hour goes 'til midnight?"

"You'd be surprised," she said and hung up.

I went back to my research. I couldn't find anything else on Bernadette Driscoll. That left me feeling sorry for her, although I couldn't describe exactly why. I read two dozen more rave reviews about Gaston before I decided to pack it in and rejoin society as I knew it, at The Spot. Madeline was nowhere to be seen, so I signed myself out in the logbook and left. On the way over to The Spot, I phoned Catherine Lindquist and left a message.

Twenty-one

It was a sunny, pleasant morning despite my lingering at The Spot until well after midnight the night before. I barely had a chance to make the office coffee when my phone rang.

"Haskell Investigations."

"May I speak with Mr. Haskell, please?"

The woman on the other end sounded clipped and precise. My first thought was, who is suing me now?

"You got him," I said, resigned to my fate.

"Mr. Haskell, I'm returning a call you placed yesterday afternoon at four-twenty-seven."

Other than calling Louie and telling him to meet me at The Spot, the only call I made yesterday afternoon was the message I left for Catherine Lindquist.

"Catherine Lindquist?"

"Yes."

She'd been on the line for all of ten seconds, and I'd determined she wasn't going to be much fun. Then again, given the fact I wanted to discuss her sister's death, that was probably a foregone conclusion, so I plunged ahead.

"May I call you Catherine?"

"What is this about?"

"I wanted to talk to you about your sister."

"Helen?"

"Yes, I'm a private investigator. I'm working on a case where Helen had a passing involvement with an individual while she worked in the HR department at Touchier & Touchier. I don't—"

"Those awful people. Are you working for them?" There was an immediate edge to her tone.

"Hardly," I said, playing the angle. "The individual I'm working for was let go from Touchier some years back. It gets rather involved from there. I just wonder if I could meet with you personally?"

"I wouldn't have any information about that situation or anything else that went on at that dreadful place. After all, Helen worked there, not me, thank God. She gave her heart and soul to those criminals, poor thing. I'm sorry, but I don't believe I can be of any assistance to you in this matter. I wish you the best of luck in your endeavor, but I—"

"Actually, I'm investigating what seems to be shaping up as a similar circumstance to your sister's. It sounds like you believe she was treated unfairly. The investigation I'm involved in may be heading in a similar direction."

There was a very long pause.

"Miss Lindquist?"

"I don't wish to discuss this matter over the phone," she said.

"I could meet you somewhere, your home or a public place of your choosing if that would help make you feel more comfortable."

"Not my home. Do you know the St. Paul Grill?"

"I do."

"I could meet this evening for a short while. Six o'clock would work best for me," she said.

"I'll be there," I said. "I'll mention you to the hostess, and she'll point you in my direction. If for some reason she doesn't, just call me at this number, and I'll stand up and wave."

"Very well, six o'clock. But, I warn you, Mr. Haskell, if this is some scam or it turns out to be another attack on what's left of Helen's reputation, I'll have no problem turning on my heel and walking out."

"Fair enough," I said.

Twenty-two

The St. Paul Grill is located, not surprisingly, in the St. Paul Hotel. The Grill is one of the city's trendier restaurants, able to comfortably cater to the casual designer-jean and golf-shirt crowd as well as the starched-collar and club-tie set. Although in these times, ties, especially club ties, seemed to be few and far between.

I arrived fifteen minutes early. My phone impression of Catherine Lindquist was a woman who wouldn't tolerate tardiness and was quite capable of sipping a single glass of Perrier with a twist of lemon for most of the night. I'd donned a sport coat and my cleanest dirty shirt for the occasion.

I was shown to a table near the large bank of windows. The table had a starched white tablecloth and two starched white napkins. Two black wooden chairs with burgundy and gold-striped-cushion seats were positioned directly across from one another. There was a small votive glass in the center of the table holding a burning candle with the wine menu resting just in front of it.

"Would you care for a beverage, Sir?"

He looked a bit like Bruce Willis, only taller and with some hair.

"I'd like to wait. Someone is joining me."

"Very good." He nodded and seemed to fade away.

It was still a little too early for the dinner rush, but the bar area was filling up. What I presumed was the courthouse crowd drifted through the door in groups of twos and threes, looking ready to relax after a long day of making life miserable for those of us less fortunate. Over the course of the next fifteen minutes, the noise level increased perceptibly.

I spotted her as she approached the hostess. She had close-cropped blonde hair and the same upturned nose as her sister's obituary photo. She was maybe five-six with an extremely slim figure. A figure most women would describe as really cute, and most men wouldn't notice. She wore some limp outfit that seemed to hang on her and effectively hide whatever slight curves she possessed. The color was so light blue it almost looked grey and must have carried the 'boring' label. She had cinched the thing around her narrow waist with a thin powder blue belt.

I waved as the hostess pointed in my direction. Catherine Lindquist nodded acknowledgment, but didn't smile. She seemed to take a visibly deep breath before plunging in my direction.

I was on my best behavior and stood as she approached. She glanced from side to side like she was walking point for a platoon in the field. No one bothered to give her or the shapeless outfit a second look.

"Mr. Haskell?" She stood with her hands cupped together, heels touching, and her feet spread at a perfect forty-five-degree angle. As she said my name, she looked like she should be in a receiving line standing next to the Queen.

"Very pleased to meet you. Please call me Dev. May I call you Catherine?" I asked, extending my hand. I felt like I was in some junior high manners class, and she was the battle-ax instructor.

"You may," she said after a short consideration.

"Thank you for coming. Please, please sit down. May I get you something?"

"Perhaps just a sparkling water with a twist of lemon."

I knew it.

"Two sparkling waters," I said to the waiter hovering just within earshot. He nodded and ran off.

She looked at me— actually, no she didn't. Her blue eyes turned into lasers, and she bored holes in me. I was thinking of asking her how she was related to Detective Norris Manning when she interrupted my thoughts.

"You said this was about my sister and someone who was at Touchier with a similar circumstance. It wouldn't happen to be Daphne Cole, would it?" she asked, then leaned back as the slightest hint of satisfaction spread over her face.

I waited for the smugness to set in, giving myself a mandatory five count before I responded.

"No. Daphne Cole? Who's that?"

"Oh, I just thought, well, I'd received a call from her maybe a year, year-and-a-half ago."

The waiter suddenly appeared and set our sparkling waters and a bowl of bread crusts on the table.

"Would you mind if I took some notes?" I asked, taking a notebook and pen from my coat pocket, hoping their appearance would make it more difficult for her to say 'no.'

"That depends on what you choose to write. I'll find it acceptable for now," she said, then took a barely perceptible sip of water.

I wrote the name Daphne Cole at the top of the page then set my pen down.

"Catherine, before I ask you about Daphne Cole or your sister, let me tell you what I'm looking into, and you tell me if any of this strikes a chord. Other than a one time mention of your sister, Helen. I know of nothing else associated with her. But there is possibly a bit of an unfortunate coincidence, I think, maybe. Let me explain, and then you tell me. Fair enough?"

She nodded and raised the glass of sparkling water to her lips. About the time the water touched her lips, she set the glass back down. I couldn't see her doing tequila shots with Marsha anytime soon.

I proceeded to tell her Desi's story. I told her about Desi's education, her hard work, and eventually, I got around to her affair with Gaston Driscoll. I explained how Desi thought she was set up, how Driscoll cut her loose, let her twist in the wind until everything she'd ever worked for was lost. She interrupted only once, just after I told her about finding Desi's body and calling the police.

"She's the woman I recently read about in the paper. I felt like calling the authorities again, but I've given up on that. The last time I phoned, they told me in no uncertain terms that I was crazy," she said.

I finished my tale by telling her about reviewing case files and finding her name listed in Helen's obituary. I didn't mention Marsha or her appointment with Gaston Driscoll, and I didn't mention Karla.

"So, then who's paying you?" she asked when I finished.

"No one," I replied, which was technically true since I still had Karla's check in my wallet. "I met with Desi only once. She told me her story with something close to a religious fervor and asked me for help. She told me I was her last shot. Looking back, I think I was her only chance. She was broke, desperate, no one believed her, and then there was Driscoll's shining reputation stacked up against her more tarnished one. So I looked her in the eye, and I told her I wasn't interested. She shook my hand and walked away. Shortly after that, someone murdered her. I was her last shot, and I blew it. Who's paying me? With all due respect, Catherine, I think I owe a God damn debt."

She didn't so much as blink at my language. "And you believe that if you catch the individual who murdered her, that will even the score?" Her eyes were back to boring in on me like lasers.

I thought about that. Would catching the bastard even the score? Not really. The damn sparkling water suddenly wasn't cutting it. I signaled a waiter then looked across the table at Catherine Lindquist.

"Look, nothing I can do is going to even the score. I believe I screwed up, big time. But I hope I can nail whoever killed Desi, and then I'm going to deal with whoever is ultimately responsible."

"Sir?" The waiter nodded. He'd heard my last statement and looked just a little nervous.

"Jameson, on the rocks," I said then looked across the table to see if she understood what I had been trying to say.

"Ma'am?" the waiter asked.

"Maker's Mark," she said. "And you can take this." She pushed her glass of sparkling water toward the edge of the table, then redirected her attention to me once the waiter departed. She suddenly seemed to relax a bit.

"I think Helen might have mentioned that dismissal. I believe it was her first experience with something like that. You know, a dismissal over the phone no less and then having to escort someone out of the building. At least I think it may have been her first experience on that high a level. If I recall, she mentioned this woman, your friend Desi, was in line to be made partner. Helen was rather upset by the whole thing. It was quite the news all around the firm from what I gather. Well, and then, of course, the charges and the poor woman's subsequent trial. Actually, I think it may have either been the beginning or the cementing of her relationship with that dreadful Driscoll although, she gave me no indication of that fact at the time."

"Relationship?"

We chatted on about things in general. Catherine did most of the talking, and although her information on Touchier & Touchier wasn't current, it was better than the information I didn't have. Eventually, we ordered dinner.

I'd finished a second Jameson and was busy cutting into my dinner steak, listening to Catherine.

"Once I learned of Helen's affair with that Driscoll person, I repeatedly warned her. In fact, I warned her so often it became a point of contention between the two of us, and we didn't need that. What we needed was one another. Then Driscoll took another bed-mate, and just like I had warned, Helen found herself on the outside looking in. The next thing you know, she lost her job and her world collapsed like a house of cards. No job, no income, the economy was shot, she had a mortgage, everyone was out of work. Do you know how many companies were hiring in those days? Let alone hiring for their Human Resources department? Exactly zero, no one."

I nodded.

"Helen told me once that she had spoken with a friend at a large insurance company out in Omaha or Des Moines or somewhere. She was one of something like seventeen-hundred people applying for the entry-level position they had. She said they eliminated her application because she was too qualified. Can you imagine? Too qualified, my Lord. She worked so hard, so damn hard."

I nodded. A couple of nearby tables were suddenly watching us.

"She eventually lost her home. Of course, her job had been who she was. It allowed her to do all the other good things that she did. And she was a good person, Mr. Haskell, a very good person."

"Is that when she began drinking?"

Catherine looked at me for a good long moment. She just stared. Actually, she was looking through me. I had the feeling she could see my very soul. Finally, she shook her head.

"My God, as if life wasn't cruel enough. Helen didn't drink."

"But they found that open bottle in her car. Her blood alcohol was almost three times the legal limit. Why else would she have gone—"

"I'm telling you, Helen didn't drink. She couldn't. She had a reaction to alcohol, almost like she was allergic to it. She would get violently ill. We used to laugh as girls." Tears were suddenly welling up in her eyes. "Helen was the perfect double date. I could pound them down, and she couldn't drink. The next morning she'd be able to tell me everything that had happened the night before. Three times the legal limit? In thirty-plus years, she couldn't drink half-a-glass of wine before she was throwing up."

"But the autopsy results . . . I mean, they were pretty conclusive."

Catherine shook her head. "Autopsy results," she scoffed. "Look, I can't tell you what happened. All I know is she didn't drink, and by the way, she couldn't swim either. She was afraid to even be around boats, scared stiff. So to suggest she consumed that quantity of alcohol and then drove out on a frozen lake in March, in the middle of a spring thaw? It's just not credible, it's preposterous."

"Did you go to the police with this?"

"I've lost count of the times I've been to the police. I hired specialists. We provided medical history and a-half-dozen different expert medical opinions. But, the fact remains she had that damn blood alcohol level, and an open bottle was found in the car, just as you said. The car with my sister in it went through the ice, and she was strapped in behind the wheel. As far as the police out in Minnetonka were concerned, it was case closed."

"Are you aware that Driscoll's wife was killed in a boating accident late one night on the same lake, Lake Minnetonka?"

Catherine nodded. "I remember reading about it in the paper. I bought a card and wrote 'It serves you right.

Now you know how it feels.' But I never mailed it. Still have the thing tucked in my desk somewhere."

"I'm wondering if there might be a pattern here."

"Well, you convinced me a long time ago, but under the circumstances, I'm a pretty easy sell."

"Tell me about Daphne Cole?" I said.

"I really don't know much, actually. Well, except she's one of the lucky ones. She's still alive. She worked at Touchier and had been swept off her feet by Gaston Driscoll, and when he grew tired of her, she lost her job, I presume just like all the others. So she gave me a call."

"Why you?"

"Apparently, there were rumors about Driscoll, and Helen and so she contacted me. Let me rephrase that, there were rumors in the ladies room. He was, and as far as I'm aware, still is, a managing partner. I don't think anyone there would dare confront the man. I suppose if you were honest, he probably represents a particular route of career advancement for a woman, and if you were really honest, it's a route that never gets you where you hope to end up."

"Seems to be the pattern. I think it might be worthwhile to talk with her, Daphne Cole. Do you have any idea how I can reach her?"

"Not really. I did see a marriage announcement for her in the paper awhile back, maybe a year ago."

"Do you remember who she married?"

"No, I do recall that she was keeping her maiden name, though. If that's what you're referring to. At the time, I thought good for you, young lady. Stick to your guns."

There might have been more to what she said than the woman keeping her maiden name, but I didn't pursue it.

I told Catherine about the Touchier & Touchier name change to Gaston Enterprises.

"Oh, how vile, how absolutely dreadful. In a way, not surprising, after all you're dealing with a tremendously gigantic ego. What's a measly seventy or eighty years of firm history and reputation next to that?"

We parted after dinner. As I was driving home, my phone rang.

"Haskell Investigations."

"Dev, Marsha. I'm on break, so I gotta make it quick. I got a phone message from Gaston Driscoll. He wants me to call him."

"For another appointment?"

"He just asked me to call him."

"So, what'd he say?"

"Hello? Are you listening? I haven't called him back yet. He can just sit there and play with himself tonight for all I care. I'll get back to him tomorrow."

"Just be careful, Marsha. This guy is beginning to look really bad."

"Gee, there's a surprise, not."

"Let me know what he says and do not meet with him until we talk further. Okay? You'll keep me posted?"

"Yeah, Dad, I'll have the car home just as soon as the library closes. God, will you F-ing relax? You're driving me crazy."

"I'm not kidding, Marsha. Don't go off like the Lone Ranger here. I can be watching you if he wants to do anything. He doesn't know what I look like."

"Whatever. Okay, hey, gotta go."

"Listen, Marsha, I don't want you—"

"Sorry Dev, that's my intro they're playing. Gotta fly. Bye."

I wondered what Gaston Driscoll's reaction would be if word got out his royal highness was expressing interest in a stripper. He'd probably come back with some line about saving those less fortunate.

Twenty-three

I couldn't find anyone named Daphne Cole in the phonebook, which probably put her age somewhere under fifty. From what Catherine told me last night at dinner, I figured she might be more around thirty-five. I found a half dozen Daphne Cole's when I looked online. There was a slim chance I might be able to locate the woman I was looking for after a day or two of long hours and some lucky guesswork.

I decided instead to call the Department of Motor Vehicles, the DMV, and talk with my friend Donna, who owed me an eternal favor. Then I could look out my office window at women boarding the bus while Donna searched the DMV records for Daphne Cole's phone number.

"Good morning, Minnesota Department of Motor Vehicles. This is Donna. How may I help you?"

"Hi, Donna, Dev Haskell."

There was a long pause before she half-whispered. "What do you want? I could lose my job talking to you."

"You'd lose it for sure if I report your torrid little night with that summer intern, but you begged me not to and promised to help me and be polite whenever I called."

"I did not say I would be polite, you jerk," she hissed.

"True. Hey, look, Donna, I need the address and phone number of a Daphne Cole. That's C-O-L-E. Her marital status would have changed about ten to eighteen months ago. I'd guess she's between thirty and forty years of age."

"I can't be acting as your dating service. You're putting me at risk here."

"Oh, okay. I'm sorry about that. Let me ask your husband. I've got his number here somewhere."

"All right, all right. I'll call you back," she said and hung up.

I had my feet resting on the window sill, scanning the street with my binoculars when Louie came in.

"Wow, you're already working. Gee, amazing."

"Just keeping this corner of the city safe," I said when my phone rang.

"Haskell …"

"I have two potential numbers. Do you have a color crayon handy so you can write these down?" Donna said. There was not a drop of humor in her voice. She proceeded to read me the numbers then growled, "Satisfied?"

"Let's hope these work," I said.

"Give the poor woman my condolences," she said and hung up.

I tossed the phone on my desk and shook my head.

"Problems?" Louie asked. He was pouring the last of yesterday's coffee into his mug and then putting the empty pot back on the burner.

"No, my pal, Donna down at DMV."

"No offense, but it didn't sound like she was really your pal."

"You're telling me. Look, I did her a favor, a big favor. So from time to time, when I need a little help, she has to come across."

"She doesn't seem too happy about it."

"If I had to guess, I'd say she's never very happy. Hey, turn that burner off, will you? The pot's empty."

"Just drying the thing out."

"Sure, you are."

I phoned the first number Donna gave me, and the recording told me to; '*Please check the number you have dialed, the number you have reached is either out of service or out of the area.*'

I called the second number. A woman picked up on the fourth or fifth ring. I could hear a baby crying. The kid sounded close, like she may have been holding it.

"Hello."

"Hi, I'm trying to reach Daphne Cole."

"This is Daphne. Who's calling, please?"

"My name is Devlin Haskell. I'm trying to reach a Daphne Cole, who at one time was employed by an architectural firm, Touchier & Touchier."

"Yes." Her response was drawn out, and you could hear the caution rushing in.

"You worked at Touchier & Touchier, Miss Cole?"

"What is this about?" she asked, then tried to quiet the baby who ignored her and kept right on crying.

"It's a bit of an involved situation. I wonder if there might be a convenient time to meet, I'm—"

"To tell you the truth, no, there isn't. In case you can't hear, I've got a baby with an ear infection, and there is nothing convenient for me where Touchier & Touchier is concerned. Thank you," she said and hung up.

I shook my head again, tossed my phone back on the desk, and picked up my binoculars.

"You seem to be having that effect on women of late," Louie said.

"No, I've always had that effect on women," I said and went back to scanning the street.

Twenty-four

It was almost two in the afternoon. Nap time. I watched the woman on the other side of the street pulling a wagon up next to the front steps. She walked back across the front yard and pushed a stroller with side-by-side seats up next to the wagon. She wandered back again and gathered up the half dozen toys scattered across the lawn and dumped them in the wagon. She looked around the yard, gave a half satisfied nod, then sat down on the steps, took out her phone, and started punching keys.

The two-story house was a tan-colored stucco affair with chocolate-brown trim and a fire-engine-red front door. Given the neighborhood and the design, I guessed it would have been built around the late 1920s. The steps and front door were perfectly centered on the front of the house. About eight feet on either side of the front door was a pair of double windows. The pair on the right would be the living room, probably with a brick-front fireplace. The windows on the left were most likely the dining room with maybe two built-in corner cabinets and a swinging door leading into the kitchen. The staircase to the second floor would be just a few feet beyond the front door.

Even when the toys were scattered across the front yard, the house had that sense of being a neat and well-tended home. I got out of my car and made it across the street almost to her front sidewalk before she casually glanced up at me.

"Miss Cole?"

She frowned as soon as she heard my voice. "You're the man who called this morning. I told you there was nothing I care to discuss if Touchier & Touchier is involved."

"If I could just get a moment of your time. I'm a private investigator, and my client has been involved in a situation that I think might show a pattern. Anything you could tell me would be a help."

"What I can tell you is run, don't walk, back to your client and tell them to get away from that place as fast as possible. That's all I have to say on the matter," she said, then stood and turned to climb the three steps and escape inside her house.

"I wish I could do that, but I can't. You see, my client is dead."

She was on the top step when she stopped, but she didn't turn to face me.

"See, she lost her job at Touchier. Things went from bad to worse, and finally someone murdered her."

"Desi Quinn," she said, but still kept her back to me.

"Yeah, that's right, Desi," I said, trying not to sound too surprised. I took a gamble. "She had an affair with Gaston Driscoll, not that I can prove it, but she trusted him, and I think he set her up. She lost everything, including her life, eventually. I'm just trying to sort things out right now. I don't have any proof, but I was hoping you might be able to help. Maybe you know something that seems insignificant, but it might be the one thing that would make a difference. If we could just talk for a bit. If you're uncomfortable, I could give you my number, and we could talk on the phone."

"What did you say your name was?"

"Haskell, Dev Haskell. I've got my card here. You could call a friend of mine in the police department if you wanted to check me out," I said, pulling out my wallet and grabbing a card stuffed next to the lone dollar bill resting in there. "Here," I said, taking a couple of steps closer.

"That's far enough," she said, then looked up and down the street. "I'll tell you what. You go around that side gate and meet me at our picnic table in the backyard. I'm going inside, and I'll have someone join us just to make me feel safe. I'll know soon enough if you're on the level." With that, she stepped inside her house, closed the front door, and then snapped the lock.

I walked around the side of the house. The heat from the sun bounced off the stucco wall and raised the temperature a good twenty degrees. The sidewalk was barely a foot wide and looked like it had probably been poured a hundred years ago. At the back of the house was a picket fence painted white. The gate was coated with dirt and grime. Beyond the gate was a swing set, with two green swings and a yellow plastic slide with green ladder steps attached to the back end. A tan stucco garage was in the back of the lot, maybe ten feet beyond the swing set.

I went through the gate and pushed it closed behind me. A brick patio flowed off the back of the house and took up maybe a third of the back yard. There was a metal table with a glass top and six chairs on the patio. An open umbrella was planted through a hole in the middle of the table. With the afternoon angle of the sun, all the shade was on the far side of the table. I walked around and pulled a chair out to sit in the shade and wait.

I was looking around the yard, not really noticing much. There was a large oak tree in the far corner of the back yard. Two squirrels were chasing one another. As they ran, they seemed to always remain the same distance apart. The one not wanting to catch, the other not wishing to be caught, they ran round and round the large tree trunk a half dozen times, then down across the yard and under the picket fence. I was focusing on a rather large pile of dog shit back near the fence just as the door opened, and a big German Shepherd bounded out the door. The thing took two or three steps toward the garage before it caught sight of me, turned, and picked up speed.

"Halt! Halt, Gunny!" Daphne screamed, and the dog did just that. But he never took his eyes off me, and I had the distinct impression he was cocked and ready to spring.

"This is Gunny, Mr. Haskell."

"Gunny?"

"My husband was a handler in the Marines. He was at the battle for Fallujah, then did two more deployments in Afghanistan," she said, putting a glass with some light-colored liquid and clinking ice cubes down in front of me.

"I was in Iraq," I said.

"Where?"

"Most of the time, I couldn't tell you, just a lot of sand and not too many friendlies."

"Marines?"

"No, Army, Second Infantry."

"Too bad." She smiled.

"Spoken like the wife of a Marine." I raised my glass to toast her and took a sip. It was lemonade.

"How's he doing, your husband?"

"We're getting there. He's out now, and he's been practicing law for a few years. His contemporaries are always complaining about the workload. He thinks it's a cakewalk after his time in the Corp."

I nodded.

"Anyway, Gunny came home with him."

"How's Gunny with the baby?"

"Babies, plural. We were blessed with twins. With Gunny around, the kids and I are the safest folks in town."

"I don't doubt it." Gunny hadn't taken his eyes off me. "Is there anything you could do to maybe get old Gunny there to stand down?"

"We'll see, you said you wanted to talk."

"Yes." I tried to focus on Daphne's face. She was pretty, with eyes so dark you almost couldn't see her pupils. Prominent cheekbones, a long thin nose. Her skin looked incredibly smooth. I was afraid to glance anywhere below her chin for fear old Gunny would tear my throat out. I could feel his breath, or was that just a warm breeze? I wasn't sure and had no desire to check it out.

Twenty-five

I began to tell Daphne about Desi. Once again, I didn't mention Karla or Marsha and certainly not Marsha's pending appointment with Gaston Driscoll. I did tell her about my earlier conversation with Catherine Lindquist. I touched on Helen Olson going through the ice, and I mentioned Driscoll's wife Bernadette and the late-night boat explosion out on the same lake.

None of what I said seemed to faze her. About the only reaction she ever gave was an occasional, almost imperceptible nod.

"So that's about all I know. I think there's a pattern or at least the sense of a pattern, but like I said, nothing I can go to the police with. At the end of the day, it all amounts to hearsay, pretty thin hearsay, at that."

She nodded, looked at the dog, which I didn't think had blinked over the course of the last twenty minutes. "Gunny, drop," she said, and the dog immediately laid down. "At ease," she said. Gunny stretched out at her feet and placed his head on top of his paws. He gave me a quick glance, just to let me know he hadn't forgotten I was there.

"I can see why you feel safe with him around. Amazing."

"Yeah, and everything you've been saying is one of the reasons he's here."

"Have you had problems? Been threatened? Anything like that?"

"No, not directly, but it was, umm, an understanding. If you get what I mean."

"I'm not sure I do."

"When you're fired, when Gaston Driscoll basically tells you you're used up, and he no longer finds you desirable, you are in complete, total, absolute shock. By the time he threatens you with exposure, public humiliation, or worse— good God, you just want to get out of there alive. Fired from your job? That's the least of your problems. At least you might have half a chance of getting another job, as long as you don't make waves."

"Tell me about his threats."

She took a couple of deep gulps of lemonade. "Let's just say, when you're crazy in love, you do all sorts of things. He tells you you're the one and you think to yourself, no, actually you convince yourself that you're the luckiest girl in the world. Of course, he's got all the images and the DVDs he made of you, of me, everything. Plus, those extra little payroll bonuses I got at yearend for those 'special' little projects— it turns out they were all written on checks from the wrong account."

"You mean your bonus checks bounced?"

"Oh, no, he's a lot smarter than that."

"Huh?"

"That bastard wrote me, I don't know, maybe a half dozen checks over twenty months to the tune of about sixty-six hundred dollars total. That doesn't really sound like much, does it?"

I shook my head. "I suppose it depends on your circumstances at the time."

"You're exactly right. See, I'd just started there. After I finished grad school, I had the national debt for student loans, and Touchier was my first real job. So, six grand plus, it was like ten-percent of my take home. It turns out he wrote the checks on some bogus account that was used for, I don't know, paying the water bill or something. Anyway, he had it set up to look like I'd stolen the things and made them out to myself. His signature wasn't forged. It was from a damn rubber stamp, so it looked like I could have printed the things off myself."

"You didn't figure this out?"

"Your boss, the man you've been sleeping with and going out of town with on business trips hands, you a check for fifteen-hundred dollars and says you're doing a great job. You tell me, who in their right mind was going to look at that check and say 'I don't think I should cash this?'"

I nodded.

"You know what sixty-six hundred comes to over the course of twenty months? Don't try and figure it out, Dev. I'll save you the time. I got it right here." She slid her watch, a small little silver thing, up her left arm. Where the watch had been was a small red tattoo, '333'.

I looked at her, puzzled.

"Yeah, I know. Three-hundred-thirty-three. That's what the sixty-six hundred, my big bonus payments were." She sat up, raised her voice slightly, and shook her head. Gunny suddenly half rose and stared up at me. "That's what it turns out to be, three-hundred-and-thirty-three dollars a month for twenty months. My ass was cheaper than any old crack-whore he could have found on any street. I was a hundred times better than he deserved and always sitting by the phone waiting for his next call. You got any doubt just call him. He'll be happy to show you the DVD, and then I'll lose my husband and my babies."

I shook my head. "That's blackmail, just for starters."

She snorted, then said, "Oh, really? Call it what you will, but when it happens, and he pulls that old trigger, you just want to get the hell out of there. And suddenly, all the rumors you'd heard and dismissed, Helen Olson, Desi Quinn, Amanda Richards… good Lord even the man's wife. What's her name?"

"Bernadette?"

She nodded. "Yeah, right. All those rumors you knew couldn't possibly be true, because he was Gaston Driscoll. A good, decent man, and he loved me and chose me to be his one and only, and suddenly all of that is just so much bullshit. He tells you to just leave quietly, or be exposed as a whore and someone who stole from the firm, and, oh, by the way, there's a good chance you'll be going to jail. That sixty-six-hundred dollars? Five grand is the cut-off. Sixty-six hundred makes it a felony. Now we're talking some serious time, even if it's your first offense. And there wasn't anybody who was going to believe me, because after all, he's Gaston Driscoll."

"He's got tapes of you or the women he's been with?"

She nodded. "Oh yeah, DVDs. He's got a way of getting you to think you've awakened something in him, and I'm guessing we all made those DVDs. He took pictures of me and everything. Jesus, if my husband knew, he'd leave me and take the kids. I would never get my babies back if anyone ever saw those damned things."

"Was this when he was deployed, your husband?"

She nodded. "We weren't married then. Believe me, I get it, okay? I know it was so incredibly stupid. But Driscoll is so good at getting you to think you're the one. That you are so special, and the two of you are just made for one another."

"Would there be some trail? You must have traded emails and phone calls."

"You'd think so, but no. There were never any emails, for exactly that reason. He didn't allow it. Funny, but I think if I'd sent him some torchy email, he probably would have dropped me on the spot. Of course, looking back, now I understand why."

I nodded. It sounded like Driscoll had a system in place, and he just inserted a new victim whenever he tired of his current one.

"The phone calls I got from him came through from some phone number in Florida, Miami or someplace. He said a friend owned the company down there and gave him a special rate. I remember it was a cute little red phone. He said it was a personal number just for me so I could reach him anywhere, anytime I wanted. Jesus, and I believed that bastard. I had a geek girlfriend who works for Verizon check it out for me after I'd been fired. As near as she could figure out, it was some pay-as-you-go thing under a false name and no way to track it. She tried to contact the thing a number of times over a period of months, and it was dead. He probably just tossed the phone in the river or something and got a new one, so his next sex-toy would be able to call him."

I was about to say something, but she shook her head.

"I used to wait for his calls so I could run right over and prove to him how good I was. If we were traveling for business, we always had separate rooms, never even on the same floor. One time we went to a conference down in the Outer Banks of North Carolina. Just for laughs, he made me walk back to my room, two floors down without my clothes. He handed me this little towel, hardly bigger than a washcloth to wrap around me. It didn't even come close to covering me. I ran all the way to my room two floors away. I don't think anyone ever saw me."

"You're kidding?"

She shook her head. "Nope, and the sad news is, I was thrilled to do it. It was just one more lovers' adventure the two of us had. We got back to St. Paul, and the next morning, he walked into my office with one of those checks made out for five hundred dollars if I remember correctly. Then he showed me about a thirty-second video from his phone of me walking down a hotel hallway at four in the morning with this little towel not covering anything. I remember he laughed and said next time he wasn't even going to give me a towel."

"You didn't…I mean—"

"Fact is, at the time, the brakes were going out on my car, and I probably would have done it. No towel, I mean. Besides, I know this sounds insane, but I thought we were crazy in love. Turns out only I was, especially the crazy part," she scoffed. "And he was just getting his rocks off whenever he wanted. Just another little test to see how low I'd go. I never found out, never reached the bottom. I just became his 'Personal whore on call.'" She looked up at me with watery eyes.

"No, you were, are, a very lovely woman. You're a good mom, and wife, and you were taken advantage of by a real nut case. To tell you the truth, Daphne, based on what I think happened to some of these other women, you just may have gotten off easy. You're here to tell the story."

"Long as he never shows anyone the DVD."

"I'll maybe see if we can't do something about that."

She looked at me, half snorted, and shook her head like I wasn't getting it.

"You mentioned a name a while back that I hadn't heard before…Amanda Richards."

"She was sometime after me, the same sort of deal, though. I guess one day she was just escorted out the door. It's always hush, hush, you know? Of course, there's that bunch of old bitties shaking their heads wondering, what's wrong with these girls? I met Amanda at the U, although I never really knew her. I think if I recall, she may have been up here from Chicago. Not sure where she is now. She may have gone back down there, for all I know.

Twenty-Six

There were sixteen individuals named Amanda Richards in the online directory for Chicago. That didn't count the suburban listings that popped up on pages two and three of my search. I started dialing a little after three in the afternoon.

I hit pay dirt on number eleven.

"I'm trying to reach Amanda Richards."

"Then this is your lucky day. What are you thinking about?" she said, followed by the unmistakable sound of ice cubes rattling in a glass.

"Is this Amanda?"

"It sure is, Sweetheart. What did you have in mind?"

"Actually, I just want to make sure I had the right Amanda."

"Oh, I'm the one darling."

I'm looking for a woman who lived up in Minnesota for a while, attended the University of Minnesota, and worked at Touchier and Touchier architectural firm."

"You looking for money? Because if you are, I can't help you," she said, then followed up with more ice cubes rattling.

"No, actually, I wanted to chat for a moment. Did you work at Touchier?"

"I don't know that I should answer that. Hold on here, Honey, I just need to get another coffee. Back in a minute," she said, and I heard her set the phone down.

I could hear her rummaging around in the background. I thought I heard more ice cubes thrown into a glass, maybe the sound of something being poured. She picked up the phone about five minutes later, but who was counting?

"Hello?"

"Hello, is this Amanda?"

"Who's this? I didn't even hear the damn thing ring? What are you looking to do, Sweetheart?" she said, then gulped loudly a couple of times.

"Amanda, were you employed by Touchier and Touchier at one time up in Minnesota?"

"Maybe, maybe not. I haven't mentioned them in years, and I don't intend to now."

I took that as a 'yes.'

"I'm a private investigator. My name is Dev Haskell. My client was employed by Touchier and Touchier about ten years ago. Her name—"

"I wouldn't know anything about that. That was way before my time, and like I said, I have no intention of talking about them now." More ice cubes clinked, and then there was a gasp as if she'd emptied the glass, but she remained on the line.

"Amanda, I understand you not wanting to chat. Could I explain a little bit about what I'm involved in, and maybe at the end of that, you might feel like talking? I'd be very interested in anything you have to say."

"What did you say your name was?"

"Haskell. Dev Haskell. I'm a private investigator."

"Really? Well, isn't that nice? How about this, Mr. Hascar, the private investigator. I'm going to go mix myself another little drink, but before I do that, I'm going to hang up so you can call some other fool and stop wasting my time."

"If you could just give me a minute to explain. I'm representing a woman by the name—"

"I'm going to go mix another drink now. Good-bye. Can't thank you enough for your time," she said and hung up.

It was the middle of the afternoon in the middle of the workweek. I didn't get the sense I'd caught Amanda on her day off, nor on her first drink. I'd have to put her down as just one more inconclusive chapter to the Gaston Driscoll story. I felt like I kept circling, but I wasn't getting any closer.

Twenty-seven

y phone rang a little before ten that evening. Actually, I couldn't really tell if it rang because the jukebox in The Spot was playing so damn loud I could barely hear. I did feel the thing vibrate, and I was pulling it out of my pocket as I waded through a crowd of softball players and made my way to the door. I could almost read Marsha's name on the screen.

"Hi, Marsha, hang on I'm headed outside so I can hear you."

"Dev, Dev?" She sounded impatient, probably off stage between numbers.

"Yeah, Marsha. Sorry, I had to step outside."

"Dev, some asshole is following me."

"What? Where are you?"

"I'm on I-94 heading back into St. Paul. This guy has been on my ass ever since I pulled out of the restaurant parking lot in Minneapolis."

"Where were you?" I asked. Not too far in the back of my mind, I had that sense Marsha hadn't bothered to listen to me earlier and had taken the initiative.

"Oh, I just had some dinner, is all. Hey, he's two cars back. I'm putting my blinker on to switch lanes and see if he does the same thing."

I waited for a couple of moments, expecting her to say something.

"Is he switching lanes?" I finally asked.

"No, he doesn't seem to be doing a thing. Sorry, looks like it was a false alarm. Just a little paranoid, I guess."

"Where are you?"

"I told you, I-94."

"Where exactly on I-94, Marsha?"

"Will you relax? I'm just coming up to the Dale Street exit. I'm going to take that and—"

"Marsha, do not take that exit."

"Come on, now who's being paranoid?"

"Stay on 94 and take 35E heading north, see if he follows. How much gas you got?"

"What?"

"Your tank, is it full, empty, what?"

"More than half full."

"Get on 35E, heading north. You know where it meets Highway 36?"

"Yeah."

"Take the exit for Highway 36 West, stay on the cloverleaf, get back onto 35E going south, and head back into town."

"Dev, I just want to get home. Tonight's my one night off this week, and oh, shit, he's pulled out. He's following me again, Dev."

I started running to my car, talking to her as I went.

"Okay, look, he's just following. We're going to deal with it. I'm coming to get you. Keep your speed at fifty-five, Head up 35E going north and take that turn onto 36 and then head back into town. Okay?"

"Yeah." She didn't sound all that sure.

"I'll be picking you up along 35E, okay?" I waited a long five seconds. "Marsha, damn it, answer me."

"This is creepy, Dev, I'm scared."

"Just stay the speed limit, don't speed up. Right now, there's a good chance he doesn't think you picked up on him back there."

"Maybe I can lose him?"

"Just do what I'm telling you. Okay?"

"God, okay, but hurry up."

I headed for the freeway. Six blocks later, I barely slowed at the stop sign, then shot onto the entrance ramp and raced up 35 toward the Maryland Avenue exit, talking to Marsha all the way. Her words sounded like she was in control, but I could sense the fear in her voice.

"God, he's right on my ass now. I'm on the cloverleaf, heading back into town," she said.

"Perfect, I'm just going across the Maryland Avenue Bridge. I'm going to get back on the freeway and pull onto the shoulder then I'll back up until I'm under the bridge. I want you to drive past me and just keep going. Give a little honk as you pass me. I'll pull out and catch up until I'm right behind you. Okay?"

"Yeah, okay, I'm just passing the sign that says two and a quarter miles to the Maryland exit," she said a moment later.

"I'm heading down the ramp now. I'll be under the bridge in a minute. You just stay in that right lane and keep it at fifty-five."

"God, how many times are you going to tell me that? I'm doing it. I'm doing it."

"Good girl, can you describe the car following you?" I asked.

"No, not really. It's just a pair of headlights, really close headlights."

Fortunately, the traffic was light. I backed up and stopped under the bridge. I reached beneath my seat and took out the Ruger I had stashed there, an LC9. I set the pistol on the passenger seat.

"One-and-a-quarter miles," she said.

"Anyone in front of you, Marsha?"

"No, least not for a good way."

"Flash your brights," I said.

I saw them flash in my rearview mirror. She was still a way's back.

"Hey, Dev, I'm flashing you. Like it?"

"Yeah, loving it, Marsha. I got you. I'm going to let you pass, then ease into traffic and come up behind. You just stay on 35 through the interchange. Okay?"

"Maybe I should pull over on the shoulder, and he'd stop behind me?"

"Maybe you should just stay on 35. Okay?"

"That's a drag," she said. But didn't argue. Her horn beeped as she drove past. I waited for three more cars to pass before I pulled into traffic.

"I saw you back there. Did you hear me honk when I drove past?"

"Yeah, I'm coming up behind you now. Stay on 35, Marsha."

"God, Mr. Broken Record, come on, let's get this guy."

"We're going to. You'll have the St. Clair exit coming up in about four minutes. If no one else is taking it, put your signal on and exit. Okay?"

"Yeah, I'm just passing the sign for it," she said a moment later. "Looks like no one's taking it, Dev. Do you want me to?"

"Yeah, take it. There's a stop sign when you get to St. Clair. Stop, but do not get out of your car, Marsha. Do you hear me?"

"Yes, for God's sake, I heard you. Will you just—oh my God, he's coming right up behind me."

"Was his blinker on?"

"Who the fuck cares, Dev? Jesus, he's getting close. Right on my ass, right on it."

"I'm coming up behind him, Marsha. I see your taillights going around the bend. Stop at the stop sign, and don't get out of the car. Make sure your doors are locked."

"Gee, really? I never would have thought of that one. Just hurry up and get here."

As we drove up the exit ramp, I gained on whoever had been following her, pulling up close enough behind the car that I could read the make on the trunk. It was a Buick LeSabre, a later model, maybe a four-door. At first, I thought it was light blue, but as I got closer, it turned out to be a light metallic green. The car looked very clean. The taillights were working, but the left taillight cover had been damaged and was patched over with what looked like red tape. I made a note of the Minnesota license plate number. It hung below the rear bumper in a frame with the words *Girls! Girls! Girls!* running around all four sides. I repeated the license number out loud to myself a couple of times.

I couldn't actually see the driver, but I could make out a silhouette of the top of his head moving just above the headrest on the driver's seat. He couldn't have been too tall, and his silhouette suggested he was wearing a strange kind of hat. He appeared to be alone in the car, and if I had to guess, I would say he was checking his rearview mirror as my lights pulled up behind him.

"Okay, I'm stopping at the sign," Marsha said.

"Stay in your car. Make sure your doors are locked. This guy comes toward you on foot, you take off. If he tries to pull alongside, I want you to duck."

"Oh, shit, Dev," she said.

"I'm right behind him, Marsha. Put your right blinker on."

"Okay, it's on, Dev," she said, suddenly sounding a lot more like a little girl as I saw her taillight flashing.

Although the freeway we just exited cut through the center of the city, the immediate area up around the exit was rather isolated. Trees and bushes on either side hid the freeway to the left while the right side was a heavily wooded ridge with houses sitting maybe fifty yards up on top. I'd actually seen a deer grazing just inside the tree line a year or two ago. You could see slivers of orange light shining out through the trees from the large homes up there, overlooking the city. The ridge was cut in half by a curving one-way street that drained traffic from the neighborhood down into the lower area. There were four highway lights illuminating the exit, but they were a good distance behind us and down a hill. For all practical purposes, we were pretty much in the dark with trees and undergrowth surrounding us on both sides.

Around a bend and a little before the stop sign, the exit widened into two lanes. The exit was actually a fork in the road, so you had to turn either left or right. Driving straight ahead wasn't an option. Marsha's car was stopped with her right turn signal on. The guy following her pulled up behind. I put my signal on to indicate a left turn and began to pull alongside the LeSabre.

"Marsha, take off around the corner and keep going. I'm going to cut this jerk off."

She didn't need any encouragement and suddenly squealed around the corner. Just as her pursuer began to move forward, I pulled in front of him, thrusting my car across the road to cut him off. I grabbed the Ruger off my front seat and jumped out of the car. I flicked on the centerfire laser and took aim at him over the roof of my car.

The red dot wiggled back and forth on his windshield. For just a nano-second, I had a sense of vague recognition as his face, lit by the dashboard lights, flashed in panic. Just as quickly, that recognition disappeared.

He was already backing up, accelerating in reverse to get away from me and swerving as he went. I was tempted to put a round into his windshield. I moved the red dot toward the passenger side but then thought better of it.

Suddenly there was a set of headlights coming up the exit ramp behind him. A van swerved sharply to the left, honking, leaning on the horn just as the LeSabre clipped the rear quarter panel on the van and screeched to a stop. It made a sharp right turn and took off racing the wrong way up the curving one-way hill, accelerating as it disappeared around the curve.

I was tempted to jump back in my car and follow him, but then what? I would suddenly be confronting some clown who was going to insist he was just on his way to the grocery store or some other innocuous place. Technically, he hadn't done anything wrong. Well, other than the hit and run. But that wasn't worth the potential trouble. Besides, I had his license number and a sort-of-willing accomplice down at the DMV. I stuffed the Ruger into the back of my belt and pulled my shirt out. I walked back to make sure everyone was all right in the van that had just been sideswiped.

Twenty-eight

There was a large, dark haired-woman behind the wheel, and no one next to her in the passenger seat. There were two car seats strapped to the middle seat in back, both empty.

"Are you okay?" I asked.

"Did you see that bastard? He could have killed me. Son-of-a-bitch," she screamed. "He hit my damn car."

"Are you all right?" I asked again.

"What? Yeah, yes, thanks. I'm fine. But that bastard. What in the hell was he doing? Did you see him? He just shot up that hill. That's a one way. He's nuts, no, crazy is what he is," she said.

"No argument from me."

"Did he hit your car, too?"

"No, he was driving erratically behind me, and I thought he might be having a heart attack or some issue, so I got out to check on him, and that's when he took off and slammed into you," I said.

"Jesus Christ," she said, getting out of the car and walking around the front of the van to see where he'd smashed into her.

She was not what you'd call trim and looked to be draped in yards of bright yellow and red fabric, topped off with large white lapels bordering a massive cleavage. There was a very wide flowered belt stretched taut around her middle. She had on yellow shoes with red toes and no heel. She stood just about my height.

"I'm just coming home from choir practice at my church and . . . God damn it!" she yelled as she spotted the damage to the rear of her van. "Oh, shit, will you look at this? Now, what the hell do I do?"

"Well, as bad as it looks, I think you can probably still drive. You might as well go home. As long as no one was hurt, the police won't come out. Call and report it as soon as you get home, and they'll send you some paperwork, or there's a form you can fill out online."

She looked at me as if she had a question forming.

"You got a pen?" I asked.

"Yes," she said, sounding suspicious.

"Here's my card," I said, pulling the last one out of my wallet. "I got the guys license number."

"You did? Oh, fantastic," she said, taking my card and looking at it. "Private Investigator?"

"Yeah, you got that pen?"

My phone rang. It was Marsha, so I answered.

"Hi, Marsha, hang on I'll be right back to you. That pen?"

"Oh, yeah, sure It's just in the front seat." She walked around to the driver's door, reached in and fished around, then said, "Okay." She stood there poised, ready to write in a leather-bound notebook.

I repeated the license number. Then said to her, "Look, if you're okay to drive, just head home and call the police to file a report. It's probably best to get it filed as soon as possible."

"I can't thank you enough. You've been so kind, Mr." She half held my card up to read my name. "Mr. Haskell."

"My pleasure, my number's there. If you need a witness statement or anything, just give me a ring."

"Thank you so much," she said, then climbed behind the wheel and waved as she went by. I watched as she drove off.

I was seated behind the wheel when my phone rang again. I'd been writing down the license number because I knew I'd probably forget it by morning.

"Marsha."

"Jesus, forget about me? Are you okay? Did you get him? Tell me you shot him a half dozen times."

"Yes and no."

"What the hell is that supposed to mean? You didn't let him get away, did you?"

"Yeah, he took off, smashed into another car coming up the exit ramp, then took off going the wrong way on a one-way street."

"Did you wound him?"

"No, Marsha, I didn't shoot."

"Didn't . . . Oh that's just great. So you mean you're telling me that nut case is still out there somewhere waiting for me?"

"Afraid so. You going to head home?"

"Are you kidding me? No. I'm staying at your place tonight. I'm not going home to my empty apartment. I mean, if that's okay."

"If I must. You know the way, or do you want to follow me?"

"If you'll recall, I've been there before. I think I know the way, Dev. Have you got something there to calm me down?"

"I've got just the thing in mind."

"I meant something to drink, you slime ball."

Twenty-nine

I figured it was going to be an uphill battle talking Marsha into eating Coco Puffs for breakfast, so I ran out to get some eggs and Wonder Bread to make French toast. I sprinkled a little powdered sugar over the French toast and then topped it off with a dollop of whip cream from the can a woman named Lori had left during a grope-and-grab session a few weeks back.

"Wow, I never pegged you for someone who cooked," Marsha said.

She was curled up on a kitchen stool, wearing one of my St. Paul Saints jerseys and sipping coffee. The jersey had never looked so good, and I made a mental note to never, ever wash it again.

"So, against everyone's better judgment and my telling you not to, you decided to have dinner with Gaston Driscoll last night."

"I didn't think it was such a bad idea at the time. To tell you the truth, he can be pretty charming, as long as you don't mind talking about him all night."

"And being followed home."

"Well, yeah, there is that, but maybe that was just a coincidence."

"Sure it was," I said, sliding a plate across the counter toward her. "Let me see, some idiot is behind you as you leave the restaurant and then follows you in a figure-eight route across town, I almost shoot him between the eyes and he sideswipes some woman's van before he takes off going the wrong way. Yeah, that's what it was, Marsha, just a coincidence."

"Mmm-mmm, this looks really good. Whipped cream, I'm really impressed," she said, ignoring me.

"Never can tell when you might need some," I said, thinking she didn't need to know its origin.

"Mmm-mmm, very good."

"But let's get back to your pal Driscoll. What did he tell you?"

"Well, he thought there just might be the chance for me to try for an entry-level spot at Gaston Enterprises. I told him I had a chemistry background, not architecture or design."

"And?"

"And he said he didn't think that would be a problem. He mentioned maybe starting in his sales division and then seeing where things went from there."

"Did he invite you for a weekend in Las Vegas or Hawaii, or maybe a topless beach somewhere to fill out the job application?"

"No, he really thought I might add something to the firm. He said they were always looking for talented people like me. I don't know, to tell you the truth it sounded like a lot better opportunity than running around on stage naked and riding a hobby horse."

"Marsha! Are you kidding me? Come on, he's setting you up to tumble into the sack with him. You should have talked with the women I've talked with these last few days. This guy is, at best, a stalker, at worst, a murderer. Did you forget what happened to Desi?"

"I know that. Of course, I remember. But it was still nice to hear."

"Did you tell him you were dancing?"

"Yeah, sure, Dev. That would have cinched the deal. Yeah, right."

"You kidding? He probably would have jumped all over it."

She studied me for a long moment then said, "Not really. You might think that, in fact most guys think that, but while some pompous bastard like Driscoll and frankly any decent guy might be interested privately, they're really just thinking, maybe a wild weekend at most. Vegas? Sure, you bet, but only because it's out of town, and no one would ever know they'd strayed over to the dark side with someone like me."

"I don't know."

"I do. I've seen it too many times. It's why I keep that aspect of my life on a more private level. It's just a lot fewer problems that way."

I decided not to pursue what she meant by 'private level.' "So where did you leave it with him? Your pal Gaston."

"I'm calling him later today, once I'm out of class."

"Class?"

"Remember? He thinks I'm a student. He's going to have someone give me a tour of the firm and interview me."

"Someone else will interview you?"

"That's what he said. Told me he didn't want to present any undue influence in a decision-making process."

"And you said?"

"I said I really wanted and really needed the job, that it would be absolutely fantastic to work there and that I'd do anything to get hired." She smiled.

"You really said that?"

"Yeah. Remember we were going to learn about the guy? Remember, we were going to try and get the guy to woo me? And then we are so going to nail him."

"And last night someone followed you home, or attempted to."

"Yeah, doesn't make a lot of sense, does it?"

"What doesn't make a lot of sense? You're getting interviewed for a job, having dinner with this jerk, or that idiot following you home?"

She seemed to consider all three possibilities.

"Well?"

"All I know is I've had two meetings with him. How 'bout you?"

"I don't know, Marsha. For supposedly just two meetings, you suddenly got someone following you. I think that guy in the car was pretty aggressive last night."

"Gee, really? You think?"

I ignored her sarcasm. "Maybe he was checking you out. You know, just to see where you lived. Although, it seems he could have just asked for your address or gotten it off your job application. Did he have you fill one out?"

"A job application? No, that's part of what I'll be doing in my next meeting."

"Do you know who you'll be meeting with?"

"A woman named Dawn something. I have it written down."

"Dawn Miller," I said. The name had suddenly popped into my head.

"You know her?"

"No. I know she works in the HR department there. I spoke to her briefly on the phone the other day for all of about thirty seconds."

"And?"

"Like I said, I spoke to her very briefly. If I had to guess, I'd say she was cautious, probably lives and breathes the company. Now that I think of it, she may be the current Driscoll play toy."

"That's rather crude."

"Yeah, it is, and unfortunately probably accurate. The stories I've heard and the lives this guy has affected, he's a real sleaze." I shook my head.

"Pity. He's pompous, but he can be a very nice pompous." She smiled.

"I can't talk you out of this, can I?"

She shook her head. "No, you can't. You know, in a strange way, he's like all those stupid guys waiting for me to bend down and pick up their dollar bills every night. They love it, but they would never want anyone to know they had any interaction with someone like me. But what he did to Desi, I'm not talking her murder, I mean before, in a strange way I think that was almost worse."

"Don't fall for this creep, Marsha. I'm telling you. Let me be on record as saying I don't think you should go to the next interview. I think you should just disappear off Driscoll's radar."

"Not to worry, Dev," she said, then pushed her empty plate across the kitchen counter toward me. "I suppose I better get dressed and head home."

"I suppose unless maybe you wanted your back washed up in the shower."

"Just my back?" She grinned.

"I think we could work something out."

Thirty

I was standing on my front porch, watching as Marsha backed out of the driveway when my phone rang.

"Haskell Investigations."

"Hi, Dev, Karla."

"Hi, Karla." I suddenly remembered I hadn't called her in the last couple of days.

"Just wondering how you're coming along with the Desi stuff."

"I've eliminated some possibilities, discovered some new ones . . . it's becoming a little multi-dimensional," I said, waving as Marsha honked, made an obscene gesture, and drove off.

"Gee, sounds like the kind of bullshit my employees would try and lay on me. I got an idea. Why don't you drive over here and tell me in person? That will give you a chance to get your story straight, and in the end, hopefully, you'll feel better, and I won't think I wasted five grand. What do you think?"

"Yeah, I think I can do that. Hey Karla?"

"Yes, Dev."

"Not to worry, you haven't wasted five grand."

"Actually, I know that. It's just my crazy sense of humor, Sweetheart. When can I expect to see you?"

"I'll be over in a bit," I said, hung up, and went to grab another shower.

On the way over to see Karla, I made a couple of decisions, one of which was to not tell her about Marsha inserting herself into my investigation. Although, I'd be the first to admit Marsha had been a lot more successful than me at getting one-on-one time with Gaston Driscoll. Amazingly old Gaston seemed to be more into Marsha than me. Who knew?

By early afternoon, the temperature was in the mid-nineties and still climbing, with the humidity not too far behind. Karla's Karwash was doing a brisk business. Two lines of vehicles, ten deep and growing, slowly made their way into the car wash. More customers were constantly driving in. There wasn't an open space in the employee lot behind the building, so I had to park on the side street about a block away.

I made a beeline for the staircase leading up to the office level, hoping to avoid that idiot Pauley. With any luck, he'd be too busy cleaning interiors to spot me. Then again, if anyone was liable to hide from doing too much work, it would be Pauley.

Karla was cutting across the small receptionist lobby just as I came up the staircase.

"Oh, hi, Dev. Wow, look at you all showered and nicely shaven. You clean up pretty well. Come on back to my office."

I followed her down the hall, giving her rear some subtle, positive appraisal as she walked ahead of me. She was wearing wonderfully tight black slacks. Just the hint of a thong outline showed through her slacks, surrounded by the tease of her wonderfully firm flesh.

Her office walls and ceiling were painted in the same off-white. Now that I thought about it, all the walls and ceilings on the entire second floor were painted the same off-white.

There were two large framed photos on the walls of her office. I'm talking three feet by five feet. One was a black and white shot of the building exterior with just the sign Karla's Karwash glowing neon red. The other, just as large, but in color, was a group of people sitting at a bar in some hotel swimming pool. Everyone was wearing large sunglasses, extremely small tops, and very recent sunburns. I guessed the shot was taken in Mexico. There was a palm frond roof over the bar, and the crowd was drinking from tall glasses with large pieces of fruit and little umbrellas. No doubt just slaving away, getting their daily requirement of vitamin C.

"So," she said, stepping behind her desk and indicating the chair I should sit in. "How's my ass?"

"What?"

"You are such a predictable pervert, Dev," she said and shook her head.

"It's very nice," I said. I could feel my face redden.

"God, look at you, caught again. I doubt you'll ever learn. So, fill me in," she said, sitting down.

"Well, like I said, I've learned some more things, or maybe I think I have. But I'm still kind of circling around. Look, before I get to all that, I want to give this back to you," I said, and pulled out my wallet and fished around for her check for five grand. I grabbed the check and handed it back to her.

"What's this? You didn't cash the thing?"

"Obviously not."

"You're quitting, not going to pursue this? Why the hell not? Don't you think Driscoll had something to do with Desi's murder?" She was increasing her volume and talking just a little faster. Her eyes had begun to flash.

"No, it's not that. It's just—"

"I can give you more money if that's an issue," she said, somewhat sharply.

"Karla, slow down. I gave you that check back because I'm not going to accept your money. I'm not going to quit. I'll find out what happened. I'll find out who is responsible and deal with things from there. You're just not going to pay me for it."

"But, Dev, I'm . . . I'm not getting this. No offense, but I'm not so sure this is your strong suit."

"What, doing something nice?" I laughed.

"No, I didn't mean that. I meant the financial end of things. You know you're… or at least can be, a little careless in that department, and maybe you should just hang onto that check and reconsider."

She opened the folded check and stared at it for a moment. The seams where I'd folded it to fit in my wallet were coated with enough dirt and grime to look like I'd drawn two dark lines from top to bottom on the thing. One of the corners on the check had somehow been torn off. It looked like it had been written a few years back instead of little more than a week ago. She reached across the desk and handed it back to me.

I shook my head.

"What happened?"

"I just can't get that picture of Desi out of my mind. Watching her become resigned to her fate, giving up and just walking out the door and around the corner because her last chance to get things put right came down to hearing me say, "No." She thought I didn't care enough or maybe not at all. Me."

"Little hard on yourself," she said, setting the check down in front of me.

"Or not hard enough."

"You are a very sweet and kind man."

"Well, don't tell anyone. I've got a reputation to uphold. Let me tell you what I've run into thus far. The more I look into this, the more there seems to be the semblance of a pattern." I proceeded to bring her up to date. I didn't tell her about Marsha inserting herself or the car following her. I finished up telling Karla about my phone call to Amanda Richards.

"I didn't learn anything talking to her, other than she wasn't going to talk. If I had to venture a guess, I'd say being drunk at that hour of the day has probably become just an everyday occurrence for her. She maybe hasn't hit rock bottom yet, but she could probably see it from where she was. Again, it may have nothing to do with Driscoll, but it would fit the pattern of him sending another life into a tailspin and then down the drain."

Karla sat there and lifted her eyes up to the right, focused on some fancy wooden box on a shelf. I followed her gaze. The box was polished wood, inlaid with a design pattern running along the edge. It was a strange shape for a jewelry box.

"Desi," she said, half pointing with her chin. "Well, I mean her ashes."

"Her ashes?"

"I guess she didn't have family. At least that we could find. I checked her employment application. She left the next of kin section blank. Anyway, not unusual in this business." She shrugged then stared off like she was rummaging through files somewhere in the recesses of her mind.

"So, like I said, there seems to be a pattern here maybe. But nothing that could be proven in a court of law. And if Daphne Cole is any indication, he's got something to hang over the head of each and every woman he's done this to. I'm guessing Desi maybe just didn't have anything else to lose. Well, except her life. And maybe it was the same thing for Helen Olsen."

"The woman who's car went through the ice?"

I nodded.

"Keep talking," she said, suddenly sitting up and turning in her chair. She began clicking keys on her computer. "Something's ringing a bell on that Amanda Richards name, but I can't place it."

"You think she maybe worked for you? I mean, she went to school up here at the U, before she worked for Driscoll."

"No, I'd remember that. I don't know. I'm just checking my files. I'm wondering, was she a reference for someone?" She finished typing and clicked a key, and then another, waited, then clicked one more and sat back, staring at her screen.

"So?"

"I must be mistaken. Probably nothing. I thought she might have been a personal reference, but that wasn't it. It'll probably pop into my head about three in the morning and wake me up."

"Let me know if you come up with something, no matter how obtuse it might seem."

"Obtuse, my, my, listen to you using a big college word. Have you been hitting on college students again?"

"No, that's one of the things they teach them in college. Stay away from guys like me. I was just at a coffee shop reserved for the intelligentsia. Fortunately, I left before I broke out in a rash."

"I don't know," she said, back to clicking keys on her computer. "God, most of my employees give their probation officer as a job reference."

"How's that working out?"

"The usual, you just learn to go with the flow. Some are good, and some always think they can con you. I have one who just moved out of the half-way house he's been in. If there's going to be a problem, this is one of those spots on the timeline where they tend to screw up."

"That wouldn't be Pauley Kopff, would it?"

Karla looked over at me, surprised. "How'd you know that?"

"Nothing related to Desi. I knew him some time back and saw him working here, awhile ago. Matter of fact, it was the day I ran into Desi. She gave me her phone number that day and then we got together. Pauley had mentioned he just had a few days left and then was going to get his own place. He sounded like he was counting the minutes."

"Yeah, Pauley. We'll see. He started just about the same time as Desi, maybe a week or so later. I don't know, I've been at this long enough that you tend to get a sense. I hope it works for him, but I think the other shoe is just about to drop, and he'll do some incredibly stupid thing."

"That sounds like Pauley," I said.

"Sounds like a lot of them," she said. "Matter of fact, he called in today. I think he was going to be late. Apparently, his car was stolen last night."

"Oh?"

"Who knows? It may be true. I mean, he did say he was coming in. He just had to take the bus or something to get here, and you know what that's like."

"You believe him?"

"Let's just say he's got all the signs of doing something stupid. We have a system that records the reasons. About the third time someone's grandmother has died, you start to get the idea you're being played."

I nodded. "That would be Pauley," I said and stood up to leave. Karla suddenly came around her desk and gave me a long, lingering hug.

"I don't care what everyone says." She laughed. "I think you're a wonderful man, Dev. I'm hanging onto this check for you. It's yours whenever you want it, just call me. And Dev?" she said, releasing me and stepping back.

"Yes."

"You be careful. I mean it."

"You keep wearing those little thongs, Karla. I mean it."

"Get the hell out of here." She laughed.

Thirty-one

It was funny, but since Pauley wasn't at Karla's yet I felt like I had some time to linger. I wondered if he had that effect on everyone who came in contact with him? Not that I wanted to hang around Karla's Karwash all day, but I felt the urge to buy a large Milky Way and eat it in air-conditioned comfort before rushing out into the oppressive afternoon heat.

"That'll be one-sixty-nine," the cashier said.

I wondered how many times a day she heard someone say, "I remember when they were just a dime?" I graciously shut up and paid, then opened the thing and took a bite as I stared through large steamy windows at the crew drying off cars.

The uniform of the day seemed to be a T-shirt, shorts and tattoos, lots of tattoos. Most of the arms were covered from the wrist up to at least under the T-shirt sleeve with non-stop artwork. Many of the legs had a calf hosting a large something or other…one snake wrapped around someone's leg, while another leg was emblazoned with a flowering vine of some sort. Quite a few names were scrawled on the side of necks. That was what the women looked like. The guys looked to be even more covered, although they also looked to have been inked up on a budget, if not just homemade. I loitered for a few more minutes, checking out the artwork while I finished my Milky Way, and then carefully licked my fingertips before I wandered back to my car.

I was actually parked on a dead-end side street in a forgotten one-block stretch just off of downtown. The street was named Islay, and you'd have to actually know it was here, and even then, it would still be hard to find. Two boarded-up frame structures covered with graffiti and housing a few dozen pigeons stood silently on the street overlooking the remnants of a once vibrant railroad switching yard. Sweat was running down my back and seeping through my shirt by the time I arrived at my car. A newspaper and a plastic bag had blown up against one of my rear tires, and as I bent down to pull them off, I glanced toward the parking lot across the street.

The lot was large, devoid of any pretense of shade, and looked like it could house a few hundred cars. It provided parking for one of three undistinguishable state office buildings. The lot was innocuous enough that a normal person would have found the litter on their car more interesting. Yet, there was something. I watched a vehicle slip into a parking place. Pretty sure I'd seen it once before. A late-model Buick LeSabre, light green in color and very clean. I was willing to bet I'd almost shot the idiot behind the wheel just last night.

I probably should have, once I saw who climbed out of the driver's side with his ridiculously spiked hair. An image flashed in my mind, the dot of my centerfire laser coming to rest just about on the tip of his nose. The nanosecond of that stupid look plastered on his face before he screeched away in reverse, slammed into that van, and then raced up the hill going the wrong way. I'd had a sickening feeling I'd recognized him last night. I must have tried to blank it out because the mere thought was so unpleasant— Pauley Kopff.

He was dressed in cut-off jeans, unlaced work boots and an olive drab T-shirt with red lettering that said 'Don't Tell Me What To Do.' He looked around cautiously once he climbed out of the LeSabre, took a quick gulp from a half-pint bottle, then lit a cigarette and cut across the boulevard lawn past the sign that said, 'Please Keep Off.' He crossed the street at an angle, causing traffic to slow and swerve. One car honked, and Pauley absently gave it the finger while taking another drag on his cigarette, multi-tasking. He stood outside the door marked 'Employees Only,' apparently in no hurry to finish his cigarette. Eventually, he extinguished the remnants of his cancer stick, leaving a blackened smudge across the white door in the process. He dropped the butt on the ground, gave a quick glance around, and then went in. I waited a couple of minutes while the sweat dripped into my eyes. I pulled the note off my dashboard with the license number I'd written last night and crossed over to the parking lot.

There was no mistaking the car. The left side taillight was still wrapped with red-tape, although maybe half the tape had come loose and fluttered in the slight breeze. The left rear corner on the car was scraped and dented. Remnants of dark blue paint ran along the side of the LeSabre and seemed to match my memory of the woman's van. By the looks of Pauley's car, I'd say the van got the worst of it.

I opened up the note. The license number didn't match. Hell, it wasn't even the same state. Pauley's LeSabre was sporting a South Dakota plate with an image of Mount Rushmore, although it was fastened in the same frame that read 'Girls, Girls, Girls' around all four sides. After a little closer examination, I noticed there were clean areas around the four screws that held the plate in place. The plate had been recently installed, if I had to hazard a guess, very recently.

I figured maybe earlier this morning clever Pauley thought he'd pulled a fast one. He'd changed the plates, maybe even reported his car as stolen. He'd probably lined up an alibi as well. I wrote down the number of the South Dakota plate.

Unfortunately for me, he'd had the momentary common sense to lock all four doors on the vehicle. I was tempted to go back to Karla's and talk to him. You'd think they'd have the proper equipment on hand at a car wash to water-board someone like Pauley. Upon further reflection, I thought it made more sense to just let the air out of one of his tires. So I did, flattening the tire on the front passenger side.

I walked back to my car, drove around the block and across the street into the state parking lot. I parked at the far end of the lot from Pauley's car and waited.

Now the question was, how did a low dripper like Pauley Kopff link up with someone like Gaston Driscoll?

While I waited slouched down in my front seat with all the windows open and drowning in sweat, I phoned my favorite person down at the DMV.

"Good afternoon, Minnesota Department of Motor Vehicles. This is Donna. How may I help you?" She sounded cheery, pleasant, exactly what you'd want in an employee dealing with the public. I knew how to change that.

"Hi, Donna, thanks for taking my call this is Dev Haskell."

"Shit," she said, making no attempt to disguise her disappointment.

"I know the feeling, believe me. Hey, listen, could you look up a license number for me? It's Minnesota plate, V-J-Y…"

"I can't continue doing this for you just because you happened to be present the night I made one tiny mistake. I've half a mind to tell you 'no,' and then—"

"And then with the other half of your mind you could start writing letters to appeal your conviction for sexual assault on a minor. How old was that kid? Fifteen?"

"No, he was a summer intern, and he was almost an adult."

"Sure he was. I'm sure the taxpayers would be pleased to know they were funding a little boy-toy exchange for state work."

"Just tell me the damn license number."

I gave her the number I wrote down the night before. Then I gave her the number on the South Dakota plate.

"This second one will take a bit longer since it's not Minnesota."

"Thanks in advance for your time, Donna. What about that Minnesota plate?" I could hear the keys on her computer clicking in the background.

"That Minnesota plate comes up as a '99 Buick LeSabre, registered to one Lester Palti Kopff."

"Lester?"

"Palti Kopff."

"Can you give me the spelling on that middle name?"

"It's just the way I pronounced it, Palti, P-A-L-T-I," she snapped.

"Huh, never heard that one before," I said absently, followed by a frustrated exhale from Donna on the other end of the line. "You got an address?"

She gave the address to me, and as I was writing it down, I realized I was just across the street from the place, Karla's Karwash. The address was bogus, but I saw no point in mentioning that fact to Donna.

"What about that South Dakota plate?'

"I keep telling you I could lose my job if anyone found out I was giving you all this information. Do you ever bother to listen to the news? They're making a big deal about unauthorized personnel accessing DMV records."

"Really?"

"Yes, really, it's been all over the papers. Of course, I suppose you couldn't be bothered with something as mundane as a newspaper."

"And it's become a big deal, accessing DMV records?"

"It certainly has, and every time I get one of your stupid calls like this one, you're putting me at risk. I've told you before I could lose my job."

"Gee, just think, and you'd lose it for sure if the state ever found out you were treating their summer interns to an all-night, sex-filled adventure."

"You can't just keep calling me like this," she whined.

"You know, you're right, Donna. Tell you what, when you get that info on the South Dakota plate, you can call me."

"Oh!" she hissed and hung up.

I slouched down in the front seat and waited for old Lester Palti Kopff to wander back out to his car.

Thirty-two

The car door slamming next to me woke me up from my nap. I glanced over just in time to see the frightened woman slap the lock down on her door as she quickly started her car. She glared at me as if to say 'some people,' then reversed out of her parking spot, almost smashing into a pink Volkswagen in the process. The Volkswagen driver leaned on her horn for an extremely long period of time. Reading her lips, one got the distinct impression she was anything but pleased.

There seemed to be a steady departure of cars for the next half hour, all racing toward the exit to just get the hell away from the office. After that, just the occasional person strolled out to the almost empty lot and drove off. By maybe six-fifteen, there were about twenty cars left in the entire lot. My sweatbox and Pauley's LeSabre were two of them. Fortunately, there were a few vehicles between us, and I was parked so far away from Pauley, I didn't think it would be an issue if the others left.

At about thirty seconds past seven, Pauley swung open the 'Employees Only' door. He stood in the open doorway, lit his cigarette, inhaled deeply, then turned and blew a large cloud of blue smoke back into the building. He crossed the street, causing traffic to slow in both

directions as he headed straight for his car and me waiting in the far corner of the parking lot.

He was talking on a cell phone, oblivious to his flat
tire, as he went around to the driver's side and slipped
behind the wheel. He started the car, lowered the windows, and flicked the butt out into the parking lot where
it sparked when it hit the shimmering asphalt pavement.
Then he pulled ahead. He stopped after a couple of
thumps and climbed out of his car to check the tire. I
heard him shout an obscenity as he scanned the almost
empty lot for a reason the tire was flat. I slouched down
a little further, settled in, and watched as he changed the
tire.

I didn't think he knew how to work that fast, but he
had the thing changed and tossed into his trunk in under
ten minutes. He fired up the LeSabre and pulled out of
the lot. I watched him disappear around the edge of a
building before I moved. I stayed a couple of car lengths
behind him as he made his way up East Seventh Street,
weaving through traffic.

He pulled into the left-turn lane and waited a couple
of minutes for the light before turning onto Payne Avenue. He stayed on Payne past the old Hamm's Brewery,
past the East Side District Police Station, and then took
a left and went down the hill on Reaney Avenue.

He pulled to a stop across the street from a seedy-
looking two-story brick building that predated the Second World War. The place looked to have been built as
a four-plex and was edged with faded, flaking brown

trim. I counted twelve doorbells with exposed wires attached to a piece of wood nailed to the side of the door frame that apparently served as the building's security system.

Pauley didn't ring one of the door-bells. He used a key to open the front door and went in the building. I felt the odds looked pretty good that this was the new apartment Karla had mentioned. I debated about walking up the front sidewalk to see if his name was posted next to one of the doorbells, but then decided to stay put in my car. I didn't want to take the chance of him glancing out the window and catching me standing in front.

A little before nine, he walked back out to his car wearing jeans, a different T-shirt, and drove off. I followed some distance behind him. He made his way on East Seventh, driving back into downtown. He drove past Karla's Karwash and turned left on Minnesota Street down to Shepard Road, which ran along the Mississippi River. He turned onto Shepard Road, heading upriver. The traffic was much lighter along the river, and I had to drop back further or risk being spotted.

There were a total of five stoplights, and we had green lights on all of them, never stopping once. Shepard Road runs along the river for a few miles, then gradually rises to the top of the river bluffs, where it eventually morphs into the East River Boulevard. Pauley continued at a leisurely pace, winding along the top of the bluffs, driving past more and more stately homes, all of which were definitely out of his financial weight class, not to mention mine. He was about two blocks from the Lake Street Bridge when he turned onto Dayton Avenue. I slowed a moment later at the same corner and glanced up the block to see if I could spot his taillights.

Instead of taillights, I caught Pauley just three doors up the street. He was walking around the back of his car on his way up to the front door of a large three-story home, stucco with a brick front. I waited at the corner and watched as the front door opened before he'd even had a chance to knock. He stepped inside, and the door closed behind him.

I resisted the temptation to let the air out of his front tire. I drove up the street past Pauley's car. He had parked behind what looked like a burgundy Corvette, but I couldn't be sure in the dark, and I didn't want to be too obvious and stop. I gave a quick glance toward the house, but other than noticing an orange painted door in the front with a yellow porch light shining overhead, I didn't see anything. I pulled to the curb in front of another gigantic house halfway up the block, parked, and waited.

Over the course of the next hour and a half, three people walked by, and all of them gave me the evil eye. All three were walking dogs.

The first was a very large woman in a grey sweatsuit walking a very small white dog that seemed to lift its leg on every boulevard tree along the street, and there were quite a few. She would wait for the dog, then give some encouraging words like 'Aren't you just the best boy ever', before the thing scampered off to the next tree and lifted its leg again. It sounded like awful high praise just for taking a piss. She looked at me as she waddled past and frowned. Her jowls seemed to sag, and her fat cheeks turned her eyes into slits. As she came into view in my rearview mirror, the word 'PINK' was stenciled across her rear in very large letters. I gave an involuntary shudder.

Fifteen minutes later, some guy impersonating a college professor, or maybe he was one, walked past. He was walking an ancient German Shepherd with a number of bald spots on its coat and a gait that suggested severe hip dysplasia. The guy was wearing wirerim glasses, sandals, Bermuda shorts, a white golf shirt buttoned to the neck, and a navy blue beret with a number of brass pins stuck to the thing. He began giving me the evil eye from two lots away. I pulled out my cell phone and pretended I was talking and taking notes. Fortunately, he didn't stop to interrogate me. He probably had to hurry home so he could fall asleep reading Elizabethan literature.

The last person to walk by was a kid. I pegged him at thirteen or fourteen. He stared at me for a bit then frowned in my direction, but not directly at me. I figured he was just mad at the world because he had to walk the family dog at night, and all the neighborhood bedroom windows were on second floors so he couldn't peek in. He was walking what looked like a black lab. The dog gave the impression it would have really preferred to not be going this fast at this hour of the evening.

I was still watching the kid and his dog in my rearview mirror when the front door opened down the block. Pauley quickly stepped out and headed for his car. I slouched down until he drove past then waited to start my car once he rounded the corner.

I followed him down University Avenue and back over to the East side of town. He pulled to a stop in front of a bar named Mr. Blue's. A place so low, it was even below my tawdry standards. Once again, I resisted the urge to let the air out of his tire. I waited down the block, watching his car in my rearview mirror until a little after eleven when I figured he probably planned to waste his time in Mr. Blue's until closing.

I drove back to the home he'd stopped at on Dayton Avenue. The burgundy Corvette, or whatever it had been, was nowhere in sight. I slowed down and scanned the front for the address numbers. I found them after a long moment, wrote them down, and then headed home.

As I crawled into bed, I could still catch the scent from Marsha's hair on the pillows. It smelled like something tangy, maybe fresh fruit. I fell asleep in minutes.

Thirty-three

The problem with going to bed somewhat early and alone was I woke up the same way, somewhat early and alone. It was a little before six when I put the coffee on, then got on the computer and did a reverse search on that Dayton Avenue address. I fully expected Gaston Driscoll to pop up. Close, but no cigar, as Dawn Miller's name appeared. Interestingly, there was no Mr. Miller listed, and I wondered if my original hunch had been correct. Dawn Miller, Gaston's current HR person, was his toy.

If I was correct, that had me worried about Marsha's safety, and that reminded me that she had an appointment yesterday with Dawn Miller for a job interview, and I hadn't heard from her. Six-fifteen in the morning was too early to call, so I resisted the temptation to do so and scold her.

I did sit there and wondered what Dawn Miller was up to, having a low life like Pauley stop by her home. Whatever it was, it couldn't be positive. And that brought me full circle to Pauley following Marsha, which made me think six-twenty wasn't as early as six-fifteen, so I called Marsha.

My call got dumped into her answering service after about eight rings. I phoned again, and I got her answering service in two rings. I phoned three more times before she answered.

"Lo."

"Hi, Marsha, Dev."

"Dev? What the hell time is it?"

"Just a little after eleven," I lied. "Just checking to see how things went yesterday?"

"Yesterday?" She was slowly beginning to come around, but it was work.

"Yeah, your appointment with Dawn Miller at Gaston Enterprises. How did it go?"

"Mrumph, mrumph." She cleared her throat, slowly becoming more awake than not. "Oh, I think it went pretty good. Course I listed you as a reference. That might not have been a wise move. Just a little lie, told them I did routine office work for you for eighteen months and that I was a model employee who made you a lot of money."

"Yeah, Marsha, that's what I want, you working at Gaston Enterprises. I'll be able to sleep nights, knowing you're safe with that jerk."

"Yeah, well, God I'm tired. I worked until close last night. Then get this, we had some dopey, bullshit meeting."

"A meeting? At two in the morning?"

"More like closer to three. Yeah, it went on for a half-hour. You wouldn't believe it. God, I bet I didn't get to sleep until close to four this morning. Hey look, I better get going, I've got a one o'clock appointment down there again today."

"At Gaston?"

"Yeah, follow up interview."

"Did you give them your address?"

"Hello? Yes Dev, its pretty standard procedure on a job application and a resume. You know, in case they want to mail you something like an acceptance letter or God forbid, a paycheck."

"Paychecks are all direct deposit nowadays."

"Yeah, well, look, I better run."

"Keep me posted. Call me after this interview thing today. Oh, and Marsha, keep an eye peeled for that light green Buick LeSabre from the other night. It's got redtape on the left rear taillight, and the left rear panel is dented, scraped and scratched."

"Tell you the truth, Dev, right now I'm so tired I wouldn't know a Buick LeSabre from a pick-up truck."

"The LeSabre has four doors, oh and South Dakota license plates."

"Gee, thanks, look gotta run and hit the shower."

"Need your back scrubbed again?" I tried not to sound too eager.

"Not this morning, but I'll gladly take a rain check," she said.

"You got it."

My phone rang about twenty minutes later.

"Haskell In…"

"You moron, what the hell do you think you're doing calling me at this hour? You jerk!"

"Who is this?" I asked.

"Shut up, Dev. Damn it. You woke me out of a sound sleep at six in the damn morning. God, no wonder I'm so tired."

"It wasn't six. Calm down, it was more like six-twenty, and besides, you should have called me after your appointment yesterday."

"Bastard," she screamed and hung up the phone.

I could have called her back. I could have explained. I could have stepped in front of a bus, too. I decided another cup of coffee was probably a much better idea. After that, I'd have to see what I could learn about Dawn Miller.

Thirty-four

I wandered into the office about ten-thirty. It was already hot and humid, and the temperature was going to climb for about six more hours. There was a love note taped to my chair from Louie that said he would be in court until early afternoon. It went on to say we were out of coffee, and while I was getting the coffee, some doughnuts might be nice.

It was too late in the morning to watch the ladies board buses for work or college, so I sat at my desk drumming my fingers and willing my phone to ring. Amazingly it did.

"Haskell Investigations."

"Hi, Dev, Karla."

"Karla," I said, and then that idiot Pauley immediately came to mind. Great minds must think alike.

"Got a moment to talk?" she asked.

"I've got all day."

"Yeah, right," she said, apparently thinking I was kidding. "Look, do you remember yesterday when you were here telling me about the people you talked to?"

"Yeah."

"You mentioned a name that rang a bell."

"Amanda?"

"Amanda Richards. But I couldn't remember how or where there was a connection."

"I thought you checked your computer files, didn't you? You were thinking she may have been an employee at one time, but nothing came up."

"Yeah, well, she wasn't an employee, but she was mentioned in some background information on one of my employees."

"Did someone use her as a reference?"

"No, welcome to my labor pool. Victim of an assault and attempted rape."

"Assault and rape?"

"Attempted rape."

"You mean one of your employees attacked her at the carwash? What the hell did he do?"

"No, not exactly, but it was how he ended up here. As a matter of fact, it's your friend, Pauley Kopff."

"That idiot?"

"Yeah, the charges originally filed against him were for breaking and entering, assault and attempted rape on a woman named Amanda Richards. The records I received had him pleading guilty to breaking and entering and the assault charge. The attempted rape on Amanda Richards was stayed provided he did the time and didn't reoffend. That's why I got the notification from his Parole Officer. Any hint of anything even remotely resembling a problem, and he's back behind bars. It's all part of the terms of his parole, well that and about twenty other things."

"Attempted rape?" I was deep in thought.

"I don't know much beyond that. There must be some way you could check on this, get a more complete picture."

"The police would have an incident file. Interesting."

"Yeah, it came to me about three-thirty this morning, just popped into my head and woke me up."

"You've been up since three-thirty? You should have come over."

"I just might next time. Anyway, interesting coincidence, don't you think?"

"Yeah. Is he scheduled to work today?"

"Pauley? Bear with me here a minute. I'll check." I could hear her keyboard clicking in the background. "Yeah, we've got him on one till seven every day this week."

"Does he usually show up for work?"

"Yeah, he's okay. I think I told you he just made the transition from the half-way house to his own place. That's potentially a difficult change for this crowd. Like I said, I'm half expecting the other shoe to drop. They usually do something like throw a party for some girlfriends and pals, and things tend to go downhill rather quickly from there."

I was deep in thought.

"Dev? You still there?"

"Sorry, just thinking for a moment."

"Look, I'd appreciate it if you decide to talk to him that you do it away from our premises. I don't want any repercussions coming down on me or the business."

"Repercussions? I'm a nice guy."

"Yeah, you usually are, but you'd be dealing with the social pool my employees come from, that always puts a little different spin on things."

"Yeah, I get it. I won't talk to him there, Karla."

"Thanks. Hey, I better get back to work. Keep me posted."

"I will, see ya."

"Bye," she said and hung up.

Pauley, Pauley, Pauley, I thought for a while. Then figured if I could look at the police file, I could study up on him, especially in relation to Amanda Richards, and then maybe just take a peek around his new pad while he was at work this afternoon.

Thirty-five

"In relation to what?" Aaron LaZelle asked. I'd phoned him as soon as I hung up with Karla.

"I told you I just wanted to see a file on a low-life named Pauley Kopff."

"Wiseass with spiked hair? A four or five-time loser?"

"Oh, I don't know that number sounds a little low."

"And let me ask again, this is in relation to?"

"Like I said, the Desi Quinn murder. I'm still gathering information, but there seems to be a consistent pattern here with Gaston Driscoll flittering out there somewhere on the horizon."

"Driscoll? You're still on that kick. Dev, you'd have better luck trying to nail the Governor."

"Yeah, believe me, I know. It's still all circumstantial, and I feel like I keep going around in circles, but the circles seem to be getting a little tighter."

"How so?" Aaron asked.

"Again, all circumstantial," I said, then told Aaron pretty much everything I knew, including Pauley stopping in at Dawn Miller's home last night. I left out Marsha getting close with Gaston Enterprises, Pauley following Marsha home, and me almost shooting him. As I was talking, I wished I'd gotten a license number on the Corvette parked in front of Pauley's car. It may have been Gaston Driscoll's. I made a note to have a romantic conversation with Donna at the DMV as soon as I was off the line with Aaron.

"I suppose we could bring him in, and I could have Manning sweat him for a couple of hours. He can be pretty good."

I knew from some very unpleasant personal experience what it was like to be opposite Detective Norris Manning in an interrogation. The guy would like nothing better than to lock me up for life, just on general principles. I didn't want to go anywhere near Manning.

"No, I don't think that would be such a good idea."

Aaron half laughed. "You still holding a grudge?"

"A grudge? Me? No, I just think the guy is a little too 'by the book' for my taste."

"This coming from someone who has no book whatsoever," Aaron said.

"And I'm not sure what it would accomplish. Pauley Kopff has probably been on the wrong side of an interrogation table since he was twelve. As good as Manning might be, I don't think it would turn up anything new. If, as I suspect, Pauley is somehow working for that squeaky clean Driscoll, it would just serve to alert the two of them that something is up."

"And you want to review our information on Pauley Kopff?"

"Yes. Maybe you could put one of your team on Kopff."

"Yeah, that sounds like a good idea. Let me see, the department is two investigators short and can't replace them due to city-wide budget cuts. Did I mention everyone over here is working under a mandatory no-overtime policy? The team I have working Desi Quinn's murder in normal times would have a caseload of seventeen other cases, all hanging fire. These days it's probably double that."

"Okay, okay, look, everything I'll see in that file is probably public record stuff, but it would save me half a day of digging it out." I waited a long minute. "You there, Aaron?"

"What? Yeah, sorry, just filling out the file review card. Stop in and see Madeline. This will be down there waiting for you in the next hour. Gotta run." I heard him say to someone, "Come in, have a seat, and close the door." Then he hung up.

I wrote Louie a note on the bottom of the note he left for me, telling him I'd get coffee and doughnuts. I stopped at the grocery store on my way to see the always smiling Madeline down in the records department.

When the elevator doors opened to the musty basement, Madeline wasn't smiling, but she was bleary-eyed. She never mentioned the file review card Aaron said would be waiting for me. Instead, I just wrote down Pauley's name on a post it note and handed it to her. She more or less directed me with a clumsy wave of her hand toward the bank of cubicles, then swallowed, smiled, and walked unsteadily back into the file area using the counter as a support, a guide, or both.

After fifteen minutes of waiting, I was ready to call out to her when she suddenly appeared with a file about a foot thick. She attempted to set the file down on the desktop, but as she did so, she lurched forward, and the contents fanned out across the Formica top like a deck of cards.

"Whoopsie." She giggled, then staggered out to her desk where she picked up her thermos and disappeared into the ladies room.

I looked at my watch. It wasn't even eleven in the morning.

I straightened the stack of forms, investigations, reports, interviews, and assessments that made up the file and began reading. It was modestly interesting and very depressing at the same time.

Pauley had been born Lester Palti Kopff in 1980. His mother was listed as a woman named Ruby Kopff, born in 1964, which made her just sixteen when Pauley was brought into the world. Things went downhill from there. There was no mention of a father, responsible or otherwise.

I had been incorrect when I suggested to Aaron that Pauley had been on the wrong side of an interrogation table since he was twelve years old. He'd actually been eleven when he was hauled in on an arson charge for attempting to burn down his school. Juvenile sentencing was staid, and Pauley was remanded to the custody of his grandmother, Emerald Mebbs. Emerald was back five months later, petitioning the court to take Pauley off her hands. Her petition was the last mention in the file of either Pauley's mother or grandmother.

In and out of foster homes for the next three years, Pauley apparently tried the patience of some extremely patient people. At fifteen, he was sentenced to the juvenile facility in Red Wing, Minnesota, on a series of burglary charges. He escaped from the Red Wing facility three weeks later. At age seventeen, he was sentenced to the Minnesota Correctional Facility in Saint Cloud, where along with honing his criminal skills, he learned the art of license plate stamping.

He was released in February of 1995 and promptly returned in November of that same year for possession with intent to distribute. This seemed to suggest a recurring pattern in Pauley's life. Namely that if anyone was going to be caught, it would be him. Unfortunately, Pauley seemed incapable of ever learning this basic lesson for himself.

There seemed to be nothing in the file that would suggest anything as serious as the murder of Desi Quinn, let alone Helen Olsen's car falling through the ice or Bernadette Driscoll's boat exploding. Still, there was a graduated series of offenses that, over the course of a quarter of a century, created a lot of problems for a good many people and in general, made their life experience a lot less than it could have been. Collectively, the societal problem could be summed up in one word, Pauley.

It was close to two in the afternoon when I finished reading Pauley Kopff's depressing biography. I needed to get out of the musty catacomb of the records area, out into the sunshine, and maybe spend some time chasing him down.

I carried the file out to Madeline's desk, but she was nowhere to be found. I was tempted to take the file with me, but then I would have to kiss my access down here goodbye. I placed the file on her purple desk chair and then pushed the chair in so the file wasn't just left sitting out in the open.

Thirty-six

I drove past Karla's and couldn't spot Pauley's car, so I drove through the state lot across the street. There it was, parked in the middle of the lot, lost in an ocean of state employee vehicles parked around him. The LeSabre was still sporting stolen South Dakota plates. Once again, I was tempted to let the air out of one of his tires but decided to take the high road and instead drove over to his apartment to break in.

When I pulled up in front, there was a hopscotch game drawn on the sidewalk, and the door was wedged open with a kid's shoe, burgundy with neon orange laces. The shoe was the kind where the heel lit up every time a step was taken.

The dozen doorbells were all labeled, except for one, unit 205. I didn't see Pauley's name listed anywhere, so I gambled and went for the unlabeled unit. The apartment was up on the rear of the second floor, the last of three filthy doors on the righthand side of a dingy hallway. Apartment 205 had, by far, the filthiest door and was located next to a rear stairwell spray painted with some illegible gang graffiti.

I knocked twice, and nothing happened. I put my ear to the door, but couldn't hear anything through the grime. I quietly turned the knob. The door was locked but seemed pretty loose in the door frame. I felt around the molding above the top of the door for a key and came up empty-handed. I pushed softly against the door, and it moved maybe three-eighths of an inch before it stopped. I could see the latch catch in the door frame, so with the assistance of my expired VISA card, I slipped the latch in under five seconds, and the door suddenly creaked open.

I listened carefully and then called a soft "hello" before I stepped in and closed the door behind me. It was a small compact unit with a no-smoking sign tacked onto the back of the door. The place reeked of stale cigarette smoke and dope. Against the far wall was a grimy grey couch with navy blue trim around the seams of the three cushions. The end cushion on the righthand side was torn along the seam, and yellowed foam rubber seeped out from a gaping slit. On the opposite end of the couch, a thin bed pillow, grayed and soiled, was wedged in the corner. The whole affair looked like it should have been out on the boulevard with a sign marked "FREE," which was probably how Pauley got it in the first place. Opposite the couch was a forty-two-inch flatscreen TV that looked shiny and brand new. The flatscreen was sitting on a stack of a half-dozen boxes, each one holding a brand new flat screen. Next to the flatscreens was a pile of maybe a dozen cellphones, and behind them, a number of Toshiba laptops piled against the wall. Funny, I'd never pegged Pauley as the hi-tech type.

The wood floor was well-worn oak, long devoid of any finish, let alone wax, not that you could really tell with all the clothes scattered around. There were two empty beer cases stacked at either end of the couch, serving as an end table of sorts. A table lamp sporting a bare bulb and no shade sat on one of the stacks. A coffee can filled with cigarette butts rested on top of the other.

Three unmatched dishes were on the floor in front of the couch. The one with the fork had remnants of what appeared to be chili or very old pasta. The other two held spoons and a grayed substance that had probably been milk at one time. An empty half pint of Jim Beam rested just underneath the couch.

A light blue four-drawer chest stood against a wall leading into the kitchen area. A bottle of Phillips gin, two different cheap vodkas, and a bottle of orange-flavored schnapps with barely a swallow remaining were scattered across the top along with what looked like a tuna fish can, filled with more cigarette butts. The remnants of a large teddy bear sticker decorated the front of the top drawer. There was a rectangular mirror hanging on the wall above the dresser. The wood frame around the mirror was missing on one of the sides.

The kitchen consisted of an overflowing sink full of dirty dishes and dirty paper plates scattered across a small greasy counter. I cautiously opened the refrigerator. The light was out, but I could see an open bottle of ketchup, three hotdogs in a package that once held eight and a half-empty bottle of Mountain Dew. I closed the refrigerator door using my foot.

The bathroom was at the rear of the small kitchen. I figured I'd need a whole slew of inoculations just to step inside the place. There was a dirty little sink with a dirtier little cracked mirror hanging above it. The tub had a shower surrounded by three walls of white plastic tile stained a rust color. Mold was growing along an area where half-a-dozen tiles were missing from the top course. Instead of a medicine cabinet, there was a dusty, white metal shelf with circles of rust probably from wet cans of shave cream or bug spray left sitting there. Pauley had deodorant, an aftershave named *Bad Boy*, shave cream, toothpaste, a tooth brush, a razor, and a container of Spiked Up Max Control that was missing the cap.

I went back to the blue dresser and searched the drawers. A couple of T-shirts were tossed in the top drawer, probably worn for maybe a day or two, and thrown back in there. The second drawer held boxers, a belt without a buckle, three photos of a much older fat woman lifting a grey sweatshirt over her head to expose herself, socks, and one sandal.

The next drawer contained more clothing, none of it folded. The bottom drawer held two pairs of blue jeans, a tube of *KY Intense Arousal Gel for Her* and two rather large vibrators still glistening with lubricant. I decided not to touch any of it.

Hanging on the corner of the mirror were three plastic bead necklaces, the sort of necklace one either 'earned' or gave away on Mardi Gras. Next to them hung a gold chain with a small gold Irish Claddagh medallion— hands holding the heart with a crown.

There was a small closet in the corner next to the couch, but nothing was on hangers. There were three jackets and another pair of jeans hanging from hooks attached to an unpainted board across the back wall. Two pairs of boots, three shoes, and a sandal matching the one in the dresser drawer were thrown in a corner. Two baseball caps sat on the shelf, and next to them was a silver roll of duct tape.

The duct tape got me thinking, and I went back into the bathroom and removed the top of the toilet tank. There was nothing in there but rust and water. I checked the back of the tank— nothing.

I looked beneath the little bathroom sink, and there on the backside of the sink was a plastic bag taped in place. Vintage Pauley, only the second place everyone would look.

The plastic bag held a small black pistol, a Beretta 950. It was maybe four-and-a-half inches long, three-and-a-half inches high, a .25 caliber. The sort of weapon you'd use for concealed back up, maybe in a coat pocket, on your ankle or in a purse.

I remembered when they wheeled Desi's body out the ME had said to Aaron, *"Looks to be a small caliber, if I had to guess I'd say maybe .22 short or a .25."*

That got me thinking about the gold Claddagh medallion hanging on the mirror. There was no way I could
ever prove it, but it sure looked like the one Desi had
worn the day I turned her down. I left it hanging on the
mirror and decided to flee the scene before I contracted
some weird disease.

Thirty-seven

I hadn't taken more than two steps back into the hallway when I heard laughing and heavy stomping coming up the front stairwell. I ducked down the backstairs and out of sight just as the voices arrived on the second floor. One of them sounded stupid enough to be Pauley.

"Just playing hard to get. I know she wants it."

"What she wants is to be left alone," another voice said, followed by guffaws and giggles.

I heard the apartment door creak open, and Pauley said, "Hey, what the fuck?"

"You don't lock your door?"

"Pretty sure I did. You guys notice that shitty de Ville parked out front?"

"De Ville?"

That was my cue to get out of there before I was spotted. I stepped into the first floor hall, just as an apartment door opened, and a rather obese woman in a purple T-shirt waddled out using her walker.

"Who are you?" she snarled.

I smiled, nodded and kept on moving.

"I said, who are you? Hey, you, what are you doing in here? I'm going to call the police," she yelled after me.

As I picked up speed, I heard footsteps thundering down the rear stairway.

"Stop him, I think he wanted to rape me," the woman growled.

"There he goes," a voice yelled just as I flew out the front door, running toward my car. I had just slipped behind the wheel when the front door to the building burst open. Pauley and two exceedingly large guys screeched to a stop and looked up and down the street, searching for their prey, namely me.

They zeroed in on my car as I fired up the engine. Pauley yelled something, but I couldn't make out what he said and didn't see any wisdom in asking him to repeat himself.

As I pulled away from the curb, the car suddenly rocked, and I glanced out the passenger window just as one of Pauley's gigantic pals kicked the door again. "Get out of your God damned car, stop damn it, stop!" he screamed and began to punch the window with his fist.

I accelerated to get away from him. A second later, I heard a loud thump above my head, and a baseball-sized rock bounced off the roof of the car and across my hood. I rounded the first corner, then zigzagged the next few blocks in case they were following. I hopped onto Interstate 94, heading east toward Wisconsin, the opposite direction from where I wanted to go. I kept checking the rearview mirror every other second, but couldn't spot anyone following me.

Thirty-eight

round ten miles out of town, I began to think about heading back. I had checked the rearview mirror repeatedly, but the coast seemed clear, and I began to feel a little more comfortable. I drove to my office and parked in front. Louie was nowhere to be found, so I wandered over to The Spot for a quick beverage just to calm my nerves.

I was on my fourth, or was it my fifth calming beer when a guy I recognized and whose name I'd forgotten wandered in.

"That your DeVille they're towing?"

"Towing? Not likely," I said, shaking my head.

"Red, with a blue passenger door? I'm guessing you had some windows in there at one time," he said, nodding as Carrie the bartender slid two shots across the bar.

I'd been half lost in some country song coming out of the jukebox. "Huh?"

"Looks totaled, Man," he said, downing a shot and nodding in a nonchalant way like my car being totaled and towed would be an everyday occurrence.

I looked out the dingy front window through the orange neon 'OPEN' sign. My car, or what was left of it, was being pulled onto the bed of a large blue and shiny chrome tow truck. There was a squad car parked in front of the tow truck, and the two cops seemed to be having a casual chat as the tow truck driver hooked chains to the undercarriage of my car.

I was out the door shouting. "Wait, wait, hold on, that's my car."

The three of them turned in unison to watch me running toward them. One of the cops said something I couldn't hear, but it brought a smirk to their faces.

"This vehicle belongs to you, sir?" the smaller of the two cops asked once I'd crossed the street.

The tow truck driver suddenly became very involved in raising my car onto the bed of his truck.

"Yeah, it is. Did someone hit it?"

"Not exactly," the other cop said, looking up to where my office window used to be.

For the first time, I became aware of a crunching sound beneath my feet and noticed glass, lots of glass scattered around the street and sidewalk. Then I noticed there was a beige, two drawer file cabinet that was wedged between my dashboard and the roof of my car where the windshield had once been.

"You want to tell us what happened here?"

"I don't know. That's my office up there, and I think that looks like my file cabinet." I nodded as my car was hoisted up toward the front of the tow truck bed. Both cops glanced up at my car then looked back at me.

"I, I just went into The Spot for a minute to use their phone," I said, realizing how stupid that sounded as soon as I said it.

"That's your office up there?" The shorter cop indicated the broken picture window on the second floor with a nod of his head. "And you don't know how that file cabinet ended up in your front seat?"

"Well, I'd say someone threw it out the window." I was picturing the idiot screaming at me and punching my passenger side window back at Pauley's just a couple of hours ago.

"Any idea who might have done this?" the other cop asked. He sounded calm, and he came across as one of those quiet, even keel types. I had the feeling he was finding the whole situation rather interesting.

"No, no idea," I said, pretty sure they knew I was lying.

"Been in an argument or fight with anyone? Maybe an outstanding debt? Road rage incident, something like that?" the short cop asked.

"No, no, nothing like that."

"Girlfriend trouble?" the calm cop asked.

"No, no girlfriend. Nothing." I looked up where my office window used to be. I guessed whoever did that had to have kicked in the office door to get to the file cabinet, and probably trashed the place for good measure.

"Well," the short cop said, glancing up at the broken picture window. "Someone doesn't seem to be too happy with you."

Another squad car pulled up with just one officer in it. He sat behind the wheel, looking at us for a moment while he had a brief conversation on the radio before he climbed out of his car. I saw sergeant stripes, and he maybe looked familiar, although I couldn't place him. Most of the cops, and especially the younger ones like the two I was talking with, were in good shape. They had physiques on them that suggested they worked out, a lot, and wouldn't have a problem handling people if it came to that.

This Sergeant wasn't like that. I put him at mid to late forties, heavy, but in that farm kid or laborer kind of way. He wasn't fat, but not a sculpted bodybuilder either, just old fashioned solid, maybe a hockey player. The 'S' curve on his nose suggested he may have held some solid opinions on occasion. He gave me a perfunctory nod and directed his question to the two officers.

"What happened?"

"We were just asking this gentleman the same thing," the short cop said, and then looked at a small notebook in his hand before glancing up at me. "Mr. Haskell?"

"I don't know. Like I said, I was in The Spot using the phone." I indicated over my shoulder where three guys were standing on the sidewalk, smoking, and watching. None of them made a move to venture over toward us.

"And this just happened? No fight, no argument, no incident?" the Sergeant asked.

"No, nothing like that. Someone said they were towing my car, and I looked out the window and, well, here I am."

He nodded like he'd been here before. I wasn't going to give him anything, and he had more things on his plate than wasting time with me. He turned to the two officers. "You check upstairs?"

"Door kicked in, place trashed, the window obviously," the short cop said and glanced up to the second floor again.

"Mr. Haskell, you better check things out up there. Look for items missing, maybe files. I don't know if you kept valuables or cash up there. Maybe there was a safe." He rattled this last bit off like a memorized line. He sounded like he wouldn't just be surprised, he'd be positively shocked if there had been anything remotely of value in my office.

Then he suddenly produced a sheet of paper from out of nowhere. "This has contact information. That's my card attached at the top along with a case number you can reference. You can file your report online. Please feel free to contact us should you have any information. Obviously, we'd like to get the person or persons who were involved, but it becomes difficult if not next to impossible without any cooperation from you, sir." He smiled then handed me the form.

They were gone three minutes later. I guessed experience told them I wasn't going to say anything, and they were just wasting their time. The tow truck driver handed me a clipboard with a form I had to sign. "You can claim your vehicle at the start of business tomorrow down to the impound lot. Course you ain't going anywhere's with no windows. You could have 'em replace them windows on site, but there's a crease where that file cabinet hit, so a body shop will probably have to take care a that before they fit a new piece a glass to her." He flashed a quick smile then spit a shot of tobacco juice off to the side.

"Thanks," I said.

He nodded, tore a pink copy of the form off, and handed it to me. "Be seeing ya," he said, then spit once more for effect before climbing into the cab of his tow truck and driving off with what was left of my de Ville.

Thirty-nine

Oscar said, "I'll total up the charges and slide the bill under your door sometime tomorrow night."

He was measuring the window they tossed the two-drawer file cabinet through. It was the window overlooking the street where I leered at all the pretty women. Oscar was our office landlord and not too happy about the state of things just now.

"Christ, I suppose everyone'll be wanting new locks and more security. I don't know how the hell I'm supposed to pay for all that." He shook his head and shot me a look.

"You better get all that glass and shit cleaned up out on the street. Someone gets a flat tire, or some little girl cuts herself, you're the guy who's liable, Dev. Saw all sorts of papers blowing into folks' yards down the block. Guessing that's from your damn file cabinet. Jesus Christ, you'd think at some point you might just catch on. I don't know what woman did this, but you must have really pissed her off."

There was no point in offering a defense. "When do you think you might be able to have the door fixed?" I asked. I was on my hands and knees, sorting through files that had been dumped all over what was left of our office. Sorting was a generous term. Right now I was just stacking things into three separate piles - Louie's pile, my pile, and an 'I don't know' pile.

The door to our office had been forced open, and it looked like whoever did it used a sledgehammer. The entire right side of the door was shattered. The trim around the door frame had an almost forty-five-degree angle to it where the wood had snapped and would have to be replaced. The benches to Louie's picnic table looked like a pile of kindling, my desk was turned over, and every one of the drawers had been damaged. I figured once they dumped all the files out, they took their sweet time kicking in the empty drawers. The coffee maker was shattered, and the pot had been thrown against the far wall.

"I called Gary, my fix-it guy. Earliest he can be here is tomorrow morning. He'll replace the door frame, and he can install a new lock. Think I might have a spare door somewhere down in the basement," Oscar said, sighing like it was one more pain in the butt thing he had to do, which I guess it was.

"Is Gary the guy who'll paint the wall?" I nodded at the 'Your next, asshole,' message spray painted in large red letters across the wall.

Oscar sighed again, then said, "You notice they spelled that wrong? Should be you're, you know, with an apostrophe and then the letters r and e. Might just be a clue."

"I don't think these were the kind of people who worry a lot about grammar and punctuation."

Oscar nodded. "Gary can paint it, but I don't know if he'll have time to do it tomorrow," he said, then wrote something down on the wall next to the broken window and stepped back. "Figures, damn it…hundred and three by eighty-two inches. It'll take two sheets of plywood, and I only got one downstairs in the shop. I suppose I'll have to go get the damn thing and figure out how to drag it back up here," he said and gave me another disparaging look.

"Gee, I wish I could help you out, Oscar, but my car is waiting down at the impound lot for new windows, if you'll recall."

"Think you might be better off just totaling that bomb."

I couldn't argue with his logic and returned to my sorting.

"I better get going if I want to get this shit installed. I got stuff to do tonight. I gotta life, too, ya know." Oscar groaned, shaking his head like a father who was very disappointed, but not at all surprised.

"Thanks, Oscar. Sorry for the hassle. Hopefully, the cops will get a handle on whoever did this."

"Yeah, sure, Dev," Oscar said as he read the measurements he'd just written on the wall. As he left, his lips were silently moving, repeating the dimensions of the window. I heard his voice mumbling something at the bottom of the stairs, but couldn't make out what he was saying. A moment later, Louie stepped in the door.

"What the hell? You forget your key? What the hell happened here?"

"I think we had a very unhappy client pay a visit."

"You okay?"

"Yeah, I wasn't here."

"You know who did this?" Louie asked just as a sparrow fluttered halfway in where the window used to be, then quickly shot back outside.

"I got a pretty good idea," I said and went on to retell Louie about Pauley, his pals, what was left of my car, and finally, I reiterated my suspicions about Gaston Driscoll.

"I'd say this comes awfully close to confirming your suspicions. It seems like you're getting under someone's skin. Jesus Christ, how in the hell do you get into these situations?" he asked, shaking his head.

"I just told you. I was minding my own business, just getting my car washed when—"

"I get that part. It's just all the other stuff. Aren't the cops supposed to check this stuff out, look for the murderer and shit? You did call them, didn't you?" Louie asked, indicating the shambles that used to be our office.

"Well, yes and no, not exactly," I said.

"Oh, God," he said, shaking his head again.

"What do you think?" I asked.

"I think I need a beer, probably more than one. I think you better not stay at your place tonight, and I think you are going to need some protection."

I remembered my Ruger was safely tucked under the front seat of my car, which was now resting down at the city impound lot. "I got a piece stashed at home I can get. Ahhh, I'm without wheels at the moment. Think you could give me a lift?"

"Yeah, but you're buying the beverages, and a piece isn't going to do it."

"Huh?"

"You need a bodyguard, someone with some real muscle. Whoever did this," he said and looked around. "Right now, it's a pretty safe bet, they're thinking you're a pushover. They're gonna come back for you, Dev, and it ain't gonna be pretty," he said, staring at the spray painted message on our wall.

Forty

The name that came immediately to mind was Tony Colli, the Dog. He'd watched my back when I got mixed up with Mr. Swirlee a couple of years ago. I hadn't heard from him in maybe over a year, but I knew how to reach him, eventually.

"Yeah." It was a three-pack-a-day rasp that answered the phone, followed by an audible drag on her cigarette. I could see her sitting at the card table set up in her living room, watching some dreadful midday game show while she chain-smoked the hours away.

"Good afternoon, Mrs. Colli, this is Dev Haskell. I'm trying to get in touch with The Dog. I, I mean Anthony," I said into the phone.

Louie was seated on the stool next to me, signaling Jimmy, the bartender, to give us another round.

Rasp, cough, cough. "Why, Devlin, how nice to hear from you. How are things?"

"Couldn't be better, Mrs. Colli," I lied. "I was looking for some help on a work project I have going on, and I thought of Anthony. He wouldn't be around, would he?" I didn't add, as opposed to being locked up in some correctional institution.

"No, I'm afraid he's unavailable, as a matter of fact." She lowered her voice as if someone next to her in the living room was attempting to listen. "He's been out of the country on a business trip."

"A business trip? Really? Do you expect him back anytime soon?"

"I'm not too sure. He's been down in Mexico for a few months, attempting to get some work organized," she said, displaying the sort of naïveté mothers around the world seemed to be capable of. I figured if The Dog was in Mexico, it wasn't to build schools or improve water quality in a village.

"If he returns anytime soon, would you please have him give me a call?"

"I will, Devlin, but you know Anthony. He can be so busy, so…" Cough, cough, cough. "…unpredictable."

So criminal, I thought. "Yes, he's quite the entrepreneur. Well, thank you, Mrs. Colli. You sound great." I said.

She never wasted time saying good-bye, so she did her usual and just hung up.

"Well?" Louie said. He was already halfway through our next round.

"He's out of town . . . Mexico."

"Mexico?"

"Business," I said, but the word could not possibly explain whatever The Dog was involved in.

"Well, you're still gonna need someone, unless you maybe want to leave town and hope things ultimately quiet down."

"Can't, man. I got Marsha out there flirting with this Driscoll creep. Karla, Catherine Lindquist, Daphne Cole, and, well, what I let happen to Desi."

"I think you've probably beat yourself up enough on that gig, Dev. It's not nice, but sometimes shit happens. You didn't do anything. You—"

"That's just it, Louie, I didn't do anything. I was her last shot, and I told her to take a hike. I couldn't be bothered. She got jacked around, set up, sent up, and the final straw was me, and I just blew her off. Then, someone decided she deserved to die. Why? I want to get whoever did that, man. I have to just to keep my own sanity."

"Look, I don't like it any more than you, but we'll get the office put back together. You can get your car repaired. We can—"

"I'm not sweating any of that shit, Louie. Were you listening? I'm talking about that pompous dickhead Gaston Driscoll, that slime ball, Pauley and his muscle-bound idiot pals. I want them, bad."

"You're heading for trouble is what you're doing, Dev."

"Probably."

Forty-one

Sometimes my best ideas are beverage fueled. It was a little after eleven, a little after the take out pizza, and somewhere in the middle of the twelve-pack we picked up on the way home from The Spot. I was sitting in Louie's ratty recliner, watching a rerun of the Blackhawks playing the Bruins in game three of the Stanley cup. Louie was snoring on the couch.

She answered on the third ring, sounding surprised she was even getting a phone call. Maybe it was the hour, or maybe she had caller ID and just panicked when she saw it was me. "Hello?"

"Hey, Annie, Dev Haskell."

"Ooh, bad time, Baby, very bad," she whispered.

"Everything okay?"

"Yeah, sure, but I mean us…you and me," I could barely hear her, she was talking so softly. "You probably shouldn't call me. At least for a bit," she whispered.

"You with Lydell?"

"Mmm-hmmm."

"Actually, that's why I called. I wanted to talk to him if it's okay."

"What about?" She was back to a normal tone, and there was a sudden edge to her voice.

"Nothing about you and me. Actually, I wanted to hire him if he's available."

I was aware of a male voice in the background, but couldn't make out what was being said. It sounded like Annie had covered the phone, and I could only pick up about every fifth word. Eventually, a soft-spoken male voice came on the line.

"Yeah?"

"Hi, is this Lydell?"

"Yeah."

"Lydell, my name is Dev Haskell. I know Annie through a mutual friend."

"Who's that?"

That caught me off guard. "Oh, I'm blanking on her name just now. But, I wanted to talk to you about a little side job, if you're interested."

"I don't do contracts or loan collections anymore," he said.

"I don't think this would be like that. This is more of maybe just having a presence. You'd just be keeping me safe while I go about my investigation business."

"Investigation?"

"Just looking up records, mostly, things like that. It would probably be pretty boring. I don't anticipate any trouble. I'm just playing it safe."

"Yeah?"

"Yeah. I'm wondering if you could meet me tomorrow morning at my office. We could talk a little further, see if it's something you'd be interested in."

"I suppose I could do that."

"Great. Would 10:30 work for you?"

It did. I gave him the address and directions to my office and fell asleep in the recliner with Boston up one zip.

Forty-two

ydell washed up on shore around eleven-fifteen, about forty-five minutes late. Not that it mattered. I was still in the cleaning mode, putting things in piles to be hauled out to the trash. What was left of my desk was out on the sidewalk along with the remnants of Louie's picnic table benches. I ran out of paint covering up the red threat spray-painted across the wall, so you could still read 'sshole' and easily jump to a pretty logical conclusion.

Gary, the fix-it guy, was working on the door frame, actually replacing the entire thing, cutting the new pieces with a table saw set up out on the sidewalk. He was one of those guys who seemed to operate with a lot of tools and little wasted motion.

Oscar had boarded up the front window with plywood the night before. Oscar's mood hadn't seemed to improve when he informed me he was charging me for the special order glass. I was going to argue with him, but figured on second thought it might be better to just apologize, yet again, and then shut up.

I was on my knees, sorting through my stack of files. Over the past couple hours about all I'd been able to accomplish was to turn the one large pile of my stuff into twenty-seven smaller piles, and I still had the better part of a file drawer to go.

"I'm looking for Mr. Hacksell," a soft voice said.

I'd only seen him once before, and that had been at night from the back when I was fleeing the scene. He appeared a lot larger close-up, but it was definitely Lydell. A nose with a large bump along the bridge, scar tissue around the eyes, a line running maybe five stitches long across the base of his chin and, of course, the shaved head. His black T-shirt was stretched taut over a muscled, 'V'-shaped upper body with bulging biceps and a flattened six-pack for a stomach. I'd missed the tribal tattoos across his massive shoulders and biceps that night, but then again, I was moving pretty fast. He looked like a muscular stick of dynamite just waiting for an excuse to explode.

"Lydell?" I said, kneeling back and looking up.

He nodded.

I groaned as I got to my feet then extended my hand. "Dev Haskell. Come on, we'll wheel these office chairs out the door. We can talk in private in the hallway while Gary's working here."

Gary gave a half-hearted wave as we wheeled two office chairs out into the hall and down by the door to the ladies room.

Lydell spun his chair around, then sat down backward on the thing, facing me with his massive arms resting across the back of his chair. He had large hands with thick fingers. His brown eyes were dark and piercing, and his gaze seemed unblinking.

"You said you were looking for protection? Someone upset with you?" He indicated the office door behind me, where Gary was busy replacing the door frame. Our new door from the basement was leaning against the hallway wall and was stenciled with the words "Fire-Exit" in red letters.

I nodded and gave a brief explanation. "I'm working a case. Some rich guy is involved, and he's got a couple of thugs who broke in and trashed the place, smashed all our furniture. They tossed a file cabinet through the office window onto my car out on the street and knocked all the windows out of my car."

"Yeah, I saw all that junk piled up on the sidewalk. You call the cops?"

"No, they were actually here when I discovered the damage."

"So you know who did this."

I nodded, thinking for a minute. "I'm ninety-nine percent sure, but I can't prove anything. Let's just say it fits in pretty neatly with a case I'm working on. I'll be honest. I think they murdered a woman. Someone I should have helped and didn't. I know they're into moving some stolen goods, flat screens, computers, cell phones, stuff like that. One of them is on probation and just out of a half-way house. They're stupid, vicious, and I suspect they'll try something again. I also think they're bullies, and a broken jaw or a little rest time in traction would probably go a long way in adjusting their attitude."

Lydell nodded, apparently seeing the sense of my argument and then asked the sixty-thousand dollar question, "You going to go looking for them?"

I shook my head. "No, I'm going to continue my investigation. I'm guessing they'll try something stupid again, maybe come looking for me. I'd just like to be prepared if they do."

"How many we talking?"

"I'm aware of three guys. One of them is no problem, little twerp with spiked hair named Pauley Kopff. The other two are big guys, maybe bodybuilders. They seemed to have some knowledge of martial arts. I don't know who they are, and I don't know anything about them."

Lydell nodded while he seemed to think everything over then gave a shrug. "I don't know. It sounds simple enough. You want me around just in case, right? You're not going to go looking for these guys?"

"I'm not going to go looking for these guys, or, if I do, you don't have to come along."

"Sounds fair enough," he said.

"What's this gonna cost me?" I asked.

"Three hundred a day just to hang around. Minimum three days, paid in advance. Any interaction with these individuals, the fee is commensurate with the results. Five hundred for a shouting match, seven-fifty for any physical contact. If they end up in the emergency room, that's a grand, per individual. Overnight stay in the hospital, three grand, per individual— all payable upon completion. You cover any court costs and my legal fees. I don't cut grass, do laundry, or help clean up. I'll work an eight-hour shift unless we arrange something in advance."

I had the distinct impression this wasn't the first time Lydell had rattled off his fee schedule. "You need a contract?" I asked.

"A handshake and three days in advance will do."

Forty-three

Marsha said, "Actually, he comes across as a pretty nice guy." But then she seemed to think for a second. "In a smarmy kind of way. Very impressed with himself, likes sports cars, made a point of telling me twice that his wife had passed away." She glanced over again at Lydell and smiled.

We were eating late lunch cheeseburgers in a corner booth at Shamrock's, out of earshot of everyone, except Lydell, who seemed focused on the NASCAR event running on the televisions overhead.

"He make you an offer?"

She shook her head and swallowed. "Not in so many words, but it was out there on the table."

I gave a questioning look.

"Believe me, it was out there. A girl just gets to know it. I want him to come out and say it, not make it look like I forced myself on him." She gave another quick glance to see if Lydell was listening.

"You run into Dawn Miller?" I asked.

"That H.R. cow, no, thankfully. At least, not in the past two days. But she was not happy to see me when I started in the office. She made a point of telling me she didn't know what Gaston was thinking, and she couldn't guarantee I would be on staff for any length of time.

God, she's one of those women who whine when they talk, really annoying and more than a little bit frosty, if you ask me. I'd be willing to bet she hasn't gotten any in quite a long time."

"Be careful around her. You remember what I told you?"

"Being Gaston's latest love toy? Oh, please, Dev. Believe me, he's got the pick of the litter in that place. He's not wasting his talents on her. Oh, icky."

"Just be careful. I think she sees herself as guarding the gate. Remember, I tailed Pauley to her house."

"Yeah, yeah, relax, will you?" she said, then took another dainty bite of her cheeseburger as she shot one more quick glance in Lydell's direction.

"What's next?" I asked.

"God, we've got some old chick dancing under the name, Cougar. Wants to hold a prayer meeting at Nasty's at the end of every shift. Yeah sure, that's what everyone feels like doing after dancing for six hours. Have a prayer meeting after two in the damn morning."

"Actually, I meant at Gaston Enterprises."

"What? Oh, sorry, you know, leading the double life and all. I'm in there for a few hours tomorrow then Gaston takes me out to lunch for my weekly review on Friday."

"Review?"

"I'm guessing lunch will be at some hotel, and he just might have a room waiting."

"You're not actually going to go into a hotel room with this guy, are you?"

"Relax, I've already got the 'mom needs to be taken for a doctor's appointment' excuse and a lab class after that lined up. I'll spring it casually on our way to lunch, use it as a reason to stay off any adult beverages. The more I know about this guy, the more convinced I am that Desi was set up."

"Just watch yourself. Lydell here has his hands full just taking care of me."

"Pity," she said and flashed a smile as Lydell looked over at the two of us.

Forty-four

We were driving back to the office in Lydell's truck. He had some country station programmed in on satellite radio. The truck, with its dual wheels and Ultimate Fight Club stickers, may have looked like a beast, but it was plush and comfortable as hell inside and a giant step up from my de Ville. I was enjoying just looking out the window as Lydell drove.

"So, Marsha works for you? Is she like a special secret agent or something?" he said.

"Actually, no. She doesn't work for me. She more or less inserted herself in my investigation and is attempting to get some reaction or a signed and notarized confession from our main suspect. Nice gal, but she's more than a little in the way, muddying the waters."

"Think the guy will sign the confession?"

I turned to face Lydell. "I was kidding. That's the problem. She's just in there mixing things up with no specific goal or end game in mind."

"Sounds a bit like life," he said.

"Yeah, I guess." I wasn't sure if he had missed my point entirely or was thinking way deeper than I had given him credit.

When we got back to the office, I phoned Karla. She answered on the second ring.

"Hi, Karla, it's Dev."

"What's the latest?"

"The latest? Well, no real progress on the investigation, although someone did trash our office and pretty much totaled my car."

"You're kidding. Was it a hit and run?"

"No, just a lot of damage…knocked all the windows out of my car. The thing is gathering dust down in the impound lot now. I'm thinking real hard about pulling the plug on it, my car."

"You need a set of wheels? I got a vehicle here just collecting dust."

"You're kidding."

"No, you can have it. I mean to use, if you want. But, I gotta tell you, it's not exactly what you'd call subtle."

"Would it fit under the category of 'pimp my ride'?

"Definitely." She laughed.

"We're on our way."

Karla wasn't kidding. The thing was a Lincoln Town Car, the kind with the suicide doors and the vinyl top. Only this vinyl top had a flame pattern emblazoned across it, Spreewell spinning rims, a one-foot diameter steering wheel that looked like a chrome chain and about a thousand coats of lacquer over metallic dark blue paint. I stood there and stared once the tarp had been pulled off.

"Sweet," Lydell said.

"Yeah, in a strange way. It's a sixty-four if you can believe it. Get this, that's actually Nightmare blue. The paint color, I mean," Karla said.

"It really shows off this gold crucifix on the trunk," Lydell said, staring at the emblazoned car trunk.

"Don't even get me started. That's six caret gold paint across the trunk. Who knew? That was the last straw."

"Where'd you get this thing?" I asked.

"Ramon, one of my ex's." She shrugged but didn't elaborate. "His toy, I just paid the bills. God, he could stand here and tell you things about this car for the next two hours, way too much information. But, it's all mine now, to do with as I please, and I'd be pleased if it can help you out. Of course like I said, it's not what one would call subtle." She laughed again.

"That's gotta be the understatement. Is it insured?"

"Up the wazoo, so don't sweat it. But let me warn you, the mileage it gets is downright sucky."

"It beats walking. Lydell's been hauling me around, and I'm sure he's had enough of my advice and direction. Yeah, Karla, if your offer is still open, I'll take it."

"To use," she said.

"To use," I repeated.

We went up to Karla's office, so she could make a copy of my driver's license and give me a copy of the company insurance policy.

"Just don't smash it up, promise," she said

"Scouts honor. Hey, how's my pal Pauley doing?" I asked.

"Pauley?"

"Kopff. Short, spiked hair, not too bright, probably attempting to scam you a number of different ways even as we speak. Last time I saw him here, he was cleaning interiors."

"The scam part could apply to just about anyone of them. But I know the guy you mean. I hope you're not counting on seeing him. We let him go earlier in the week."

"Oh?"

"The usual. They get out of the half-way house, and suddenly, they just don't seem to be able to handle the responsibility side of things. You miss three days work here, and you're out. That's my policy. He missed four. I think he used up both grandmothers and an elderly aunt or something. Amazing how all the funerals seem to land on a Friday or a Monday and just happen to extend the weekend."

"What did he say?"

"Say? I don't think he even bothered to come in. We finally just called and left a message, told him his final paycheck was in the mail."

"You know where he might be working now?"

"I doubt he's working anywhere, Dev. Guys like that are always too busy planning the next scam."

Forty-five

Louie had his feet up on the church basement tables he'd found somewhere and brought in for my desk. My feet were up on the window sill. Lydell looked to be dozing in the corner.

"I don't like it," Louie said.

"The car? Yeah. I know, I'm getting a lot of strange looks, and it's a bit of a gas hog, but that's still cheaper than renting or buying some bomb."

"I meant your lady friend firing that jackass."

"Oh, Pauley. You can't really blame her for firing the guy."

"I get that part. I just don't like the fact that he now has twenty-four hours a day free to come after you, Dev. His last visit worked out so well for us," he said, then jiggled his chins in the general direction of the plywood still over the front window.

"Except that, don't you think he would have tried something else by now?" I said.

"Possibly," Louie said. "But does he know you're even doing anything? I don't know. Maybe he thinks he scared you off. As a matter of fact, are you? I mean, doing anything?"

"I'm reviewing facts and shit."

"In other words, no, you're not doing a thing."

"Things are momentarily at a standstill, and I'm not exactly sure what to do, to be honest. Which reminds me, I'd better get in touch with Marsha. She's supposedly getting a work review by none other than Gaston the slime ball, tomorrow."

"A review?" Louie said, then seemed to stare off into space.

"That's his term. She thinks he'll try and ply her with drinks over lunch and then get a hotel room."

"That actually works?"

"Not with her."

Forty-Six

Either all was forgiven, or he'd forgotten he'd kicked me out for a month. It didn't matter. Benny the bouncer took a quick glance at my ID and motioned me inside Nasty's. Marsha was dancing tonight, and I figured it might be the only time I could talk with her before she went to lunch with Gaston. She hadn't bothered to answer any of the phone calls or text messages I'd left for her over the course of the day.

I couldn't spot her working the room, so I ordered a beer that turned out to be both warm and flat then grabbed a back table. Marsha, aka Brandi, came on stage about thirty minutes later with her hobby horse, wearing a pair of leather chaps and a cowboy hat. She danced to three songs, then gathered up her tips and exited the stage. As I looked around, I had the distinct feeling the crowd seemed older than the last time I was in here. A lot of salt and pepper hair wearing loosened ties and un-buttoned starched collars mixed in with the baseball cap and T-shirt crowd.

Marsha appeared a few minutes later. I was attempt-ing to wave her over just as applause and ear-splitting whistles erupted throughout the place.

"And now for your viewing pleasure, the infamous Cougar, *growl*," the announcer screamed over the sound system as the old Pat Benatar tune *Treat Me Right* blared out.

"Dev, oh my God, what are you doing here?"

"Looking for you, Marsha. Sit down for a second so we can talk. You get any of my phone messages?"

"Yeah, but . . . look, you're going to have to slip me a twenty if you want to talk," she shouted over the catcalls directed toward the stage then glanced around nervously.

"What?"

"House rules, Dev. Otherwise, they can ban me. They'll think I'm giving freebies."

"Okay, okay." I pulled a twenty out and set it on the table.

She picked it up in one quick, practiced motion and stuffed it into the side of her thong. "Thanks," she said and sat down. "Is, ahhh, Lydell with you?" she asked, looking around and sounding hopeful.

"No, sorry, just little old boring me."

"So, what'd you want to talk about?"

"Well, your meeting with Gaston tomorrow, for starters. I want to be there."

"Be there?"

"Just watching your back. Me and Lydell."

She nodded and smiled like Lydell's presence would suddenly make it acceptable. "Okay, but how do you plan on doing that?"

"He's taking you to a restaurant?"

"I think so."

"We'll just be sitting at a nearby table. Simple."

She said something, but the sudden applause and cheering drowned her out.

"What?"

"God," she groaned. "It's that damn Cougar. She's the one who wants us to pray once we're finished for the night. She's an absolute nut case, driving all of us crazy. Remember? I told you about her?"

"She seems to pack them in, that's for sure." More than one idiot was on his feet, giving Cougar a standing ovation as she exited the stage. "Look, you'll have to tell me where Driscoll's taking you for lunch."

"That's just it, I have no idea."

"So we'll be near your office. Find out and call me, or when you get to the restaurant or hotel, run to the ladies room and call me from there."

"You can't follow us?"

"I'm driving a somewhat conspicuous vehicle," I said. "Look, maybe if—"

"Well, Dev Haskell, must be your lucky day, Sweetie. Here to see about another three-way?"

A cloud of cheap perfume seemed to descend on us like mustard gas. She was close enough that her see-thru leopard skin nightie brushed my cheek as she twirled in front of our table. I was afraid I might have contracted some hideous social disease when it brushed across my face. I knew her from another time when she had been just plain old despicable, Swindle Lawless. But tonight she was 'Cougar,' the star attraction at Nasty's.

"You, you, you actually know her? You know Cougar?" Marsha looked shocked.

Cougar grinned. "Me and old Dev had a three-way one night 'Member, Dev? With that little girlfriend of yours? What the hell was her name? Holly, Helen?"

"Heidi," I said. "And if you'll recall, nothing happened. You were intoxicated, so drunk, you passed out as a matter of fact, and you simply needed a safe place to spend the night."

"Yeah, so you say, Bad Boy. But, you know, the three of us in bed. Well—"

"Believe me, nothing happened, Swindle or Cougar, or whatever it is you're going by nowadays. Marsha, it was just a case I was involved in some time ago," I said, ignoring the interruption and trying to save the moment.

"It's Brandi, and I gotta move to the next table," Marsha said, jumping off my lap and stalking off.

"Hmm-mmm, guess she's not too eager when it comes to sharing. Least not yet," Cougar cackled. "Good seeing you, Dev, but it's gonna cost you twenty to have me sit down. Sorry. Course, on the other hand, you already know I'm worth it," she said and cackled again.

"Tell you what, Swindle. Maybe you'd better attend to all your fans." I indicated a number of intoxicated and formerly distinguished gentlemen waving twenty-dollar bills in her direction.

"Your loss, Hassel baby. But don't you worry, Honey, you always got a raincheck just for old time's sake," she said, then winked, like she meant it, turned, took two steps, and sat down at the nearest table.

Forty-seven

We were parked around the block from Gaston Enterprises, ignoring the stares from curious passers-by when we weren't out plugging the meter. If they didn't walk past pointing and laughing, people literally stopped and stared at the flame-decorated vinyl roof and the gold crucifix emblazoned across the trunk. We'd been sitting there for the last three-and-a-half hours, accomplishing absolutely nothing.

"I don't know, Dude, it's after two-thirty. We wait much longer, and he'll have to buy her dinner instead of lunch," Lydell said.

"God damn it."

"Think maybe she stiffed you, just blew you off? You said she was pretty pissed off last night. You know how they can get."

"It's entirely possible. Not the first time some woman vowed never to speak to me again. I just hope she didn't think she could handle this creep by herself. I'm thinking if he's on to her and he's got Pauley and those other two thugs involved, well, there's no telling what they might do."

"And you called their office?"

"Lydell, you were right here next to me when I phoned. They said Driscoll was in meetings all afternoon and couldn't be disturbed. Not like I can really leave my name and number."

"Maybe they're going at it in his office right now. You know, all torched up and maybe—"

I looked over at him but didn't say anything.

"Only saying, man."

"I'd be lying if I said I wasn't worried about her."

"Maybe give her a call?" Lydell said.

"I've sent her four text messages already. You know many women who ignore one text message, let alone four?"

"Mmm-hmm."

A little after three, I pulled away from the curb and drove back to my office, where we sat and continued to accomplish absolutely nothing. While Lydell sent a text to Annie, I phoned Gaston Enterprises, but I didn't ask for Gaston Driscoll.

"Marsha Norling, please."

"Just one moment, I'll connect you."

Maybe I'd been worried for no reason. All this time sweating it out, and she had just been pulling a bad atti-tude. It figured. Lydell and I wasted the better part of the day worried about her, and she's been in that damn of-fice, probably flirting with that jerk, Gaston.

"Dawn Miller," a voice answered a moment later.

"I'm sorry, I was holding for Marsha Norling," I said, wondering what the H.R. witch was doing on the line. My mind was racing through a variety of scenarios, none of them very promising.

"Miss Norling is no longer with us. May I ask what this is in regard to?" I could feel the ice coming across the line. I hung up the phone as the rest of the color drained out of my face.

"That doesn't look like it went any too well," Lydell said.

"It was that wench from their HR department. She said Marsha was no longer with them."

"Like she took the day off and went home?"

"No, more like she didn't work there anymore."

"That doesn't sound all that promising, man."

I couldn't disagree. I also couldn't think of what to do next. We tossed some ideas back and forth. One of the best was Lydell running to Fast Pizza for a couple of sandwiches. He wasn't gone two minutes when my phone rang, and it was Marsha's number, thank God.

"It's about time, damn it. I've been worried sick. You okay?" I answered.

"I don't know, Sweetheart, you tell me," a male voice I didn't recognize said.

"Who's this?"

"Just a charming guy who found this phone lying on the street. I'd like to return it to you. Maybe be out in front of your office in three minutes, sitting behind the wheel of that pimp-mobile with the flames on the roof you've been driving around town, and we'll pick you up."

"Where's Marsha?"

"Dude, pull your head out of your ass and listen up. Be outside your office in the next three minutes, sitting in that car. Got it?"

"I don't think you—"

"That's right, don't think. Just get your sorry ass out there," he shouted and hung up.

I phoned Lydell to get him back to the office. His phone rang at the far end of the table exactly where he'd left the damn thing. About all I had on hand for a weapon was a letter opener. I bounded down the stairs and out onto the sidewalk. I'd parked the Lincoln out on Randolph, virtually right in front of the door. I quickly ran through my options. I could be shot, stuffed in a trunk, the victim of a car bomb, or maybe I could get to Marsha.

I sent a quick text to Lydell so he'd know what was up, while I sat behind the wheel with the air conditioner on. I'd barely finished hitting send when a black SUV screeched to a stop along the curb behind me, and two very large guys jumped out. I cautiously stepped out of the Lincoln.

"Leave that piece of shit running and get your ass back here," a shaved-headed idiot said. He was wearing a white T-shirt with red letters spelling *Budweiser* across the chest. He stood and held open the rear door of the SUV while the other guy wearing a black T-shirt walked toward my car. He gave me a cheap shot with his elbow as he passed, then started to climb in behind the wheel of the Lincoln.

I half turned, ready to shout something.

"Don't be stupid, just get over here," Shaved Head said.

"Where's Marsha? I need to know she's all right," I said as I climbed in the back.

"Shut up and get your dumb ass down on the damn floor, dipshit," Shaved Head yelled, then grabbed me by my belt and yanked me onto the floor of the back seat.

As I wiggled between the seats, he jumped in and stomped his feet down on top of me. He slammed the door closed as we sped away from the curb. I looked up at him, pretty sure he was the same jerk who'd tried to kick and punch in my car window when I was attempting to get away from Pauley's apartment the other day.

"What do you think you're looking at, Shithead?" he said, then stomped his feet on me again.

"Uff."

"Keep your hands where I can see 'em. Nothing would please me more than to pop your dumb ass right here," he growled, then pointed a small pistol at me. It looked an awful lot like the one I'd discovered taped beneath Pauley's bathroom sink. Except now that it was pointed at me, the end of the barrel appeared to be about six inches wide.

"You seem to have a real talent for being a pain in the ass." This from whoever was driving.

Shaved Head kept his feet on top of me and began to frisk me with his free hand, all the while pressing the pistol barrel against my forehead. I prayed we didn't hit some pothole in the road.

"If you're carrying anything, you better tell me now. I don't like surprises," he growled.

"Nothing, I'm clean. I swear. Just a phone in my front pocket."

He patted me down, reached beneath me, and checked my belt line. He pulled the phone from my front pocket and tossed it onto the seat. I remained focused on the pistol barrel pressed against my forehead and prayed the road remained in good driving condition.

Forty-eight

We hadn't driven all that far before we made a couple of sharp right turns and stopped. I was aware of what sounded like an automatic door opening just before we pulled into a garage. Based on the rakes and snow shovels, I saw hanging neatly on the wall, I guessed we were at a private home. There was that garage smell, a combination of fertilizer, gasoline, and grass clippings. Lying on the floor of the car with a pair of size fourteen boots on me, I could just catch the top of what looked like two side windows.

Shaved Head opened the door and climbed out, but not before giving me one final stomp and chuckling, "Come on, get your worthless ass out here. Haskell, so help me, you try one of your stupid moves, and you'll wish you'd never met me. I'll be your worst nightmare. I promise." With the gun pointed at me, he already was my worst nightmare, so I saw no point in disagreeing with him. Why argue with perfection?

The garage was one of the largest ones I'd ever been in, a spotless floor with a light grey finish, four car stalls, and a workbench area with rows of tools hanging in an orderly fashion and arranged according to size. In the far stall, a car was covered with a fitted beige tarp. Whatever kind of vehicle it was, the thing was built close to the ground and looked sleek even with that tarp draped over it. I could just make out tires with chrome spoke rims and the hint of a highly polished burgundy body.

"Just keep moving, Asshole, straight ahead through that door." He pushed me toward a door in the corner of the garage that the driver was just opening. Now, I was sure these two were the same idiots I'd seen with Pauley Kopff the other day. I was just beginning to wonder where that idiot Pauley was. Unfortunately, I didn't have to wait long to find out.

"Problems?" Pauley asked as we entered the house. He was sitting on an elegant kitchen stool, looking worse than usual and drinking something that resembled iced tea, but clearly wasn't. There was a pistol lying on the granite kitchen counter within easy reach. A fifth of Jack Daniels and a cell phone sat off to the side.

Marsha was seated across from him. Her left eye was a dark purple and very swollen. A strip of duct tape was wrapped around her head, covering her mouth. What looked like the remnants of a bloody nose stained her face. Her cream-colored blouse was torn at the shoulder and soiled like she'd fallen and skidded for a few feet across the pavement. A number of large drops of dried blood had worked their way down the front of her blouse. She raised her head as I entered the room, and her eyes grew wide. She'd obviously been crying and looked scared out of her wits.

"Marsha?"

"Shut the hell up, dickwad," Pauley said, then gave a nod as he reached for his drink. Something slammed into the back of my neck, and everything went black. When I came to, my hands were wrapped with duct tape, and I was lying in a corner on the floor. It looked like Pauley had a fresh drink, and Marsha was nowhere to be seen.

"Anyone ever tell you, you're a major league pain in the ass, Haskell?" Pauley asked, then followed that up with a couple of hefty gulps from his glass.

My mind was foggy, and I tried to clear my head. A bolt of pain shot up the back of my neck and pierced my skull the moment I moved.

"You seem to have a knack for making things very difficult for very important people. Should have quit while you were ahead, dumb shit."

I was focused on taking deep breaths in an effort to keep my stomach down while my head continued to explode.

"Hey, you hear what I said, bright boy?" Pauley half-shouted, then kicked me hard on the side of my face. There was a hollow sound as my head bounced off a cabinet door. I desperately swallowed a couple of times in an attempt not to get sick. I failed and suddenly vomited across the tiled floor.

"What the...? Jesus Christ, watch what the hell you're doing! Look at the mess you made, Haskell. Don't expect me to clean that up, you piece of shit."

I wasn't sure how long I sat there. It could have been a few minutes or over an hour. I still wasn't thinking clearly. I became vaguely aware of footsteps on the other side of the room and then another voice. I couldn't seem to raise my head to see who it was. I just sat there, taking deep breaths, inhaling deeply in an attempt to calm my stomach, all the while wondering what in the hell I'd gotten myself into.

Forty-nine

They had been arguing back and forth for some time, and the voices had gradually become raised.

"Are you crazy? This has gotten completely out of hand. What in God's name do you think you're doing? I tell you to eliminate the problem, and you think it's a good idea to bring them here? You God damn idiot, you can't keep them here. I don't want anything to do with this. Do you understand? Now get out, damn it, and get him the hell out of here."

It was a male voice, deep and booming from the far side of the kitchen counter that brought me around— a command voice. I attempted to lift my head, and another wave of nausea washed over me for my trouble. Fortunately, my stomach was empty, and nothing came up. Stars seemed to flash along the edge of my peripheral vision, and the arguing back and forth was sending waves of pain up my neck before they exploded somewhere along the base of my skull.

"Stay cool, man, I told you, I've got it under control. We're going—"

"Under control? Look at you for the love of God. You're drunk again. You actually brought them into my home? What the hell were you thinking? You idiot. What if someone saw you?”

“No one saw us. I made sure of that. Take a chill pill, dude.”

I thought it sounded like Pauley, who spoke, then slurped more of his drink. But I was still having trouble focusing and couldn’t be sure.

“What aspect of ‘I can’t be seen to have anything to do with this’ do you not seem to grasp? You seem positively incapable of following directions, of doing anything right. Do you realize that you have jeopardized everything, absolutely everything? Now for the last time, get out of my home before I summon the police myself, you stupid, brainless moron.”

“What the hell did you just say? What’d you call me?” I was pretty sure that was Pauley’s voice. As banged up as I was, I recognized his slurred words.

“Oh, please, spare me any of your self-righteous indignation. You heard me. I said, get out of here before I call the police. Your brain is so fried you’re completely incapable of rational thought. You’ve put everything I’ve worked for at risk with this latest idiotic stunt. You were given a simple task to accomplish, and yet, somehow, you’ve managed to screw it up. What the…? Don’t you dare point that thing at me! What exactly do you think you’re doing?”

I think I’ve heard just about enough of your bull—”
Boom.

It was quiet for half a second before something slammed onto the floor just a few feet from where I lay. I was close enough to feel the vibration when it hit the floor. I opened my eyes, attempted to focus, and watched as a dark puddle of blood began to flow toward me across the glazed floor tiles. I instinctively attempted to roll out of the way, and suddenly I was staring into Pauley's face.

He lay motionless on the floor, just the hint of a surprised look plastered across his face. His mouth was open ever so slightly as if he was just about to make one more idiotic statement. There was a small hole in his forehead, maybe an inch above his right eye, and a small amount of blood had pooled in his eye socket before it ran partway along the bridge of his nose. The pool of blood on the floor seemed to flow from beneath his chin and must have been from the exit wound. If Pauley ever actually had any brains, they'd just been blown out. He was dead before he hit the floor.

"Good Lord, what an absolute jackass," a deep voice boomed. "Well, it would appear it's just the two of us, Mr. Haskell. Pardon me for a moment. Don't go anywhere." I heard what sounded like the clang from a toilet seat being raised a moment later.

I strained at the tape around my wrists, which only succeeded in sending waves of pain jangling up my neck and exploding once again along the base of my skull. I heard a toilet flush, and then footsteps entering the kitchen.

"I suppose we better get you out of here. Actually, know what? This is going to work to my advantage. I'm afraid Mr. Kopff had become the inevitable loose end. Unfortunately, now we're going to have to aggressively address the problem of you and Miss Norling. Pity that, such a waste. I suspect I would have found her rather enjoyable."

He suddenly appeared, stepping around the kitchen counter to tower over me as I lay on the floor. He looked lean and fit with snow-white hair and a neatly trimmed beard surrounding his tanned face. Piercing blue eyes held my gaze, and it was clear he wasn't about to flinch. It had to be Gaston Driscoll.

"Here, let me help you to your feet. I wouldn't want you to strain anything." He half laughed then reached down to yank me up off the floor.

I waited until I was halfway up, thought I might have a chance at kneeing him in the groin and took a shot. I missed, but Gaston didn't.

"So, attempting to play it rough, are we?" he said and then caught me with an uppercut to my chin that he must have learned on an Ivy League boxing team. My jaw slammed shut, and my teeth clicked audibly, as I sailed back against the kitchen counter. Before I knew what happened, he kicked my feet out from underneath me, sending me crashing back to the floor. I half landed on Pauley's body and gasped as the wind was knocked out of me. I tried to inhale deeply in an attempt to refill my lungs and, at the same time, fight off the urge to erupt all over the place again.

"You want to play it tough, I'm more than willing to oblige," Driscoll shouted, as he delivered a sharp kick to my ribs, just in case I wasn't getting the message. "Now, get up on your feet. You try anything stupid like that again, and I promise you I won't be so gentle."

He clamped his hand in an iron grip around the back of my neck and squeezed hard, causing my stomach to threaten to retch once again as he hoisted me back on my feet. I couldn't focus, my head felt like it was ready to explode, and I had to fight to keep the contents of my stomach down.

"Just move out the door, Haskell, and please don't attempt any foolish heroics. If you insist on doing something stupid, I'll simply take your spine out," he said, then shoved a pistol into my back. I attempted to focus and somehow made it out the door and back into his garage. Driscoll steered me around the side of the SUV by pressing the pistol against my back. He opened the rear door. "Get down in there," he said, then shoved me into the vehicle.

I attempted to crawl onto the rear seat, but just as I brought my knees up to curl into a semi-fetal position, he pulled me down and onto the floor between the front and back seat. A moment later, something heavy was thrown on top of me. Guessing from the smell, I thought it was a large bag containing fertilizer or weed killer or something. I couldn't be sure, but whatever the contents were, they stung the raw areas on my face and arms. I had to close my eyes to keep them from burning.

A minute or two later, I heard the car door slam and the engine fire up. The vehicle backed up quickly, and almost immediately, there was a loud snapping noise. "God damn it," Driscoll shouted and screeched to a stop a moment later. He paused and mumbled something, then seemed to regain control before he accelerated and took a hard left. The bag of whatever was on top of me shifted slightly, and I immediately felt a stinging sensation as more of the contents poured out of the sack and over me.

Fifty

We drove for a bit, not that I had any idea where lying on the floor of the rear seat with a bag of some kind of toxic material draped over me. Eventually, we came to a stop. Driscoll seemed to just sit there with the engine running, until I heard him say, "I'm out back. No, I've got him with me. No, there's been a change. That won't work. Just help me bring him inside, and I'll explain."

The door of the SUV opened a moment later. Someone grabbed my ankles and pulled hard. The bag resting on top of me split open as I was suddenly dragged upright. The contents spilled over me and inside of the car as I was forcibly yanked out the door. A cloud of chemical dust filled the air, causing me to choke and gag. I gasped for air and felt like I might be sick all over again.

"You idiot, what the hell did you do that for?" Shaved Head growled, then punched me hard on the side of my face, bouncing my head off the door frame. "Jesus!" He coughed, stepping out of the cloud of toxic dust as I fell onto the ground.

I choked and closed my eyes from the burning chemical particles. Too late. I exploded into a coughing jag, my eyes watered and I couldn't see. A pair of heavy hands grabbed me by the shirt and belt, and hauled me up, pushed me forward a few feet then threw me down on the ground.

"Bring him inside before someone spots him," Driscoll boomed from somewhere. I caught a glimpse of him just as he headed up some steps and onto a large back porch.

Heavy hands yanked me effortlessly off the ground then threw me forcefully up a couple of steps. I stumbled in through a rear door into some junk room. "Just cool it in here," Shaved Head said and pushed me down on a wooden floor.

"Tie this around his feet. I don't want him getting any ideas," someone said. It wasn't Shaved Head, although the voice sounded just about as stupid. The next thing I knew, Shaved Head was wrapping an electrical extension cord around my ankles, then tying the cord off on a hook screwed into the wall.

I felt like I was hanging upside down, my head throbbed, my eyes continued to burn, and I thought I might throw up, again. Slowly I became aware of voices arguing in the next room. Occasionally I could make out Driscoll's deep tones, but I didn't recognize anyone else. One of the voices was a woman's, shrill and screeching, sounding very agitated, but all I could tell was it wasn't Marsha. I'd no idea where she was, not that I was in a position to do anything about it.

The sounds coming from the kitchen suggested arguments that seemed to be growing more and more heated as time wore on, although I was still unable to make out what was actually being said.

Sometime later, Shaved Head came out and checked the electrical cord wrapped around my legs then left the room, exiting out through the back porch. A few minutes later he returned, and knelt down next to me, but there was something different. My eyes still burned, and I tried to focus on the white T-shirt with the red *Budweiser* letters. It took a moment, but it slowly dawned on me it wasn't Shaved Head. Actually, the head was shaved, but it wasn't the jerk I was expecting. It was Lydell.

He glanced toward the voices drifting out from the kitchen, then quickly unwound the electrical cord from my legs. "You okay? Can you move?" he whispered as he pulled the duct tape off my wrists.

I nodded, and he helped me to my feet then guided me out the back door. We moved quickly and quietly across the back porch and around the corner of the house. We stepped over Shaved Head face down on the ground minus his T-shirt. I couldn't tell if he was alive or dead, and I didn't really care as long as he just stayed where he was.

"Lydell, you do that?"

He nodded, then pulled a brown wallet from his front pocket and opened it. "Says here, his name is Dempsey, Donald Dempsey. Ring any bells with you?"

I shook my head no.

"Bush league…he seemed really impressed with himself, but Annie hits harder than that pussy."

"How the hell did you find me?"

"I was coming out of Fast Pizza with our lunch when they passed me, that black SUV and your pimp ride. You better thank your lucky stars for that damn crucifix on the trunk and those flames on the roof of the Lincoln. It's pretty hard to miss."

"I think they still have Marsha back in there with them," I said.

"Marsha? You mean you found her?"

"Yeah, in a manner of speaking. I saw her wherever we were before. Lydell, we can't just leave her in there," I said.

"How 'bout we just call the cops like the responsible citizens we are and not push our luck?" Lydell said, pulling out his cell phone.

Fifty-one

aron shook his head and said, "I gotta tell you, Dev. You're really pushing your luck here." We were in an interview room on the fifth floor of the police station. I was seated directly across the table from Aaron. Detective Norris Manning sat next to him. We were all sipping coffee, Aaron was shaking his head. Manning was tilted back in his chair with a smug, self-satisfied I-told-you-so look on his face.

"Come on. You've got my statement. You've got Lydell's word."

"Yeah, your pal Lydell Hammer, a known felon who has now been accused of assault," Manning said and casually took another sip.

"Assault? You gotta be kidding me. Who in the hell do you think beat me up? I told you, that jackass with the shaved head and that worthless piece of shit, Pauley Kopff."

"Frankly, the only reason you're not under arrest is you haven't been specifically named in the assault charge. At least not yet," Manning said. He looked to be enjoying himself.

"That jerk with the shaved head had it coming. They were going to kill me."

"I take it you're referring to Mr. Donald Dempsey, the gentleman hospitalized with a broken jaw, a concussion, a broken nose, two broken ribs, and a laundry list of lesser injuries too numerous to mention. Apparently he was assaulted by your pal Lydell Hammer when he went out to retrieve a file from his vehicle parked in Dawn Miller's driveway."

"I think he's maybe some gang enforcer or something," I said.

"Actually, wrong yet again. Mr. Dempsey is an architectural student enrolled in the graduate program at the U of M. Did I mention he happens to be an honors student? Of course, I can see your point. Usually, a pretty vicious lot honors students."

"Architecture? Come on. The guy's a thug who was going to kill me. I told you they shot Pauley Kopff in the head, Driscoll did. I sorta saw it."

"Sorta saw it?"

"Well, I heard the shot, and then I was staring into Pauley Kopff's face, dead and bleeding out on the kitchen floor."

"That's another problem, that so-called shooting. You see, we can't quite seem to find the crime scene, not to mention locate a victim." Manning smiled.

"Dev, there was no indication of that kind of activity in Dawn Miller's home," Aaron said.

"Get real. It's not like I was able to run outside and check the address on the front door. Besides, it didn't happen at Dawn Miller's home. Did you even bother to check out Gaston Driscoll's place? Is someone questioning that guy?"

"We did speak with Mr. Driscoll. As a matter of fact, I spoke with him personally. He's out of town on business, but he was kind enough to take the time to return my phone call," Aaron said.

"Out of town?"

"On business," Manning said, clearly enjoying the moment.

"Down in Florida, actually. He's at a conference for underprivileged children as a matter of fact. The conference started yesterday in case you're interested," Aaron added.

"And you talked with him? How do you even know it was him?"

"You mean, aside from the fact that we traced the call to Florida. Exactly where he's supposed to be. Exactly where he told his office they would be able to contact him. The phone number was his personal cell phone." If it was possible, Manning seemed to look even smugger than a moment ago.

"I'm telling you guys, Gaston Driscoll is the guy who shot Pauley Kopff right in his kitchen. At least I think it was his kitchen."

"Your shooter look anything like this?" Manning said as he began clicking the keyboard on his laptop. He waited a moment, then turned the thing around so I could see the screen. An image of the well-groomed white-haired guy with the beard I'd last seen shoving a pistol against my spine stared back at me.

"Yeah, that's the guy that shot Pauley Kopff. It's him. I knew it."

Manning shot a quick glance over at Aaron.

"Understand our problem here, Dev. We don't have a body, we don't have a location, and we're dealing with a Grade-A upstanding citizen who is eighteen hundred miles away and took time out of his business day to contact us after being accused by a convicted felon and, well, you."

"But, Marsha?"

"That stripper?" Manning said. "We've been looking for her. Apparently, she was dismissed from her internship at Gaston Enterprises a couple of days ago. Inappropriate behavior, according to the head of their HR department, that, and the fact she apparently falsified her qualifications right from the start." He glanced down at a yellow legal pad with notes written across the top page.

"Seems she lied about being a graduate student in chemistry and then conveniently failed to mention she gets her kicks taking off all her clothes for dollar tips down at Nasty's. Mr. Driscoll had a vague memory of her, said he met with her for a few minutes just before he left for Florida. He suggested we speak with his HR person to get all the facts. She gave us some general info then suggested we would need a subpoena just to cover ourselves and them."

"Great, I'm guessing Dawn Miller was the HR broad, right? She's in on this whole deal. Now she's stalling for time, hoping you won't go to the trouble of actually getting a subpoena."

"Well, first of all, her response is exactly what I would expect from someone in an HR department. By the way, please note, she didn't refuse, she just needs to cover herself and the firm from an insurance liability standpoint. You're suggesting a pretty big conspiracy group, Dev. That's an awful lot of people, all upstanding citizens by the way, who are supposed to keep something like this a secret. Odds are someone, somewhere would eventually screw up and open their mouth, right?" Aaron suggested.

"Someone did screw up. Pauley Kopff. And I told you what happened. Gaston Driscoll shot him."

"Great! Pauley Kopff, another loser. We are not going to drag good people through the mud based on pure fabrications," Manning said.

"Fabrications? You got a guy dead, and a woman who's missing. What the hell else do you need?"

"Maybe some proof for starters," Manning said. "Credible proof. We can't locate this Kopff character or your friend, Miss Norling, for that matter. You'd think someone would have reported them missing. Well, other than yourself. Maybe they just went off together for a little privacy," Manning said.

"But my bruises," I said.

"Yeah, your bruises," Manning replied. "God only knows you've been dropped on your head at least one too many times. I wonder, if we examined you closely, would those bruises be consistent with selfdefense on the part of Donald Dempsey, who's sitting in a hospital room right now?"

I looked at Manning for a long moment, and he stared back, unblinking. I gradually turned my eyes toward Aaron.

"Dev, we really can't do much more here." Aaron shrugged and held his hands out, palms open.

"Can't or won't? What the hell do you think they were doing at Dawn Miller's home?"

"Gee, I don't know. An architectural grad student and the head of HR for an architectural firm, just maybe they were working. Well, at least until one of them was assaulted and robbed. We found Dempsey's wallet in the possession of your friendly felon Lydell Hammer."

"What about Pauley Kopff? How does he fit in if everything is so upstanding?"

"Good question. Of course, he wasn't there, was he?"

"Wasn't there? What did you guys do? Stand out on the street and just yell through the windows? He was there. I saw the guy, damn it. He had the back of his head blown off."

Manning just shook his head and looked the other way.

"Well, could you at least maybe check out Driscoll's house? That's where I think he shot Pauley. For all I know, his body is still lying on the kitchen floor," I said.

"We've already done that, Dev. As I said, Mr. Driscoll is out of town and the place is locked up tighter than a drum. The place has a fairly advanced security system."

"Was the thing on?"

Manning shot Aaron a quick glance, then turned his laptop around and closed it, all the while shaking his head. "I suppose all of this could have happened at the governor's mansion. They've got a big kitchen there. Maybe we should check that place out, too."

"What about Lydell?"

"Hammer? He's being held overnight pending assault charges," Manning said.

"I don't believe this shit."

"You need a lift?" Aaron asked, apparently ending the conversation. "I can have a squad take you home."

"You guys gotta believe me," I pleaded.

"We're checking things out," Manning said, then got up from the table. "Look, I've got an awfully full plate. I have to get moving."

Aaron nodded as Manning picked up his laptop and walked out of the room.

I waited until he closed the door behind him. "So, you spoke to Driscoll?" I said.

Aaron nodded.

"Did you actually see him, or was it just some voice on the phone."

"I spoke to him."

"Aaron, in the next few hours, this thing is gonna blow up, and you and your entire department are going to look like absolute idiots. These bastards are probably racing out of town now. Come on, man, they're getting away."

"Actually, no. I believe Miss Miller is over at Regions Hospital as we speak. Most likely, she's still in Mr. Dempsey's room meeting with an attorney and drawing up a laundry list of charges against you and your pal Lydell Hammer. Do I even want to know how you met that guy?"

"Lydell?"

"Are you aware he's making a name for himself on the Ultimate Fight Club circuit?"

"Gee, I had no idea, and I met him through a mutual acquaintance."

"Don't say another word. You should probably have counsel present. Dev, there's a pretty good chance there'll be a warrant out for your arrest by sometime tomorrow morning. Now, do you need that ride home?" Aaron asked, standing and apparently concluding our discussion.

"I suppose I do, since they stole my car. God, they even stole my phone."

"I thought you said your car was totaled and in the impound lot."

"It is. This was another one I borrowed from a friend, and no, you don't want to know."

Aaron shook his head, puffing his cheeks out as he exhaled clearly frustrated. "I'll get someone to give you a lift home. Don't venture too far from your front door, Dev, and you'd better get in touch with your attorney. I'd be prepared for a laundry list of charges to come your way sometime tomorrow."

"I can hardly wait," I said.

Fifty-two

If Aaron said the charges were in the process of being filed, that gave me the night to try and get things sorted out. I didn't really feel like calling Karla and telling her I'd lost her car, not to mention losing Marsha.

I found a couple of quarters in a dresser drawer and made my way across the street to the payphone in the lobby of Fabulous Ferns, a bar within sight of my front door.

"Dev?" Louie answered.

"How'd you know it was me?"

"Your call came through as 'payphone.' You're the only guy who calls me from a payphone, and when you do, it means things probably aren't going your way."

"That's the understatement. Look, you free to pick me up at home? I'll explain once you get here. It's a mess."

"Gee, surprise, surprise."

I was waiting in front of my house when Louie pulled up. I'd cleaned up somewhat, and my stomach seemed to have settled, but my head was still pounding.

"That a rash all over you? It's not contagious, is it?" Louie asked as I gingerly climbed into his passenger seat. My skin was still red and a little tingly from that toxic chemical stuff Driscoll had dumped over me. I caught the slightest hint of an afternoon bourbon wafting off Louie's breath.

"Not to worry. Besides, there isn't the germ that could live in your bloodstream. I'll tell you about it as we drive. Mind if I borrow your phone?"

"Anything else you need? Bills paid, paperwork filled out, maybe scrub your back?" he asked as he handed me the phone.

I phoned Annie and brought her up to speed on what had happened to Lydell. It was not the most pleasant conversation.

"Oh, God, you and that damn Lydell. I just knew this wasn't going to work out well," she said ten minutes later when she opened her front door. She'd had just enough time after my phone call to get really worked up.

"Annie, I told you, Lydell didn't do anything wrong. He helped me. Actually, he saved me as a matter of fact."

"Sure, Dev, that's why they've got him in jail, again," she said, then crossed her arms, cocked a hip, and made it very clear we weren't going to be coming inside.

"Jail might just be the safest place for him right now. Kind of like he's under police protection, at least until I get some answers," I said, trying my best to soothe a volatile situation.

"Yeah, sure, that's what it is, police protection. I'm not buying it, Dev. Anything else? Cause I got a lot of things to do."

"Well, actually, I was just wondering if he maybe kept a spare set of keys around. You know for his truck."

"Well, since he's been arrested, again, and you seem to know way more than me, why don't you just go and get them from him? Apparently, he won't be going any-where, so he doesn't need them now, does he?"

"They're probably locked up in a property room and, well, it gets complicated. It might be better for eve-ryone if I just stayed away. You know, let the cops do their job and all that."

She seemed to think about that. "Wait here," she fi-nally said, then slammed the door closed.

"I see you haven't lost your touch," Louie said.

The door opened a few minutes later, and Annie tossed a set of keys over my head and out onto the front sidewalk. "Next time you see the big dope, you can just inform Mr. Lydell Hammer that all his worthless shit will be out on the curb with a sign on it that says 'free.' So, if he wants anything, he better get his ass over here, and you can tell him I'm changing the locks again, too. So he can just not bother trying to contact me, ever! By the way, that goes double for you, too, Dev. Now, both of you get as far away as possible from my front door."

"Annie, maybe you—"

She just glared, looked like she might yell some-thing, and then slammed the door again. We both felt the vibration standing on her front steps.

"Nice work, Dev, real nice," Louie said.

"I can't worry about her right now. Let's grab those keys and see if we can just find his truck."

It took a while, but eventually, we did find Lydell's truck.

"What a great bomb," Louie said, admiring the dual rear wheels and the Ultimate Fight Club bumper stickers. The truck was parked up the block and around the corner from Dawn Miller's house, sporting a recent parking ticket on the windshield.

I drove the truck down the alley, then around the block, but didn't see Karla's Lincoln anywhere. I was thinking maybe they stashed it in the garage or in Gaston Driscoll's garage. I drove past Driscoll's house, hoping I might check things out. At the very least, I could verify that was the place where Pauley Kopff was shot and where I'd last seen Marsha. Unfortunately, there was a squad car parked in front standing guard, so I just kept moving.

There was one other place I hadn't checked, Pauley Kopff's grungy little apartment. I drove over to the Eastside to take a look. It was a little after midnight when I cruised past the building. Since Pauley's unit was in the back of the building, I really couldn't see anything, except that there wasn't a squad car parked out in front. There were three people, two guys and a woman smoking and drinking beer on the front stoop, probably attempting to catch what little breeze there was on a sweltering night. I drove down to the next block, parked then walked back, trying to act like I belonged in the building.

As I walked up the front sidewalk, I looked directly at the people lounging around the front door. I nodded at the largest in the group as if we were casual acquaintances. He had close-cropped hair, a tattoo around his neck, and looked to be Hispanic. I gave him a nod that suggested we knew each other, made my way around all three of them, and pulled the front door open. There was an empty beer bottle wedged in the door frame so the door wouldn't lock. As I reached for the door, the smaller of the two guys said something in Spanish, which brought a chuckle from all three of them. I pulled the door open and laughed along with them, pretending I got whatever the joke was, then took the stairs to the second floor.

The hallway didn't smell any better after midnight than the last time I'd been here. I moved as quietly as possible down toward the last door on the right, Pauley's apartment. There was a dim blue light coming from under the door. The sound of either a radio or a television playing drifted out through the door and into the hallway. I guessed the light and sound probably came from the flatscreen TV I'd seen in there the other day. A baby cried out from one of the units behind me, but the hallway remained empty and the three people on the front stoop were still out there, sipping beer.

From what I could tell in the dim light, Pauley's door was secured by the same lousy lock system. I pulled out a card, ran through the layout of the place in my mind, and then figured there was nothing like the element of surprise. I slipped the card under the door latch, then ran the card up along the door frame and barged into the room.

I'd been correct. The room was illuminated by a large flat screen TV casting a blue light over everything, including Marsha, bound up with tape wrapped around her legs and arms lying on the floor in front of the couch. Her eyes went wide as I swung the door open. She started to shake her head, then seemed to indicate the back kitchen area just as the bathroom door opened, and a large figure in boxer shorts stepped into the room, dabbing his face with a dirty towel.

He took one look at me and lunged toward the window. It caught me off guard for half-a-second. I thought he might be planning to jump out when I spotted the pistol resting on the window sill. I was right behind him, slamming into him full force just as he got his hand around the grip and began to raise the pistol. The thing fired, booming through the silence and flashing in the dark the moment we collided. It all happened in a nanosecond. I felt him going out the window before I actually heard any noise. I definitely remembered shoving him hard, rather than trying to hang onto the guy. The next thing I knew, he was spread out on the ground below. I heard bits of glass tinkling around him, and he lay very still with a dazed look across his face. I recognized him as the jerk from the SUV who gave me the elbow shot just before he climbed into the Lincoln in front of my office.

I didn't waste any time worrying. I stepped over Marsha, who was making noise and rolling away from the couch. I checked the bathroom to make sure it was empty then looked around the kitchen. The light didn't go on when I flicked the switch, but I couldn't see anyone in the light filtering behind me from the bathroom. My heart was still pounding too loudly to really hear anything.

I rushed back out to Marsha and pulled the tape from around her head, then tore it off her wrists. I was aware of a baby crying from somewhere out in the hallway.

"Bout fucking time. Jesus, where the hell have you been? I thought you were dead," Marsha gasped.

"Let's just get your ass out of here," I said.

I helped her up. "Just a second," I said, then stepped over to the little mirror hanging on the wall, grabbed the gold chain with the Claddagh I was sure was Desi's, and placed it in my pocket.

The two guys from the front stoop were standing at the end of the hallway, watching us as we fled down the backstairs. They didn't appear to have any intention of getting closer. We ran out the back door. The guy in boxer shorts was still lying on the ground and hadn't moved, so we sidestepped him as we ran down the block to Lydell's truck. I had to slow down and take Marsha by the arm, pulling her along. I wasn't sure if that was because she'd been bound up for a long time, or I was just more frightened and moving faster. Fear had always served as a big motivator for me.

By the time I got her in the truck and myself behind the wheel, she was sobbing. I reached over and clicked her seat belt into place. I was still too frightened to cry myself, so I just fired up Lydell's truck, and we drove straight to the police station.

Fifty-three

We were back in the same interview room where we'd been earlier. Manning needed a shave, and his usually pink bald head had taken on a decided shade of scarlet. He also appeared a lot less smug than he had in our earlier meeting. For my part, I was still shaking.

"That's your description?" Manning asked.

"I've told you a half dozen times it was some guy in boxers reaching for a gun. A pair of boxer shorts was all he had on. I can't even tell you the color, and he had a gun, an awfully big gun. That's really all I remember before he jumped out the window to make his escape."

"Jumped? Through two panes of glass?"

"I guess he was in a hurry or thought there were more guys than just me."

"Any identifying characteristics?"

"Honestly, the whole thing happened way too fast, Manning. I just remember the bathroom door opening, and the next thing I knew, he was two stories down on the ground, and I heard all the glass kind of tinkling around the guy."

"Including that very convenient shard that just happened to slice through his carotid artery," Manning said.

I shrugged. "I really don't know anything about that. I just wanted to get Marsha and me the hell out of there. I didn't know if anyone else was going to show up, and I sure as hell wasn't planning to wait around and see."

"The paramedics transported her to Regions Hospital. She'll get the standard examination, and they'll keep her there under observation for at least twenty-four hours. Any update on her condition, and we'll pass it on."

"She gonna be safe? That's where that other idiot is, the guy with the shaved head."

"Donald Dempsey?"

"Yeah, your graduate student."

Manning ignored my comment. "Not to worry. We've got a twenty-four-hour guard on Miss Norling's door, and we've moved Dempsey into custodial care. He's still unable to get anywhere under his own power. Probably will be for the better part of a week."

"Custodial care?"

"He's cuffed to the bed while he's in traction and recovering. I wouldn't worry too much about him."

"What about Driscoll and Dawn Miller?"

"We're working that aspect."

"Meaning?"

"Meaning I'm not going to comment on an ongoing investigation. I can tell you this much. It looks like his phone call with Lieutenant LaZelle may have actually been through Skype or Viber or some pay-as-you-go online long-distance system. He somehow programmed the thing to show a Florida locale."

"You know they're both guilty as sin, and you know Driscoll railroaded Desi Quinn and was tied into that Federal Reserve robbery some years back."

"And I think I just told you, I can't comment on an ongoing investigation."

"What about Lydell?"

"I suspect there's a pretty good chance the assault charges won't be coming through." Manning half chuckled. "I'll get the paperwork started, and he should be released later this morning."

Fifty-four

I was in Karla's office, giving her an update as to the whereabouts of her pimped out Lincoln town car.

"So, it will eventually be released from the BCA lab in another seventeen days. I didn't realize they actually hold them for a month. The good news is the thing's tucked away all safe and sound. The bad news is, you can't get it for another two and a half weeks," I said.

"Not like I want to be seen driving that thing around town," she said. "I don't know. This whole sorry scenario just seems like such a waste. Poor Desi, she was telling the truth all along, and no one believed her."

"You did."

"Me? No, to be honest, I chalked her up as a really nice woman who made a really dumb mistake and was going to do everything she could to correct it. But to tell you the truth, I wasn't completely convinced she was without sin."

"Maybe more a case of naïve accomplice?" I said.

"Maybe. All I know is she didn't deserve any of this, and she sure as hell didn't deserve to die."

"I'm not sure she deserved much of anything that happened to her in the last ten years, including me turning her down when she needed help," I said.

"Still beating yourself up on that one? I'd say you've made some pretty decent restitution. Come on, Dev, you were almost killed."

I just looked at her for a long moment before I spoke. "Well, at least they got Dawn Miller before she fled the country."

Karla nodded in agreement. "And Gaston Driscoll? They still figure he's hiding somewhere down in the British Virgin Islands?"

"It's almost a sure bet he hid his share of that Federal Reserve heist down there in some offshore account. I'm sure he's all lawyered up by now and just sitting pretty for the rest of his life."

"I can't see him keeping a low profile down there. He's bound to turn up sooner or later."

"And then what? It's not like they'll ever be able to extradite him. With that kind of money, he'll be able to fight any attempt to bring him back here to face charges. As a matter of fact, if he has any brains, he's kept his accounts down there, but he's out partying somewhere else in the world we'll never think of, South America, Singapore, the Greek Isles. We may not like it, but it looks like the son-of-a-bitch pulled it off. Rich crooks somehow manage to do that," I said.

"Behind every fortune, there's usually a crime," Karla said, then shook her head and stared off into the distance.

After a long moment, I followed her stare then said, "There is one other thing I'd maybe like to do."

Fifty-five

I stretched as I waited, bending at the waist to touch my toes a number of times after sitting for so long. Most of the people in line looked a lot older than me. The few who weren't were holding small children, barely awake at this hour. Eventually, I made my way to the front of the line. I got the signal to approach the glass booth from the woman seated there. She seemed to study me as I walked toward her.

"Anything to declare?" she asked, scanning my passport.

"No, ma'am."

"First time here?" She smiled, paging through looking at the various stamps on the different pages.

"I was here once before, but we weren't allowed off the plane."

She glanced up with a quizzical look.

"U.S. Army, coming home from Iraq. We stopped to refuel. I guess there were demonstrations."

She gave a slight nod, but I couldn't read her reaction.

"How long do you plan to visit?"

"Just three days. I'm heading back on the twenty-fifth."

"Enjoy your stay," she said, then stamped my passport somewhere on a middle page and signaled for the next person in line.

I grabbed my suitcase from baggage claim, changed dollars to Euros, and followed the directions to the car rental. I was driving out of the Dublin airport thirty minutes later and heading west. I had Desi's map of Ireland opened on the passenger seat next to me. The little village her grandparents had emigrated from was still circled in pencil, and next to that was the heart she'd drawn with a red marker around the town of Boyle where Gaston Driscoll's family hailed from.

Three hours later, I was out in the west of Ireland, driving through the village of Ballyfarnon, in County Roscommon just a few minutes from the village in Sligo where Desi's grandparents left after the Second World War. I traveled along for a bit more as a large mountain hillside rolled along on my right. As I drove across a small stone bridge, I had to slow for a little blonde girl who seemed to be just staring at the water. I turned right as soon as I saw the sign for St. Joseph's church.

There was a low wall, not even three feet high, surrounding the churchyard. The church was a pale yellow stucco affair, simple, yet graceful in its own way. The small graveyard was located in the rear. Probably no different than hundreds of other churches scattered across this part of the country, except for the one thing that brought me here.

It was a little after two in the afternoon, Irish time. I was starting to feel the effect of the time change and happy to pull over. I grabbed what I needed from the back seat then made my way around the rear of the church and into the small cemetery. It took me a few minutes, but I found them. There they were under a large stone Celtic Cross, Desi's grandparents. Their names carved into the stone, Emmett, and Elizabeth, born in 1922 and 1926. A number of Quinn headstones were scattered around, some of them so old and weathered they were next to impossible to read, the final resting place for the generations that came before Desi.

At this time in the afternoon, I was pretty sure I was the only one around, but I checked just to be sure. I didn't see anyone, so I opened the box of polished wood with the inlaid design pattern running along the edge— Desi's ashes.

"Sorry, Desi, but I guess this is the best I can do. At least you finally made it here. I'm, I'm really sorry. I screwed up. Please forgive me," I pleaded. I waited for the answer that I knew could never come. Then I just drew a blank and stood there feeling awfully stupid and probably sleep deprived. I didn't know if my tears were for Desi or for me. I stood for the longest time and watched as the breeze picked up her ashes and gradually scattered them on the Irish wind. I fished the gold chain out of my pocket, her Claddagh. I hung it on the edge of that Celtic cross and mumbled, "Sorry."

I wasn't just tired, I was exhausted and in no condition to drive back to Dublin. So I drove the short distance to the town of Boyle, where I got a hotel room and crashed until close to eleven that night. I dreamt of Desi, although I can't recall more than that, just that I woke with a strange sense of her presence. I figured it was just the emotion from the graveyard earlier that afternoon.

I was ravenous and completely screwed up with the time change. I dressed and went out to look for something to eat. Where's a McDonald's when you really need one?

After finding nothing, I ended up going to the Glass Slipper pub next to my hotel. It seemed like a quiet little place and looked like it could have stood next to the hotel for the past hundred years. All it lacked was a thatched roof. Well, and a kitchen that served food. I'd always had a fondness for Guinness, so I thought I would grab a pint and, God forbid, mingle with some locals. Serendipity is a funny thing. By definition, I guess it's supposed to be a surprise.

The entrance to the pub was actually two doors, one off the street, then the second door maybe three steps inside a small entry. You had to make a sharp left to enter the pub itself.

I heard the voice the moment I stepped in off the street. Deep and booming out the door, a command voice. I paused and cautiously peeked inside.

He was seated at the bar, holding court in an American Midwest accent, enthralling a young, red-haired woman who looked to have stars in her eyes. He was laughing and standing just a little too close to her to be casual. I was sure it was him. I'd never forgotten the uppercut he'd delivered to me in his kitchen when my hands had been tied. Though his hair was dyed midnight black and the beard was gone, it was still him, Gaston Driscoll.

In a weird way, it made all the sense in the world. Here he was, hiding in plain sight. While everyone expected him to be down in the British Virgin Islands, here he was, apparently free to come and go as he damn well pleased. I backed out of the doorway and ran to my rental car. Two minutes later, I was parked out on the street, hoping there wasn't a back door to the Glass Slipper.

I'd waited the better part of an hour before the red-headed woman came out all smiles and walked down the street. Fifteen minutes later, Driscoll exited and walked in the opposite direction. He slipped behind the wheel of a Jaguar parked a few doors down. I watched him in my rearview mirror as he made a U-turn on the quiet street, then drove past a moment later, not giving me a second look.

I followed him out of town at a distance, painfully aware we were the only two cars on the narrow country road this late on a weeknight. He drove over a slight rise, and his taillights disappeared. I gambled and turned off my headlights, then caught sight of his vehicle just as I made the rise. He was maybe a half-mile ahead, and I continued to follow with my lights off. A few minutes later, he pulled into a farm yard and parked. I pulled over and waited.

A moment later, a light came on in a house and a bit after that two more lights from second-floor windows. I turned my headlights back on and drove past the house at a normal speed. I stopped around a bend some distance past and shut off my engine, not exactly sure what to do. I knew one thing. I didn't intend to lose him this time.

Fifty-six

I walked along the edge of the paved lane. Although there was no shoulder to speak of, I didn't want the sound of footsteps on gravel to carry through the quiet night. This side of the house seemed dark, so I could only hope Driscoll wasn't watching me through a night vision scope or a laser sight.

As I approached, the house appeared to be two stories of dressed stone painted white with a tile roof, pretty typical for the area based on what I'd seen earlier in the day. There was a stone wall across the front of the property, with a driveway leading into the yard. There was also the standard white metal box hanging just under the eaves with a blinking blue light indicating an alarm system had been activated. Driscoll's Jaguar was parked directly in front of the door.

I held back in the dark. The last thing I wanted to do was alert him. I studied the place for a long time, adrenaline still coursing through my system, keeping me alert. Eventually, I walked back to my car and drove on, not wanting to return past Driscoll's house.

I thought I'd be able to sleep in the next morning, but I was wide awake just after eight. I checked out of the hotel by nine, paying with cash, then found a sport and camping store in town, along with a hardware store that would fit my needs. I kept a low profile for the remainder of the day, attempting to advertise my American accent as little as possible.

Dusk in the Irish summer arrived a lot later than in Minnesota. I approached Driscoll's farmhouse a little after ten-thirty that night. His Jaguar was parked in front, exactly where I'd last seen it. As far as I could tell, it hadn't been moved since the night before.

I approached cautiously. No lights seemed to be on in the front of the house, but that didn't mean he wasn't watching. I was closer to the house than last night. I stopped to study the place, but couldn't see anything that looked like cameras or motion detectors, and the light on the alarm system box wasn't blinking.

I thought about just knocking on the door, waiting for Driscoll to answer, then returning the favor of that uppercut the moment he opened the door. But what if he didn't answer? What if I missed? What if he just beat me to death? There seemed to be too many options, none of them going my way, so I decided to just stick with my basic plan and quietly drew alongside his car and slit the rear tire.

About two hours later, the light on the security system began blinking, and a moment after that, a light upstairs flashed on. A second light I took to be from a bathroom came on a few seconds after that. Ten minutes later, and the place went dark. I guessed Gaston Driscoll was tucked in for the night. I hunkered down in the shadows along the side of the house and waited.

It was damn near daylight at four-thirty the following morning. I wasn't as worried about Driscoll spotting me along the side of his house as I was some neighbor driving past and reporting me or simply pulling in to ask what the hell I was up to. Fortunately, no one drove past, and a little before eleven, Driscoll stepped out of the house. I must have dozed off, but the front door opening snapped me awake.

"God damn it," he shouted from the front stoop. Then he paused and looked around, scanning the area out to the road and back. He was dressed in what looked like a blue silk bathrobe with little gold crowns all over the thing. His hair appeared wet, like he'd just stepped out of the shower, and even from this distance, his face appeared freshly shaven.

I was crouched and remained pressed against the corner of the stone house. He waited a moment before he walked to the back of his car, dangling car keys and wearing a pair of flip flops. He gave another cautious look around before he unlocked the trunk, then lifted the lid, and began to rummage around.

It was barely twenty feet and seemed to take half-a-day as I charged across the open yard to grab him before he had the chance to reach for a tire iron or worse, a gun. I caught him completely unprepared just as he heard my footsteps and instinctively looked up. I slammed into him full force with a body check. The thump I heard was the sound of his skull bouncing off the edge of the raised car trunk. I was up and caught him as he fell, throwing him to the ground before his eyes had a chance to cross. I slammed my fist into his face three or four times before I realized he wasn't offering any resistance.

Based on the blood running down and around his mouth, I figured I must have broken his nose. The left side of his mouth was bleeding and already beginning to swell. I quickly got to my feet and grabbed him under the shoulders, dragging him back into the house, where I laid him out on the stone floor of the front entry.

I took lengths of rope out of my pocket, tied his wrists, tied his feet, then sat down on the staircase, and waited. He blew the occasional bubble of blood out his left nostril as he gradually came around.

"Well, Gaston Driscoll. Gee, who would have thought?" I said.

His left eye was puffy and already beginning to discolor, but that didn't hide the shock that washed over his face as he recognized me.

"You?"

"Yeah, too bad. I guess sometimes things just have a habit of not going your way."

"What . . . what? Who are you? What do you . . ."

"Shut up, you stupid bastard," I said and slapped him hard, twice.

"I have no idea . . ."

I raised my fist, ready to hit him again.

"Don't, Haskell, don't. All right, okay. What do you want?"

"What do I want? I want your head on a platter. I'm calling the cops, Driscoll. You're finished."

"Hold on, son, hold on! I wonder if we can't work something out here. I can make this worth your while, hang on. Take a moment and think about it. Just think, you'll never have to work again. You like the sound of that, don't you? I can tell. Doesn't that sound nice? You can take it easy, never have to worry about another cent, ever."

"Yeah, I'm sure I can trust you, not a problem. No, you know what I'd like?"

"Name it, Haskell, you just name it."

"I want to see that DVD of Daphne Cole having sex with you."

"Daphne Cole?"

"Don't, please, don't tempt me. I'd really enjoy causing you pain, Driscoll. Now, I'm tired, crabby, and let's just use this as a test to see if we can get along. What do you say?"

"Well, little Daphne. So she's your hot button, is she? I had you figured wrong all along, Haskell."

I nodded.

"Just untie me here, and let me get the disc for you."

"I got a better idea. Why don't you tell me where it is, and I'll get it."

"That's not going to—"

"Trust, Driscoll, this is all about being able to trust you."

"All right, all right, upstairs," he said. "In the spare bedroom, the red room, there's a rack full of CDs. They're all stored in the cases at the bottom marked holiday music."

"One chance, that's all you get. So you're sure?" I said.

He nodded.

I hurried up the wide staircase, taking the steps two at a time, then down a hallway. I almost passed the door to the small red room as I heard Driscoll calling from down below.

"I don't blame you, Haskell. They were all fun. We might get together, maybe make a good team. You certainly seem intelligent enough."

The CD rack stood next to a small, carved antique desk and appeared just as Driscoll had described, with at least a dozen CD cases labeled 'Holiday Music' arranged at the bottom. I pulled one out and opened the case. The DVD disk was labeled 'Helen' in blue indelible marker. I opened the next case and saw a name I didn't recognize. I'd gone through six or seven before I came across one labeled 'Daphne.' Two cases after that I found the one labeled 'Desi.'

It was suddenly quiet, and I realized I hadn't heard Driscoll shouting for a moment or two. I grabbed a crystal candlestick off the desk and went back into the hallway. Driscoll was just creeping up the staircase, unwinding the last of the rope for around his wrists as he reached the top.

"Driscoll, damn it," I shouted and charged.

He half jumped as he looked up, surprised. I slammed into him, automatically, liked I'd done a thousand times to guys in high school on the hockey rink. He fell backward, tumbling head over heels down the staircase, picking up speed before coming to a stop once the back of his head bounced off the stone floor.

I followed him down the staircase, ready to club him with the candlestick. I needn't have hurried. He lay still, looking off to the side, but with his head cranked at an odd angle. He didn't appear to be breathing. I sat down on the staircase and waited until discoloration began to appear around his lips. The blue silk robe had wrapped around his waist, and the small Ace of Spades tattoo Desi had mentioned was just barely visible.

I stared at him for a few minutes. I didn't have any feeling one way or the other, except that I knew he'd caused a lot of harm to a lot of people, and in the end, he deserved far worse than a brief tumble down the stairs.

So that was it. After all the schemes, all the lies, all the careful planning, it came down to a full body check from an old high school hockey player who was too tired to drive and just happened to see you in a pub one night. Serves you right, Gaston.

Fifty-Seven

When I landed in Detroit the agent asked, "Anything to declare?" He stamped my passport and handed it back through the slot in the window before I even had the chance to answer.

"No, nothing," I said, taking my passport and walking toward a domestic flight concourse. I had three hours to kill, and it felt good not to be sitting after almost eight hours on the plane. I landed in the Twin Cities later that afternoon and gave the taxi driver the address.

I saw her down the block the moment we turned the corner onto the street. She was out in her front yard, picking up toys and putting them in the wagon. The double stroller was parked next to the front steps. We pulled up, and I told the taxi driver to wait a minute.

"Daphne," I called as I climbed out of the back of the taxi.

She looked at me but didn't smile. She quickly glanced back toward the house behind her, maybe double-checking.

"Sorry to show up unannounced, but I've got something for you," I said then handed her the DVD with her name scrawled across in blue marker.

She glanced at it, then up at me with a questioning look.

"I didn't watch it. See you around," I said, then climbed back in the taxi, and we drove off.

Fifty-eight

I arrived home and opened a beer, then checked my phone messages.

Beep.

"Hi, Dev, Lydell. Thanks for putting in the good word and getting me out. Ah, hey, don't bother to call back. You can just send the check down to my new Chicago address. I'll text it to you. Annie's being Annie again, and I'm kinda tired of it. You ever need Ultimate Fight Club tickets, look me up. Thanks, man."

Beep.

"Hi, Dev, Marsha. I'm down here spending some time with my sister in North Carolina. Probably best if you don't contact me. I've got a lot of thinking to do."

Beep.

"This message is for butthead Devlin Haskell. Please do not attempt to contact me ever again." Click. I was pretty sure it was Annie's angry voice.

Beep.

"Haskell? Pick up." Followed by a long pause, then, "Haskell? This is Detective Norris Manning. Please get in touch with me. The sooner we can talk, the better."

Great, three people who didn't want to talk to me, and the one who did want to talk, I'd just as soon never hear from. I was on my third or fourth beer when the phone rang.

"Haskell Investigations."

"Hi, Dev, Karla. So you're back. Everything go okay?"

"Yeah, I guess I accomplished what I needed to do."

"You mean, Desi?"

"Yeah, Desi."

"You're so sweet. I don't care what everybody says."

"Thanks, Karla."

"Hey, I got some chilled white wine. I was thinking of stopping and getting some takeout. You interested?"

"You mean dinner?"

"Maybe for starters." She laughed.

The End

Thanks for taking the time to read <u>Last Shot</u>. If you enjoyed Dev's adventure please tell 2-300 of your closest friends. I'm indie published and a review really helps. Even if it's just a sentence or two it really, really helps.

Check out the sample from the next book in the Dev Haskell series, <u>Ting-A-Ling</u>.

Sneak Peek

Ting-A-Ling

Second Edition

MIKE FARICY

One

My phone rang out in the dark, *ting-a-ling, ting-a-ling*. The sound indicated an unknown number, and I debated answering as I came awake.

"Hello, hello." I cleared my throat a couple of times and looked over at the digital clock glowing on top of my dresser. It was after two in the morning.

"Oooh, is this Den?" A woman giggled. I couldn't place her sexy voice, but I guessed from the slurred speech she wasn't feeling much pain.

"Actually, it's Dev, Dev Haskell. I'm wondering if maybe you might have the wrong number."

I heard what sounded like a distant toilet flushing before she said, "I don't think so, honey, is this…" She repeated my phone number back to me, sounding an awful lot like she was reading it.

I glanced over at Heidi lying next to me in a 'two bottles of Prosecco' induced sleep. She was breathing deeply and wore a contented smile on her face. "Yeah, that's my number. What can I do for you?"

"That maybe depends, you tell me. It says here to call if I'm looking for a good time."

"What?"

"Right here on the door, it…"

"The door?"

"Yeah, in the ladies room. Someone wrote your number on the stall door. Well, unless you snuck in here."

"Ladies room?"

I suddenly heard a loud *whoosh*. "Yeah, I'm down here at Bunnies. I'm in the middle stall," she said as if that explanation would somehow clear things up. "Your number is right below the hook to hang your coat on. There, all finished. Anyway, I'm calling for a good time. Believe me, I could use it right about now."

"Actually, much as I'd like to help you out, I'm wondering if I could get a rain check. I'm actually in a meeting right now."

"Oh yeah, figures, someone called ahead of me, right? My whole night has gone that way. The guy I was with ditched me about ten-thirty, stuck me with the bar tab, and left me here. They had last call about fifteen minutes ago, now I gotta grab a taxi home. Oh well, you can't blame a girl for trying."

"Yeah, unfortunate timing. How 'bout I give you a ring tomorrow?"

"I'm not sure I'll remember."

"I will. Okay if I call you?"

"I suppose."

"What's your name?"

"Danielle, but everybody calls me Danielle."

I waited for a punch line, but there didn't seem to be one coming. I heard a squeak that was most likely the stall door opening. "Well, I better get going, it's gonna take forever to catch a taxi."

"Thanks for the call, sorry I can't help. I'll talk to you tomorrow, Danielle."

"Promise?"

"Yeah, I promise."

"You won't forget?"

"I won't."

I set my cell back on the dresser. Heidi's heavy breathing was beginning to grow dangerously close to a snore. I figured if I woke her, there was a chance it could lead to better things, and she was probably still Prosecco'd enough not to remember in the morning. I shook her shoulder gently. She rolled halfway over on her back and gave a little grunt. I moved back under the covers, snuggled up against her, and lightly ran my hand along her side a few times. Each time I roamed just a little further down until my hand began its final approach launching off her hip bone. She rolled over, and just as I was thinking, 'success,' she rocketed back with a quick, sharp elbow that caught me on the cheekbone. I saw stars, literally, and had to shake my head a few times to get my bearings.

Heidi returned to her regular deep breathing.

Once my head cleared, I decided to leave 'well enough' alone. Just to play it safe, I took an extra pillow and placed it between us.

It was early morning. The sun was up, and I guessed it was sometime before seven. I was vaguely aware of Heidi climbing out of bed and walking down the hall into the bathroom. I drifted back to sleep. Maybe ten minutes later I heard the shower running. Sometime after that, she walked into the bedroom. I half-opened my eyes, hoping she might climb back in bed. I rolled over, thinking I could lend some encouragement.

She had her thick white bath towel wrapped tightly around her and my bath towel wrapped around her hair. She wore a surprised look on her face that suggested something like I had two heads. She stopped and stared.

"What?" I said.

"What the hell happened to you?"

"Huh?"

"What do you mean, huh? That black eye, dopey. You walk into a door or something in the middle of the night?"

"Black eye?" I sat up and turned to face the mirror over my dresser. It looked like I'd stepped in the ring with someone a lot faster than me. My left eye and cheek were swollen and purple.

"Oh, God. Thanks for this."

"Me?"

"Yeah, I just tried to pull the blanket over your shoulder last night because you seemed to be cold, and you gave me the elbow. I guess no good deed goes unpunished."

"I didn't do that. Did I?"

I nodded.

"Really? I couldn't have," she said, then tenderly felt her elbow.

"Yeah, and that's about all the action I got."

She stared at me for a moment, then said, "Oh, so that's it. The sympathy vote. You probably did that just to talk me into climbing on—"

"Yeah, Heidi, that's right, I beat myself up so you'd feel sorry and crawl back in bed with me," I said, then waited. I counted silently, wondering if it might just work. I could see the wheels turning inside her head. I made it to nine before she spoke.

"You know, you're so stupid, Dev. But that's kind of sweet, in your own warped little way. Oh, God, I really shouldn't, I'm just out of the shower."

"I don't mind."

"Amazingly, I wasn't thinking about you."

"I was just hoping it might relieve some pressure. God, I think I've got a headache coming on." I gently touched my swollen cheekbone.

"Okay, okay, but make it fast," she said and dropped the towels.

TWO

When we finished Heidi lingered just long enough to drink the last of my coffee and eat the one remaining blueberry muffin I had saved for myself.

"Actually, I was gonna eat that muffin."

"Too bad, you should have thought about that when you made me stay and work up an appetite."

"I didn't tell you, you had to stay. I was merely thinking that after I picked up the tab for dinner last night, your two bottles of Prosecco, and the after dinner-drinks you couldn't seem to live without, that maybe you felt guilty about falling asleep on me. I certainly put in the time."

"Guilty? No, not really."

"Well, you should be."

"Sorry. Not. Look, I had a great time, and then I was tired from a really long day. Did I tell you I closed that Buchner deal?"

"Yeah, at least a half dozen times, and by the way, you weren't tired from an exhausting day at work. It was the two bottles of Prosecco, *'your best,'* if I recall your order correctly. And then those after-dinner drinks. What was it?"

"Did I order a dessert Manhattan?" She sounded like she really couldn't recall.

"No. You ordered two of them. You sure needed those."

Heidi shrugged.

"No doubt, you remember the ride home."

Her blank look said otherwise.

"I had to keep pushing you off. You were crazy, wanted me to pull over so we could *'make impetuous love'*…was how you phrased it. I think."

"Oh, sorry about that. Maybe I did have a little sip too many."

"Yeah, followed by that second bottle of Prosecco and then . . ."

"Okay, okay. Look, I gotta run, I've got a luncheon meeting. Hey, if you find my thong, it's red, hang onto it for me. I couldn't find it, unless you did something typically stupid and crude, you perv."

"Actually, I think it's down on West Seventh, right near the stoplight at Grand Ave."

"What?"

"Yeah, you said you felt imprisoned or something along those lines, and you threw it out the window. I can't remember exactly. It was just before your *'impetuous love'* suggestion."

"Are you kidding me? Damn it, that was about a twenty-five dollar thong."

"There you go, I'm always telling you not to wear one in the first place. See what happens when you ignore my common sense suggestions."

She shook her head and said, "You really are a perv. See you later. I gotta run." She scooped up her purse and the rest of my blueberry muffin and ran out the door.

"Thanks, Heidi."

"My pleasure." She waved over her shoulder but never bothered to look back, hurrying to her car in the cold weather.

I had my phone out as she pulled away from the curb. No rush, I ended up leaving a message. "Hi, Danielle, this is Dev Haskell. We spoke last night, actually this morning, early. Just calling back. You can reach me at this number. Thanks."

Three

I showered and took my time getting into the office. It was close to noon before I was able to stare out the window at The Spot bar and ignore the files on my desk. I was supposed to be doing some fact-checking on job applications for an insurance company. The work was boring, but it paid the bills, at least for this week. I just had to make phone calls and verify periods of employment, some references, nothing too heavy. I figured I could put off making the calls for a few more hours and still complete everything by about four in the afternoon. I planned to call late enough so I wouldn't get an appointment with my pal Eddie Bendix until tomorrow at the earliest.

Eddie was an old high school buddy and the HR guy at a major insurance company. I think they were gearing up to handle the influx they expected from Obamacare, although things were so screwed up on the government end no one seemed to be in a hurry.

It was winter or would be officially in a couple of days. We'd already had ice and snow for three weeks, and temperatures had hung below freezing since Thanksgiving. The day was cold and gray and seemed to match my mood. Oh, and we were out of coffee in the office.

I was staring out the window when Louie came in the door. We shared the office. Louie was fast becoming the man to talk to in town if you got nailed on a DUI, a driving under the influence charge. I think a combination of his personal experience, along with a pretty sharp legal mind, were beginning to serve him well. The personal experience wasn't the sort garnered in the courtroom. Louie had been pulled over enough times and never yet been charged, making him a bit of a legend, at least with the liquid diet crowd.

"I think you were doing that the last time I saw you," he said, then threw his briefcase on the picnic table that served as his desk. He discarded a grimy ski jacket on top of the briefcase and tossed his Minnesota Wild stocking cap on top of the jacket, it fell on the floor where he ignored it. All of his suits seemed to be permanently wrinkled. He was in the same wrinkled gray suit he'd worn the previous two days.

I suddenly came back to the present and stopped staring out the window long enough to answer him.

"Just thinking. I'm not at all excited about checking out those employment applications for Eddie." I indicated the two untouched stacks of files on my desk.

"What the hell happened to your eye? And you haven't done those yet? The files, you've had them for at least a week."

"Actually, I just got them last Monday."

"Yeah. And today is Friday. That's a week. Right?"

"I was thinking seven days, you know, not five. Anyway, I'm not all that excited about making the calls. Most of the time, I'm lucky if they'll even confirm employment, let alone the dates. These companies are always worried about being sued by some jack-ass lawyer and don't want to say much of anything beyond 'hello'."

"Tell me about it. And the eye?"

"Nothing really, just grabbed some dinner last night with Heidi. She bumped into me with her elbow. It was an accident. Hey, get this I got a call in the middle of the night from some chick. She was reading my phone number off of a stall door in the ladies room."

"The ladies room? Okay, I'm ignoring your Heidi explanation for the moment. You wrote your phone number in the ladies room?"

"I wasn't the one who—" My phone rang, and I answered.

"Haskell Investigations."

There was a momentary pause before a voice said, "Hello, I'm returning a call left for me from a Mr. Haskell?"

"That's me." I recognized her voice from last night and nodded at Louie. "Is this Danielle?"

"Yes." Her response suggested our conversation wasn't going much further.

"I'm returning your call from last night. Actually, it was early this morning, just after two," I explained.

"My call?"

"Yeah."

"I've had a lot going on lately, and I'm wondering if you might have me mixed up with someone else." She was suddenly sounding just a little unsure.

"You phoned me from the ladies room. I think you said the middle stall. Apparently, my phone number was written on the door, and you called."

There was a long pause, and I had the sense the event was slowly coming into focus. "Oh, God. Look, I apologize. I'm really sorry I bothered you. It won't happen again, I promise. I may have had a little too much to drink and I—"

"I think you said some guy ditched you, and you got stuck with the bar tab. Hopefully, you found a taxi home."

"Yeah, I did. Not my boyfriend, by the way. But back up for a minute, you're an investigator?"

"Yeah, Haskell Investigations."

"So, what do you investigate? Is it like in the movies and on TV?"

"Usually, it's a lot more boring." I glanced over at the stacks of untouched files on my desk.

"Do you ever take on new clients?"

"On occasion. It depends on what they want me to do. Sometimes they would be better served by an attorney or the police."

"You ever investigate cheating partners and that sort of thing?"

"You mean like a husband or boyfriend?"

"Not really, I was thinking more along the lines of a business partner."

"I have."

"Really, gee, maybe we should talk." She made it sound like I had just passed some test.

"Do you want to set up a time when we could meet?"

"All right." She suddenly sounded guarded. "Maybe a public place where we would both feel comfortable."

I took that to mean where *she* would feel comfortable. "You pick the place," I said.

"How about the St. Paul Grill? Could you maybe do tomorrow, say about sixish?"

"I could. I'll plan to see you tomorrow, about six. I'll be seated at the bar."

"How will I know you?"

"I'll be wearing a brown bomber jacket, I've got dark hair combed back, and right now I've got a black eye."

"A black eye," she said, but didn't comment further. "Okay, I'll see you tomorrow, about six, at the bar."

"Right," I said, but she'd already hung up.

Four

It was way past six and getting closer to seven. I was headed toward the bottom of my second beer. It was standing room only at the bar, and I must have been the only person in the place not attending a Christmas party. Everyone was dressed to the nines in silk Christmas ties or long fur coats and talking about five octaves too loud. Between my blue jeans, bomber jacket, and the black eye, I stuck out like a sore thumb.

"Excuse me, do you work here?" She was an attractive brunette with a chest fighting to escape the confines of her dress. I had to concentrate to focus on her face.

"No, sorry, I'm actually waiting to meet someone. She's running a little late." I didn't see any point in mentioning the close to an hour part.

"Are you Dev?"

I think I blinked or half jumped. "Danielle?"

She nodded and held out her hand. "Danielle Roxbury, nice to meet you." The extended hand gave me the opportunity to glance down her dress. Yeah, they were really trying to jump out and get some air.

"Sorry I'm so late, my car wouldn't start. I think it's that stupid battery again and so I— Yo-hoo, excuse me, Dev, up here. Hello."

"What? Oh, sorry, I have a hearing impairment. Service-related." I took a sip of my beer and let that seep in.

She looked like she wasn't buying it and had probably heard something along that line a few thousand times. She studied me a long moment before she spoke. "Actually, I'm really running late. I'm on my way to somewhere else, another get together, you know the Holidays. I had to taxi down here. God, I feel like I've been running late all day."

"Look, we're not going to be able to talk, let alone hear one another in this place. I could give you a ride, and we can talk on the way. It'll save you a taxi fare."

She seemed to consider my offer for a moment before she finally nodded. "Okay, I guess." She sounded less than enthusiastic.

Some fat guy with a red face and an empty martini glass began to ooze onto my bar stool before I was even off the thing. We made our way through the crowd and were almost out the door when she stopped.

"Hold on, I just want to make a call and let them know I'm on the way," she said. Her cell was already up against her ear. "Hey, Karen. Yeah, I know, stupid battery again. Anyway, a guy is giving me a lift." She looked at me and nodded. "I'll be there in fifteen. Dev Haskell. Yeah, I'll tell you later. Can't wait. See you shortly. Okay, yeah, bye."

I wasn't sure there had even been someone on the other end of the line, but I couldn't blame her for playing it safe. "I'm parked just around the corner. You want to wait here, and I'll pick you up? It's pretty cold."

"Oh, that's sweet," she said and looked surprised.

I didn't waste any time walking to my car. It was damn cold, and I hoped the heat would begin to kick in by the time I drove around the block. There was a parking ticket frozen onto the windshield of my Lincoln Continental. Merry Christmas from the city of St. Paul and the parking Gestapo. I fired up the engine, tossed the box holding Eddie's files into the back seat, then made a half-hearted attempt to scrape the frost off the inside of the windshield. I had the heater set on defrost and blowing cold air full blast. It didn't seem to be helping. I thought of running the wipers until I remembered I was out of washer fluid. By the time I drove around the block I think it had actually gotten colder in the car.

I pulled into the circular entry and stopped opposite the door. A valet with a questioning look on his face bounced out the door. I lowered the passenger window. "Just picking up."

"Good luck, man." He gave my car a quick once-over, chuckled, and bounced back inside.

I think he said something to Danielle standing there with her hands in her coat pocket because she gave a disgusted grimace when she looked out the window. She took her time then seemed to grit her teeth and stepped out into the cold, taking quick, tiny steps toward my car. I had to reach over and open the passenger door because the handle was broken on that side. The door was frozen closed, and I pounded on it a few times before it creaked open.

"Hop in."

"You sure?" she said, then cautiously climbed in. She stayed as close to the passenger door as possible. She thrust her hands deeper into her pockets, then pulled her coat around her like it was a hazmat suit, and she might contract some incurable disease from the interior of my car. Her chin was buried about four inches beneath the collar. Just her eyes peeked out.

"Heat's just about to kick in," I lied. "Where to?"

"Up the hill to Summit Ave., about two blocks this side of Dale. Do you know how to get there?"

"Yeah," I said, pulling onto the street. "I live up there."

"You live on Summit?" she asked, sounding incredulous. It was the toniest street in St. Paul, and she didn't bother to hide her surprise.

"No, but close, just a couple of blocks away."

"Oh," she said, then followed up with, "Brrr-rrrr."

I drove down West Seventh to Grand Ave and turned right. Fortunately, we didn't have to wait at the stoplight.

"Oh, God, how old is this thing? Is your heat on?"

"It's a classic, and I think the heat's getting ready to start. So, you said you needed some investigative work done?"

"Mmm-mmm, God. It's so cold." Her shoulders looked to be up around the top of her ears, and her voice came out muffled from somewhere deep within her heavy coat.

"Would you care to expand on that?"

"God, I'm freezing to death. Are you sure the heat is on? I can't feel my toes."

"Almost. What did you want me to look into?"

"Oh, God, I can't stop shivering."

"We'll be at your party in about three minutes. I think you'll survive." I felt the vague hint of warm air beginning to bounce off the windshield. As we approached Ramsey Hill, the light turned yellow, and I stepped on the gas. It turned red about the time I reached the intersection, then sailed through. The hill was extremely steep, so I gave the accelerator another push about halfway up the hill. The Lincoln sputtered then coughed a couple of times before it sprang back to life.

"Oh, God no, please," Danielle whined to herself from somewhere deep down in her coat.

"We were discussing your investigation."

"Huh? I was thinking of having you check out a guy who owes me a lot of money."

"The guy who left you stranded the other night?"

She grunted a noncommittal response.

"Why does he owe you money? I mean, did he just take it, drain your bank account or use your credit cards?"

"No, nothing like that. Matter a fact he's a banker, or at least he was. He's a lawyer too now that I think about it. I lent him some money for his business."

"Which is?"

"His business? He's into all sorts of rubs and barbecue sauces and things. He went commercial last spring. He has an industrial kitchen, somewhere. He's developed packaging or something. He's moving the stuff into stores, the farmer's market, some trade shows."

"Is it any good?"

"I don't know. To tell you the truth, I never tasted it. I'm a vegan."

"A vegan who invested in barbecue sauce . . . interesting."

"That's it, up there on the left. The brick house with the white trim and dark shutters. See, where all the candles are. Oh, God, brrr-rrrr."

The place was a large, three-story, brick colonial with a double front door centered on a long porch with lots of pillars. There were maybe a dozen large, round ice globes on either side of the front sidewalk with candles burning inside that illuminated the way. It looked pretty upscale, and although I'd been past the house a million times, I'd never been inside.

"Let me just turn around here, so you don't have to cross the street. It's slippery, and you're in heels."

"That would be nice," she said, sounding unconvinced.

"I'll walk you to the door," I said, thinking I could at least scam some free drinks and who knew where that might lead.

"No thanks," she replied in a tone that suggested no further discussion.

"Look, Danielle, I might be interested in the investigation. Why don't you call me and we can chat some more." Then I made the u-turn and pulled ahead so she could exit the Lincoln, step out onto the candle lit-sidewalk and another world.

"Here's my card," I said and handed it to her.

She kept her hands buried in her pockets, and her shoulders raised close to the top of her head. I held my card out there for a very long moment before she reluctantly snatched it and thrust her hand back into her coat pocket.

"Give me a call if I can help," I said.

"Yeah, look, thanks for the ride. I'd ask you in, but well, you probably wouldn't know anyone. Better get that heater looked at," she said, then shouldered the door open. She quickly got out, turned, and ran as fast as she could in heels toward the front door.

Nothing like a first impression. I leaned over and pulled the door closed then headed down to The Spot for my own brand of Christmas cheer.

To be continued...

Grab a copy of **Ting-A-Ling**, the seventh mystery in the Dev Haskell Private Investigator mystery series.

Books by Mike Faricy
Crime Fiction Firsts

A boxset of the first four books in four crime fiction series:

Russian Roulette; Dev Haskell series
Welcome; Jack Dillon Dublin Tales series
Corridor Man; Corridor Man series
Reduced Ransom! Hot Shot series

The following titles comprise the Dev Haskell series:

Russian Roulette: Case 1
Mr. Swirlee: Case 2
Bite Me: Case 3
Bombshell: Case 4
Tutti Frutti: Case 5
Last Shot: Case 6
Ting-A-Ling: Case 7
Crickett: Case 8
Bulldog: Case 9
Double Trouble: Case 10
Yellow Ribbon: Case 11
Dog Gone: Case 12
Scam Man: Case 13
Foiled: Case 14
What Happens in Vegas… Case 15
Art Hound: Case 16
The Office: Case 17

Star Struck: Case 18
International Incident: Case 19
Guest From Hell: Case 20
Art Attack: Case 21
Mystery Man: Case 22
Bow-Wow Rescue: Case 23
Cold Case: Case 24
Cash Up Front: Case 25
Dream House: Case 26
Alley Katz: Case 27
The Big Gamble: Case 28
Bad to the Bone: Case 29
Silencio!: Case 30
Surprise, Surprise: Case 31
Hit & Run: Case 32
Suspect Santa: Case 33
P.I. Apprentice: Case 34

The following titles are Dev Haskell novellas:
Dollhouse
The Dance
Pixie
Fore!

Twinkle Toes
(*a Dev Haskell short story*)

The following are Dev Haskell Boxsets:
Dev Haskell Boxset 1-3

Dev Haskell Boxset 4-6
Dev Haskell Boxset 7-9
Dev Haskell Boxset 10-12
Dev Haskell Boxset 13-15
Dev Haskell Boxset 16-18
Dev Haskell Boxset 19-21
Dev Haskell Boxset 22-24
Dev Haskell Boxset 25-27
Dev Haskell Boxset 28-30
Dev Haskell Boxset 1-7
Dev Haskell Boxset 8-14
Dev Haskell Boxset 15-19
Dev Haskell Boxset 20-24
Dev Haskell Boxset 25-29

The following titles comprise the Jack Dillon Dublin Tales series:
Welcome
Jack Dillon Dublin Tale 1
Sweet Dreams
Jack Dillon Dublin Tale 2
Mirror Mirror
Jack Dillon Dublin Tale 3
Silver Bullet
Jack Dillon Dublin Tale 4
Fair City Blues
Jack Dillon Dublin Tale 5
Spade Work
Jack Dillon Dublin Tale 6

Madeline Missing
Jack Dillon Dublin Tale 7
Mistaken Identity
Jack Dillon Dublin Tale 8
Picture Perfect
Jack Dillon Dublin Tale 9
Dublin Moon
Jack Dillon Dublin Tale 10
Mystery Woman
Jack Dillon Dublin Tale 11
Second Chance
Jack Dillon Dublin Tale 12
Payback Brother
Jack Dillon Dublin Tale 13
The Heist
Jack Dillon Dublin Tale 14
Jewels To Kill For
Jack Dillon Dublin Tale 15
Retirement Scheme
Jack Dillon Dublin Tale 16

Jack Dillon Dublin Tales Boxsets:
Jack Dillon Dublin Tales 1-3
Jack Dillon Dublin Tales 4-6
Jack Dillon Dublin Tales 1-5
Jack Dillon Dublin Tales 1-7
Jack Dillon Dublin Tales 6-10

The following titles comprise the Hotshot series;
Reduced Ransom! Second Edition
Finders Keepers! Second Edition
Bankers Hours Second Edition
Chow Down Second Edition
Moonlight Dance Academy Second Edition

Irish Dukes (Fight Card Series)
written under the pseudonym Jack Tunney

The following titles comprise the Corridor Man series:
Corridor Man
Corridor Man 2: Opportunity knocks
Corridor Man 3: The Dungeon
Corridor Man 4: Dead End
Corridor Man 5: Finger
Corridor Man 6: Exit Strategy
Corridor Man 7: Trunk Music
Corridor Man 8: Birthday Boy
Corridor Man 9: Boss Man
Corridor Man 10: Bye Bye Bobby

Corridor Man novellas:
Corridor Man: Valentine
Corridor Man: Auditor
Corridor Man: Howling
Corridor Man: Spa Day

The following are Corridor Man Boxsets:

Corridor Man Boxset 1-3

Corridor Man Boxset 1-5

Corridor Man Boxset 6-9

All books are available on Amazon.com

Thank you!

Contact the author:

- Email: mikefaricyauthor@gmail.com
- Twitter: @Mikefaricybooks
- Facebook: Mike Faricy Author
- Website: http://www.mikefaricybooks.com

Published by

MJF Publishing